MEET THE FORCE RECON TEAM . . .

JACK SWAYNE

The leader of the team. A brilliant tactician and superb soldier. For him, failure is not an option . . . ever.

GREINER

The Boy Scout. In the infantry battalion he won Marine of the Month—every month. And he's all too ready to test his mettle in the field.

NIGHT RUNNER

A full-blooded American Indian. Even with the cutting-edge technology used by the team, the deadliest thing about him is his senses.

FRIEL

An ex–street thug turned disciplined Marine. A natural-born killer with no remorse. Possibly the deadliest shot in the world.

FORCE RECON

The explosive military action series by
James V. Smith, Jr.

FORCE RECON

FATAL HONOR

James V. Smith, Jr.

BERKLEY BOOKS, NEW YORK

FORCE RECON: FATAL HONOR

A Berkley Book / published by arrangement with
the author

PRINTING HISTORY
Berkley edition / May 2003

ISBN: 0-425-18991-0

BERKLEY®
Berkley Books are published by The Berkley Publishing Group,
a division of Penguin Group (USA) Inc.,
375 Hudson Street, New York, New York 10014.
BERKLEY and the "B" design
are trademarks belonging to Penguin Group (USA) Inc.

PRINTED IN THE UNITED STATES OF AMERICA

10 9 8 7 6 5 4 3 2 1

EVENT SCENARIO 20

"GUILTY."

Gunnery Sergeant Robert Night Runner sat up in his rack at the sound of the word rattling around inside his head like a BB in a bathtub. He tensed his muscles to cancel out the trembling left over from his nightmare and sanded away at his gooseflesh with a corner of his rough wool blanket.

The wool left him itchy, so he threw off the blanket and tossed his legs over the side of the bunk. He stared at the puke-green tile, speckled in black and red. *Dream or reality? Which was it?*

The cold deck against his feet told him. No dream, but a nightmare. A nightmare of reality. A reality that literally did bite. If you were a Force Recon Marine convicted of misconduct on the battlefield. Today in the courtroom, reality had devoured him in gulps, a great white thrashing in the water, the better to saw off his body parts. By night, it nibbled him to death in his nightmare, like ducks with shark's teeth.

This very afternoon the judge had delivered the court-martial verdict with his name on it. *Guilty.*

A word to rewrite a life.

All he had ever been, either in the eyes of others or in his own opinion, meant nothing. All that he had ever wanted to be and all he had ever expected to be was lost, stuck away on a shelf out of reach, out of sight. If only he could get it out of his mind too. He could not. Because he'd known he was guilty before the judge had told him.

He walked to the doorway, his feet making less noise than a stalking cat. He shook his head in disgust. Once he had been proud to walk silent as any warrior in the line of his family all the way back to Heavy Runner and beyond. What did it matter now? If the military judge sentenced him to Fort Leavenworth, the lineage of pure Blackfeet warriors would end behind bars. All this time in the Marine Corps. All the fighting on foreign soil. All the tempering of his spirit both in the rites of his people and in battle. All his striving to live up to the heroic deeds of his ancestors, all forfeit in one moment of stupidity.

Instead of honoring those ancestors, he had shamed them. Instead of advancing a fighting tradition, he had buried it beneath an avalanche of his disgrace.

Guilty.

He opened the door to his bachelor enlisted quarters room. True to his word, the judge had not stationed guards outside the BEQ. Night Runner's defense lawyer, a Navy JAG officer, had asked that he be released from custody. The judge had granted the ensign's motion. Night Runner was free until sentencing tomorrow—he looked at his watch—make that later today. His last day of freedom if the judge gave him hard time in the brig.

Probably not. The judge was soft. If Night Runner were judging himself, he would have thrown his own ass in jail. Let himself sweat it out for a couple of years before even passing sentence.

He began to ease the door shut, but suddenly didn't feel like being a Blackfeet warrior any longer. He did not deserve to be one. So he slammed the hatch and strode back to his rack, the soles of his feet slapping the pukey tile, walking in the white man's style.

He picked up his uniform from the deck where he had tossed it. For a moment he felt drenched in a wash of shame. As a Marine noncom he should not tolerate such a disgrace to the uniform, either from one of his men or from himself.

Maybe he did not even deserve to be a Marine either. Better they sentence him to death. Give him a dishonorable discharge. Line him up before a firing squad. He wondered, *Did they do that anymore?*

He shook his head. No. Not in a summary court-martial. Only a general court-martial conviction carried the death penalty. The summary court? It was little more than a glorified captain's mast.

In fact, nobody had even been in the courtroom but four people: Night Runner, the judge, his defense lawyer, and a reluctant prosecutor—the trial counsel. The grizzled Marine major treated him more gently than he should have been. If *he* had been the prosecutor . . .

No. He should take his JAG lawyer's advice, he told himself. *Stop beating yourself up,* the ensign had told him. *It gets you nowhere.*

Besides, the ensign assured him, the court-martial was a formality, a way of handling a report of misconduct under the legal system. "The Department of Defense can't sweep the incident under the rug," the ensign had said.

Night Runner had trouble taking the man seriously, first because he was barely a man at that. If he shaved more than twice a month, it was overkill. The kid looked like a high school sophomore, manager of the volleyball team at best—the girl's volleyball team at that.

"Because of the satellite pictures, people know about it," the ensign said, the light from behind his face turning his peach fuzz into a facial halo. "The whole thing could blow up into a scandal. People could say it was a cover-up. So they examine the evidence. The Corps orders an Article 32 investigation. A summary court tries the facts. For all we know, the judge will toss the rap on a technicality. No harm, no foul. Your personnel jacket squeaks. You'll be back in the field with your Force Recon team in a week. In a month, everybody will forget about it."

I won't, Runner thought.

The ensign failed to notice a pall rising to darken Runner's already dark complexion. "If somebody drags up the issue later, there'd be no grounds for any legal action because double jeopardy would attach—in layman's terms—" The ensign caught himself. "—Sorry, I'd forgotten you've been to law school. You already know that you can't be tried twice for the same offense."

Night Runner sighed. *You don't get it, Ensign.* "This kind of thing. It shouldn't be swept under the rug."

The ensign shrugged. "It's not going to be. I told you how the system is going to handle it. It's perfectly legal."

"Not perfectly. *Technically.* Your word."

The ensign bit one corner of his lower lip. "Fine, if that's how you want to think about it."

"That's not how I want to think about it."

The ensign cocked his head. *What then?*

"I want to plead guilty," Night Runner said.

"Are you out of your mind?"

"The ensign means, 'Are you out of your mind, Gunnery Sergeant Night Runner?'"

"Okay, are you out of your mind, Gunnery Sergeant Night Runner?" A flash of pink brightened the boy's peachy cheeks. "You don't have to plead guilty. The burden of proof will be on the prosecution. I'll argue that you were dealing with a disciplinary problem under battlefield conditions. I have Friel's record, military and civilian. A bad actor like that, you couldn't be expected to operate under the same standards that troops in garrison—"

"With all due respect, Ensign—"

"Don't give me that crap, Gunny. Every time a Marine tells me he means all due respect, he's pulling my chain because he doesn't even have a leaky piss-pot's worth of respect for me. So don't screw with me."

"Yes, Sir," said Night Runner, finding new, true, respect for the young Navy officer. Still, he was not going to back down. "I did what I was accused of doing. I did it knowingly. It was not a mistake. I did try to teach a man a lesson. It doesn't matter that Henry has a history. I used improper methods. Methods that might of been good in the frontier Army or the Civil War Navy. Not in today's Marine Corps."

The ensign shook his head. "You know that. I know that. Everybody else knows it, but under combat conditions, we don't second-guess the troops in the field. *What*? What are you shaking your head about?"

"My captain was in the field, and he knows it. The man I mistreated in the field knows it. The private who was on the mission with us—in the field—knows it. I would rather go back to my Force Recon team as an honest man with a conviction for using bad judgment than somebody who got over on the system by a technicality."

The ensign stared at him a long time before he said, "If you get the conviction, you may not be going back to your unit at all. Ever think of that?"

Night Runner had thought of it. *May not be going back.* Hearing the words spoken struck him speechless.

"Gunny, I'm trying to understand where you get your ideas. Is this a Marine thing or an Indian thing?"

Night Runner could not bring himself to say the words: *No, it is a thing of honor.*

Honor. As a way of doing business, honor had gotten its pink slip. In politics, honor belonged only to the stump speeches and party platforms. In the military, honor meant something.

Or was that only among the fighting services? Didn't the young man understand the concept? Or was it that lawyers, uniformed or not, used honor as a mere legal strategy?

Come to think about it, what was honor? Nothing more than a word to defile? Did nobody live it anymore?

Night Runner tried to search the ensign's soul, gazing deep into his eyes. How could he expect somebody so young and inexperienced to get it? Among lawyers, the practice was to decide all things using technicalities. The kid had said as much. Lawyering was the ability to express things by a shading of words and roundabout reasoning, to see things the way the lawyer wanted to see them. Not this kid's fault. He thought the way the law schools had taught him.

Night Runner had spent enough time in Yale's law program himself to learn it before he dropped out. He had intended at one time—a time less cynical than now—to practice law on the Northern Montana reservation on behalf of his tribe. To do that he would have had to put aside all notions of decency. No matter what the truth, you had to argue the position that you were paid to argue.

Faced with that, he had refused, turning down a whopping scholarship that would have funded his final year, paid off his other school loans, and financed his living expenses as a clerk to a federal judge in Montana. Back on the rez, his friends had mocked him for turning his back on the payola. So he had stopped going back to the rez, except when he could visit quietly to talk to the elders, to learn from those who had the medicine, who knew the ways, especially those who would teach him.

Back at Yale, he had looked for truth in history, but found only the truth that the winners of wars had written. He had studied science and economics. The few truths he did believe there, he found pointless. So he had tried languages, four of them. French and Spanish were no more truthful than English. Latin and Greek at least let him read the classics unfiltered through other tongues.

In the end, he found a sixth language, Pikuni, his native tongue, taught to him by Oscar Deep Snows, a sub-chief, whose parents had refused to speak English to him. Snows had gone to a school of the Black Robes, the Jesuits, who beat him when he tried to speak his native tongue. So he had learned both languages by total immersion, without reference from one language to the other. He spoke in both. He said he could think in both. More than anything Night Runner had wondered about in his Ivy League schooling, thinking in his own language aroused his curiosity. He asked the old man—he could have been eighty or two hundred eighty—to teach him the language by immersion, the same way that Snows had learned it.

The old man laughed and said something to him in the language of the Blackfeet. Night Runner joined his mentor in the laugh. He did not understand the words as they were spoken to him, but he got the gist of what the old man had told him: *Fine, like it or not, that's what you're going to get.*

They never spoke English to each other again. From Snows, Night Runner learned how to speak and think in his native language. He found the way of the warrior, studying it not through books but through the teachings of the elders of the tribe. He learned that the truth, if he found it, would be in him and not in the world around him. Truth as he defined it would not be lived by others as they defined it.

Only if he denied the truth in himself could he be disappointed.

What he had learned had brought him to where he was at the moment, arguing with his lawyer about how to plead in court.

How could he explain it to the young man? To plead *not guilty* to a crime he did commit would be a lie. Such a lie would be the ruin of all that he had left after disgracing himself in the eyes of his ancestors. In his mind's eye, he saw them assembled on the horizon, the way Hollywood showed them before a mass suicide attack. In his vision, they were even more frightening. Not that they would attack, but that they had come to watch how he would behave under this trial of honor.

So he would not—could not—plead innocent.

He saw dismay in the eyes of the ensign. Runner knew he could not explain himself in a day or even a year. Perhaps not even if he sent the young officer to Snows to learn how to think like a Blackfeet warrior.

Some things could not be learned in a lifetime. So he told the man flatly, "I will plead guilty."

The ensign opened his mouth as if to argue, but decided against it.

IN COURT THAT day, the judge had acted as if he had someplace else to be, as if he expected to be there soon, when he asked, "How do you plead?"

The ensign answered. "Guilty, Your Honor." He made his face into an abashed grimace as if to add *honest*.

The trial counsel made a sound in his throat, as if he were about to object to a guilty plea, and barely stopped himself.

The judge stood up behind the bench and stamped one shoe as if trying to put out a hotfoot. "I beg your pardon?"

The ensign repeated himself. The prosecutor shook his head. The judge sat down and did not speak for a long time. When he did, it was a rambling lecture to the ensign, both chiding him for acting against the interests of his client and suggesting that the accused should speak up to say it had all been a mistake.

Night Runner saw what had happened. Between the lines. Behind closed doors. Beneath the technicalities. These three men, including the prosecutor, had spoken in secret council. They had decided what the outcome of this so-called trial would be even before the court had convened.

Night Runner was no virgin. He understood that lawyers and judges decided all trials, to some degree, in advance. Attorneys exchanged depositions, witnesses, and the evidence. They revealed their strategies. Unlike the Perry-Ironsides-Matlock-Mason television shows, surprises on the stand did not happen. Unlike the pulsating recent courtroom shows with lawyers so despicable as almost to be authentic, trials were uneventful, even boring, affairs.

Night Runner could see that in his case, they had decided to let him walk without even getting into the specifics of his behavior that night in the middle of an attack against an Iranian terrorist camp.

Too bad that he could not be as easy on himself. He had let down a fellow warrior in battle. That was his crime from the Blackfeet point of view. He had mistreated a man under his command—and that was his sin in the Marine Corps point of view.

He saw no technicalities to it. He would have to pay for his sins. He would have to do penance for his crimes. Let these men decide his punishment. To him, the issue of his own guilt spoke for itself. Owning up to his crime was part of the cleansing.

He had heard enough. He spoke up to spare the ensign any further reproach from the judge. "I plead guilty, Your Honor. My lawyer advised me otherwise."

The judge was on him like the bobcat pulling down the ruffed grouse from a low branch. "This is your idea of a joke then?"

"No joke, Your Honor."

"So you're not just testing the patience of the court?"

"No, sir," Night Runner said, for the judge was also a Navy captain.

"You truly want to plead guilty?" The judge practically

shouted the question, making no effort to hide the tone of *You moron, you.*

"Yes, Your Honor."

The judge turned his fury on him. Night Runner stood stiff, as if gazing at the horizon a kilometer away. The judge began to lash him, not with the whip, but with his tongue. Night Runner knew that he deserved it, and this too was part of his atonement. When the judge saw that he could not make him change his plea, the captain spoke to him as if he were an ingrate for not playing along with the legal game. Night Runner nodded his understanding. This was the white man's game, this way of thinking. He would not play it, no matter what the cost, because at the moment, he was thinking in Pikuni.

Finally, the judge tired of it too.

"Guilty," he barked. "I sentence you to—"

"Your Honor," the ensign blurted.

The judge turned on him, "You want me to sentence you as well, mister? For contempt?"

"No, Your Honor. I beg the court to postpone sentencing—"

"Why? Are you planning even more surprises?"

"No, sir. I'd like to arrange for character witnesses to speak on the sergeant's behalf before the court passes sentence."

The judge wanted to deny the request. He wanted to rap Night Runner's knuckles. And hard. Now, while he still had the fire in his belly. Night Runner could see it, and he thought it a good strategy for his lawyer to ask for a delay. Even if nobody spoke on his behalf, it was a good idea. Better the judge render his sentence after he cooled off. Atonement was one thing. No reason Runner should be a masochist. No reason to invite abuse from a testy judge.

The ensign might be pissed at his client for not taking legal advice. He would not allow him to be thrown into the brig in a fit of judicial anger.

A good kid, Night Runner thought, regretting his first appraisal. Too bad he wasn't a Marine. He'd be the type Night Runner would want to have on his Force Recon team—if he ever had a Force Recon team again.

NIGHT RUNNER SQUINTED at himself in the mirror above the sink in the one-room BEQ. Was he just feeling sorry for himself again? Was it because the court had accepted his guilt? Or because he was an idiot for insisting that ruthless honor be his judge instead of a Navy captain?

He could not say. So he slapped at the wrinkles in his uniform and pulled his cap down over his brow. He would walk. Walk until dawn. Or even forever.

Maybe by staying in motion like the whale shark filtering plankton, he could sieve something more substantial than guilt through his mind.

As he walked, he funneled his thoughts toward the team, where he wanted to be. Tomorrow the judge would determine whether the Marine Corps would allow him to stay. After that, he would have to deal with Force Recon. Would his command want somebody like him on their sensitive missions?

What about his team leader, Captain Swayne?

What would he think?

UZBEKISTAN
10SEP01—0230 HOURS LOCAL

AS FAR AS Marine Captain Jack Swayne was concerned, the Marine Corps was out of its mind. Breaking up his Force Recon team. Putting perhaps the best noncommissioned officer in the entire Defense Department on trial. Sending his best shooter off on rehab furlough. Sending him and Greiner here to hell.

The sun had a ways to go before it could get up over the horizon and scale the mountains that were Afghanistan to the south and east. Swayne and his tiny detachment of misfits and mismatches had camped in a gulch within a wadi inside a coulee nestled in a valley bleaker than death.

Swayne had been inside Iraq, Iran, Saudi Arabia, and North Africa, as well as the Canadian Rockies and the mountains bordering Death Valley—inviting in contrast to this. He had never seen anything so jagged and barren as Afghanistan. On the map, the tiny brown contour lines lay so closely massed they looked solid. The lines, showing the steepness of the inclines and irregularity of the topography, ran into each other as if somebody had spilled a can of brown paint and swirled it around with his fingers.

From the air, the terrain looked like rubble. As the plane had come in for landing, Swayne doubted the C-141 could find a stretch of level ground long enough to put off him, his team, their equipment, and the platoon of Marine regulars that would provide security.

On the ground by day, as he looked into Afghanistan from Uzbekistan, the ground lay jumbled. He felt half-dizzy, as if watching an earthquake in progress, except without the movement.

As he stood in the dark outside the squad tent that he and Greiner shared with the three scientists, he was glad that he did not have to look at the chaos of the land. It was too much to see the boulders stacked on boulders, landslides lying dormant—temporarily—on top of avalanches. Cliffs looked like skyscraper walls on mountainsides, ready to peel away and topple to reveal new cliffs. Peak after peak, each one scraping the sky a little deeper, stacked up toward the interior of the terrorist Taliban country, a land so fierce that only fierce people could inhabit it.

At least when he was inside the tent, he was dealing with chaos of his own without having to see it displayed as reality.

Chaos was sending him and one green Marine with only a single combat mission under his belt into possibly the most hostile territory on the globe. This was their jumping-off point, Uzbekistan, on the border with Afghanistan—if anybody could identify where the border was. For all he knew, he already stood deep inside the Taliban badlands. The way these tribal bandits and militias figured—and there was no way to tell the difference between the good, the bad, and the ugly—even a well-defined boundary was up for grabs. Was the line the center of a river? The left bank or the right? If the stream flooded, did the boundary move too? If it dried up, where did the border then go?

Hell, everything in this land was up for grabs. The cheapest commodity of all was life.

Even so, just being in a hostile territory didn't bother him. He and his team had spent a good part of the last two years of their lives sneaking into places where they were not wanted and, often as not, fighting their way out. As long as they were well armed and watching each others' backs, they had survived. Except for a few setbacks, including two very terrible ones, they had accomplished all their missions and left the field of battle with both honor and their skins.

Now he and Greiner had landed in south central Uzbekistan with a trio of tekkies and a Conex shipping container full of military toys to test under field conditions. They had bounced in trucks to within mortar range of the border with Afghanistan. A conventional Marine platoon would provide security as the two Spartans helped the scientists with their high-tech, highly classified experiments.

Swayne had been around the block a few times. He knew there was more to this than just field experiments. This was an excuse to get his Force Recon team—the half of it left intact—out of the States while Night Runner faced his court-martial.

The Marine Corps did not want him and Greiner around to testify, either for or against. They didn't want character witnesses to impede the wheels of justice. In fact, they really didn't need witnesses—satellite pictures could give all the testimony required in a top-secret trial by court-martial. The fewer the witnesses and participants, the less likely any details would be overheard by some nosy journalist trolling for tidbits in the bars outside the gates of bases. Beyond that, the Corps just wanted a serious problem to go away, never to be brought into the open, even after top-secret files were declassified fifty years hence.

Talk about serious. Swayne's Force Recon Team 2400, the Spartans, had gone into Iran on its last mission to strike at a terrorist encampment and training ground. Just one of a dozen around the world that were to have been hit the same night. Swayne's team had gotten one of the low-priority targets. The team had gone in at less than top form, nursing wounds from a previous mission.

Not all of the damage carried into Iran by members of his team was either physical or visible. Sergeant Henry Friel had developed an attitude problem. Night Runner, the team's top noncom, had decided to give him an attitude adjustment. When Friel became belligerent toward Greiner, Night Runner had disabled him with a blow to the head. He had tied him up so he could watch the battle but not participate, probably a more severe punishment than any court-martial could levy.

They had set up to strike at a camp full of amateur terrorists sleeping off a feast. It should have been a day at the fish barrel for his team.

But a band of real terrorists, led by one of the world's most notorious leaders, had tried to infiltrate the camp just as the Spartans struck it. Moments after the team had triggered the ambush, the terrorists snatched the helpless Friel. Leaving Swayne's Force Recon team to risk their lives to recover him. In the end, the terrorists had shot Swayne through the chest. Friel came back a shell of himself. The terrorists had tortured him in a way that the term *post-traumatic stress syndrome* did not do justice to.

Worse, he had felt betrayed by his own kind.

The team's secret had stayed under wraps, Friel not willing to report it, insisting he would not testify to it if it were brought to a court. Swayne had wrestled with his conscience. As an officer, it was his duty to report such misbehavior of a noncommissioned officer toward a subordinate.

Swayne had agonized for days. He'd let himself put off the decision while his wounds healed in the hospital. Afterward, he took medical furlough, promising to file his report later.

When he returned to duty, he called a one-on-one with Night Runner to tell him he'd made the most gut-wrenching decision of his life. Before he could say it, the gunny took him off the hook. He had made his own decision, and Swayne could not sway him from it.

"Captain, I have to report this. If they ever look at the satellite imagery in detail, they'll find out. They'll come down hard. Not only on me, but you. Because you knew about it and didn't do anything." For Night Runner, the speech was a long one, the gunny's equivalent of a State of the Union Address.

Swayne argued. "I could talk to Colonel Zavello. He could give me some advice, maybe let me have a look at the imagery first—"

Night Runner shook his head. "Okay, sir, forget the imagery. There's more to it than worrying about my getting busted. It's me—my duty. I can't carry this around. I can't risk your career—"

"Not your job to worry about my career."

Night Runner drew his lips into a tight line and clamped down on them from inside his mouth. He would not add defiance to his sins. "You're right. I'm not out to save your career. I'm doing this for me alone." He held out both hands, fingers splayed, clenching his gut to force out the tempered words that lay at the core of a Marine's soul. Words to live by. Words to die by. Words so cher-

ished where they rested in the heart. Words defamed by
any Marine who needed to speak them in self-defense.
"My—personal—honor."

Swayne nodded. He understood honor, of course.
Honor was a word that had lost its meaning in the civilian
world, if it ever existed there. Night Runner had to redeem
himself by first restoring his honor. Swayne could do
nothing to stop him. More than that, he must do nothing.

So Night Runner reported himself, and the system went
to work on him.

Zavello had grabbed Swayne, literally snatching the
front of his shirt. Swayne winced, not fully recovered
from a bullet to the chest.

Zavello released him, a curse word his apology. "You
couldn't talk any sense into the man? You couldn't get
him to withdraw his statement? Amend it? Anything?"

Swayne, his chest still smarting, shrugged.

Sending the one-eyed colonel into a spasm of rage, his
speech spraying mist into the air around Swayne, his
string of obscenities salted with barely half-a-dozen non-
curse words.

When he had finished, his good eye looked as if it
might squirt out of his skull. White froth edged his lips.
His pained expression was itself a curse word.

Swayne told Zavello the brief truth that ended in only
the one word: *honor*.

Leaving Zavello speechless. Whatever else Zavello
was, he was, first of all, a Marine. He understood honor.
End of discussion.

Or so Swayne thought. How could the end of discussion be Night Runner's conviction? No telling what courts
would do. What chance would Night Runner have with
his own statement to condemn him? How could he get
off with only a military lawyer to defend him, some kid
just out of ROTC?

Swayne thought he might as well face it. He would

have to put together a new Force Recon team. One without Night Runner. How could he do that? He had always preached that no one man was indispensable, least of all himself. In his heart he'd always known it to be an empty maxim. He could name the exception to his own rule. Its name was Gunnery Sergeant Robert Night Runner.

The man could track anything, even insects. Swayne had watched him do it, had knelt on the ground as Night Runner pointed out the marks with a straw of grass. "Spider," he had said.

Night Runner had followed it for six feet, Swayne watching in disbelief. Then Swayne knelt down beside him again when Night Runner beckoned. Under a magnifying glass, he watched as the straw flipped over a leaf of sage. As a spider no bigger than the primer on a round of 5.56mm ammunition reared back on its legs, ready to fight the two monsters hovering over it.

Once an officer had a man like that in his platoon, he knew the meaning of words like vital, crucial, key, essential—and, yes, indispensable. Night Runner could navigate without electronic devices, see in the dark, and walk without lights at night. He could detect the enemy by his smell, and take off his head with that sword he had carried since Iraq. How did you settle for anybody else? If he was not indispensable, then Swayne thought Force Recon should send at least two men to replace him.

And Friel. Once they had finally gotten clear of Iran, it didn't take a psychologist to see that Friel was damaged goods. All you had to do was look at the wildness in the eyes of the kid from Boston. Swayne wondered if he could ever heal, if he would ever return.

He knew Friel was on medical furlough—*psycho-pass,* the man called it. He doubted Friel would ever return to active duty. How could he ever get a clean mental exam? No, Swayne decided, Henry would never return.

BENEATH THE STREETS OF BOSTON
09SEP01—1837 HOURS LOCAL

AFTER HE RETURNED home to the mean streets of Boston, Henry Friel had begun riding the subway system daily because he liked the atmosphere. Lately, he lived on the MTA, riding daily ever since the moment he heard the Kingston trio sing about it on a golden oldies radio station.

Well, did he ever return? No, he never returned, and his fate is still unknown. . . . He may ride forever 'neath the streets of Boston, he's the man who never returned.

As he rode, Friel sang it to himself, swaying from side to side with the car's motion. Amazing. The train rocked in time with the tune inside his head.

Whoa! What would the boys in the hood think about him thinking things like that? *A-a-ah-h-h-h-h, screw them.* Anyways that was better to think about than the other things that kept scurrying through his head like rats in a sewer.

For instance, the question that he woke up today with on the tip of his head: *How many people did you have to kill before you were a serial killer?* He didn't want to think about it, but he figured four. Two was too few. Three would be a triple homicide. Once you got to quadruple homicide, the words got too long. *What, octagonal-homicide? Nah.*

From three on, the term serial killer covered all the ground from four to four hundred.

No matter what the number, from what he had seen on the court shows on television, he would—

No, not him, *man. He* was not the serial killer, *they* were. He was just thinking of for instances. *They* would have to be enough to establish a pattern. Did that mean *they* had to kill each victim the same way? No, probably not. Richard Ramirez had varied his technique from victim to victim. A little variety was the spice of death for him.

Speaking of patterns, did the victims have to look alike? Did crimes have to be committed within the same area? Were you a serial killer if the cops never put it together that the same person killed all the victims? *Shit, man*, he had to admit. If he—*anybody*—was going to get into that game, *they* had a lot to learn.

Poor Charlie. In the song, he couldn't afford to get off the train. For the want of a nickel, he had to ride the MTA forever.

Friel had a pocketful of money. Yet he couldn't afford to get off the train either. Not for the want of a nickel, but for fear of himself. So he rode it day after day, worried he might never return to the Marines. Riding, riding, every day from morning till midnight.

Did he ever return? No, he never returned, and his fate is still unlearned. Poor-er Henry boy. He's the man who never returned.

NORTHWEST AFGHANISTAN
10SEP01—0805 HOURS LOCAL

"SHIT!"

Swayne's Force Recon team used a well-practiced system of one-word codes to alert each other about the presence and severity of danger from an enemy. Not including *shit*.

Since he and Greiner huddled in the close confines of an observation post inside Afghanistan, Swayne granted himself the lapse in discipline.

Greiner and Swayne sat back-to-back so they could watch in a complete three-sixty. Greiner kept still, so as not to alert an enemy by a sudden movement. His response was merely a whisper into a boom microphone he kept at kissing distance from his lips.

"Sir?"

Swayne granted himself a smirk. If Greiner kept it up, he would soon be a better Force Recon soldier than his boss. For now, both of them had better get good at being odorless and fast.

Because half a mile below them, a squad of men had appeared from behind the boulders. Bouncing ahead of them, a dog darted along a trail hidden by the boulders and rubble of the slope. It had the long hair of a goat and the mane of a lion. It lifted its leg to pee on every rock, plentiful as they were, and to mark every bush, sparse as they were. At the rate it made water, the dog would dehydrate itself into a prune by noon. Swayne wished he'd already done so, because by noon, the animal would have wrecked their little mission.

Hours earlier, Swayne had ducked back inside the tent, and pinched the soft plastic flashlight clipped to his uniform pocket. The device was no larger than his thumb and less than half as thick, all battery and a red lens. The glow lit up Corporal Nathaniel David Greiner.

"Sir, I'm up, Captain, sir," Greiner said. He sat at the edge of his cot, hunched over his boots, cinching the laces.

One hell of a Marine, Swayne thought. So earnest. A slave to his training, steady in combat. Greiner never faltered. Swayne felt bad for the kid. Usually, a trained Force Recon Marine came to the team on trial, hoping that he would not let down the unit. In Greiner's case, on their last mission, Swayne had to wonder: *Wasn't it the unit that had let the kid down?* If so, Greiner had class, never letting on that the Spartans failed him.

Swayne and Greiner left the three scientists sleeping, and together slipped through one of the Marine security force guard posts to cross half a dozen gulches, wadis, coulees, and a couple of valleys, one or two ridges, and a mountain. They went as deep into Afghanistan as the darkness allowed. Then, at before morning nautical twi-

light, about an hour before sunrise, they holed up to watch
the day go by. Hidden by camouflage and the shade, they
looked for any terrorists from the Al Qaeda network or
members of the Taliban military, considered terrorists as
well.

Unless Swayne and Greiner screwed up, there would
be no fighting. The idea was simply to see whether any
enemy troops from Afghanistan had learned of the landing
of Swayne's group in Uzbekistan. He didn't want anybody trying to infiltrate the tiny encampment just three
miles beyond the border between the two countries. He
didn't want anybody setting up to toss mortars or rockets
their way.

Now they had the dog to deal with. Swayne shook his
head. No matter how well he prepared, no matter how
many contingencies he set his mind to avoiding, his enemies never stopped surprising him. Roseanne Rose-
annadanna came to mind: *It's always something.*

Swayne did not care so much that the men had come.
His job was to see without being seen. The mission was
a simple S&W recon, sit and watch. Take note of what
went on within sight and sound. Report any activity or
any lack of activity, which was also significant. Overhead,
satellites would collect data, and the human intelligence,
HUMINT, would be compared and contrasted with the
SATINT to establish a baseline for tomorrow night's
scheduled trial of the drone intelligence craft.

So, the men were no problem. The problem was the
fickle breeze blowing across the Spartans' shoulders,
carrying their scent down the slope. The dog might pick
up the scent. Swayne had worked with a dog himself two
missions ago. He could assume that the men below were
not out aimlessly walking their pet goat. He saw how it
worked ahead of them as a scout. When it picked up the
strange smell of intruders from another culture, the dog
would be a problem.

They had been in position for less than two hours.

Swayne had chosen a prime tactical site before they had even left the tiny, half-military, half-civilian, half-assed camp inside Uzbekistan. On his digital topo map, he had picked a ridgeline that would give them a view of as much of Afghanistan's territory as the washboard terrain would allow.

Swayne's mind ran through the options open to him. During his mission planning, he had already mulled every risk, including getting spotted by the enemy. During the march to this spot, he had reviewed every aspect of the mission again, then again. He'd had a lock on it by the time they arrived. No patrol would catch them here— unless they showed up with a dog. He wanted to kick himself in the fanny pack for overlooking that contingency, but that wouldn't help. Surprises were the fortunes of combat. Events always overtook plans. No matter how well a leader scripted things in advance, the best-laid mission planning went to the dogs on enemy contact.

A quiet voice in his head told him to relax. The voice reminded him that he'd made his name as a combat leader, not in the planning of missions, but in the execution. He'd never frozen in the face of a sudden turn of events. He'd always steeped himself in the tactical situation, left himself options, war-gamed it in his head. Hit by changes, he never had to stop and think. Men marveled at his instant ability to adjust to the flow of battle. Nothing instant about it, and nothing instinctual. He'd already done the thinking. So well that an idea always cropped up between one option or another. All he had to do was act on it.

Still, Swayne wondered: What would Night Runner do in a pinch like this? Night Runner. For the thousandth time since setting off in the dark at 0309 hours—nine damned minutes late—he wished he had the Blackfeet warrior with him. Swayne couldn't name any kind of scrape where Night Runner would not be his first choice of a fighter at his side. Runner not only understood the workings of the natural world. He was part of the natural landscape. Runner wouldn't have let him start off nine damned minutes late.

Swayne shook his head to put the gunny out of his mind. He did not have Night Runner. He had Greiner. And himself. Feeble though it might be, he was going to have to work with the hand dealt by events. He'd have to cope with the dog and those ten men. ASAP.

His options? He reviewed them once more, factoring in the dog. Could he and Greiner hold and wait, hoping that the fickle breezes would carry their scent away? Was it possible that, even if the dog scented them, the breezes down below them would be swirling, so the animal could not locate them?

Swayne shook his head. Now was not the time to depend on luck to save them from contact. That was like trying to get a mortgage by using a fistful of lottery tickets as collateral. Life didn't unfold that way, even if plenty of people functioned—or dysfunctioned—under such false hopes. Most people could afford to. In civilian life, believing in fairy tales didn't get you killed. Here in Afghanistan, hoping for the best might well have ten guns, including the two light machine guns he'd tallied, pouring bullets on him and Greiner as if the enemy were watering a garden with fire hoses.

He considered springing an ambush. He and Greiner had the firepower to take out at least half the force below before they could hit the ground and orient themselves. Swayne had picked more than one ambush killing zone already after first light this morning. In less than a minute, the soldiers below would walk into an open area. If things went right for him and Greiner, none would walk out.

Not an option that he wanted to take a chance on either. If it came to a fight, he and Greiner could hit them hard, extract themselves from their fighting positions, primary, alternate, and tertiary. They had already chosen those.

What they could not know was how many other such

squads were within hearing distance of the ambush. He didn't want to commit to a firefight with so much daylight left to the enemy for fire and maneuver.

No, if a fight could be avoided that would be best.

Could they extract themselves, creeping along one of their preselected escape routes? They would have to go uphill. Only about ten meters. Thirty feet of crawling, keeping boulders between them and the khaki-dressed soldiers below. Greiner would go first, trying to get to the ridgeline while Swayne provided security. Then Greiner would cover Swayne's move. That would put them in position to get away, unless the dog scented or spotted them.

That dog. Face facts and deal with the dog.

It could track them. Perhaps it was trained to do just that. If so, they couldn't run fast enough or long enough to escape it.

Swayne put the crosshairs of his telescopic site on the animal. He and Greiner were lightly armed. Greiner carried the experimental light machine gun called the BRAT, a 5.56-mm knockoff of the famous 7.62-mm M-60, a workhorse of the Vietnam War. Swayne carried a modified M-16, the M-4 "chunker," which could toss 40-mm grenades from the tube beneath the barrel. The name came, not from the sound of the exploding HE rounds, but the noise it made when it spat the grenade, about the diameter of an ordinary saltshaker. The gun's rifle barrel and firing action were milled to tight tolerances. Up to five hundred meters, about a third of a mile, it was almost as accurate as any sniping rifle.

So. Shoot the dog?

Not now, Swayne decided. The animal still hadn't picked up the scent. Maybe he could hope for the best and still prepare for the worst. At least for another minute or so, as the squad approached the killing zone of the ambush site.

He scoped the men one at a time, recording their images on the digital vidcam in his rifle sight. They looked as if they'd crawled out of a sack of homemade jerky, tough, dark, irregular. There wasn't a spare ounce of fat in the whole squad. Tough customers, lean, hard, and bearded, with no uniformity in dress. They traveled light, with weapons, canteens—and what he did not want to see among them, portable radios. He could see at least three handhelds, and perhaps two digital telephones attached to pack straps. Not good. Too much commo to take out—somebody would put in a call to the cavalry before all the radios could be put out of action.

He saw signs of discipline in the group. No chatter. No smoking or joking. Swayne guessed they were Al Qaeda fighters. If only—

Swayne shook his head. Maybe, just maybe they wouldn't have to.

"Greiner," he murmured into the boom mike, "I'm going to paint these guys. No shooting unless I say." They sat close enough to speak to each other without the radio, but Swayne used the radio as a way to send a report to higher headquarters. His radio scrambled his words digitally and shot the data to an overhead satellite. The KY-19 satellite compressed the data and shot it as a burst from one relay station to another halfway around the world. The last satellite fired the data burst into a dish above a hole in the ground under Quantico, Virginia.

Swayne turned on the laser designator attached to the scope of his rifle. By default, it sent out an infrared beam invisible to the eye. On previous missions, both by day and night, he and his team had kept hidden while splashing the beam on targets, including terrorists like these. Overhead, bombers flying so high and so far away nobody could hear them, pickled their smart bombs. Two-thousand-pounders identified the spots on the targets below and flew down the chute to deliver their destruction, killing suddenly and completely, leaving no clue as to the source of the attack.

Until enemy leaders—dictators like Saddam Hussein—

turned on the television news and watched bombs streak onto the grainy television screens and obliterate buildings, bridges, convoys, and troop concentrations. Not many eyewitnesses had lived to tell about such lasers painting them. All they knew were the explosions, the Free World's version of the surprise terrorist strike.

Swayne switched to a visible beam, a high-tech flashlight that cast a candy-apple red spot no bigger than a nickel at a mile. He murmured his signal for Greiner to move out. Greiner tapped his teeth twice, rogering without words, and crept toward the ridgeline.

GREINER HAD BEEN with the outfit for only one previous mission, which had turned into two. The mission itself had had mixed results. Of course, the attack on the terrorist training site had been too easy. Over in five minutes of fighting. Piece of jake, to use one of Friel's expressions.

Friel. What a piece of jake he was. The terrorists had picked off Friel, carrying him away to the Iranian holy city of Masshad. The entire rest of the mission had been devoted to rescuing Friel, in keeping with the code of Force Recon.

He thought: *The people who had written the code? If they knew Friel? They'd rewrite it. They'd make an exception: Leave Friel behind; let him rot in hell.*

After they recovered Friel, the team no longer existed, except in name. Greiner wondered whether the unit would ever get squared away.

First the months of recovery for the captain. Physical healing followed by getting his body back into shape. Night Runner yanked away during his Article 32. Friel shipped off to the nutcrackers. Zavello had detailed Greiner to a training cadre. Greiner helped test Force Recon volunteers. Before long, he realized that the graduates who went out to join Force Recon teams would get more experience than him.

Hell, until now, he didn't think of this as a real mission. Even the name they gave it—Toys R Us—showed that nobody took it seriously.

Except now. With the enemy soldiers skipping across the desert below them. A thrill coursed through him. For months all he did was train or train somebody else. Finally, some action.

At Swayne's signal, he backed away from the fighting position. He put down the BRAT for a second and fitted the pack straps over his shoulders, snapping all the buckles so they fit snugly. Only after he was positive that he could freely move and shoot and fight did he change positions. Then he moved like a Force Recon Marine, sometimes crawling, sometimes walking like a duck, and sometimes, when he found boulders tall enough to shield him, running bent over, to get to the ridgeline. He moved the way Gunny Night Runner taught him. Quick, halting, each movement followed by a few seconds of freeze-frame. As his eyes scoped the area around him. So he might detect any enemy spotters. So he could see whether a flurry of activity from an enemy meant the shooting was about to start.

Thirty meters seemed like a long way to move that way. Finally, he eased over the ridgeline. He kept belly-crawling until he could be sure he was well out of sight of the enemy. Then he lay still, checking the other side of the ridge to be sure that nobody had sneaked up from that way.

Satisfied that their six o'clock was clear, he turned back toward the ridgeline. He showed his head at a spot different from where he had gone over the crest. Anybody who had seen him might have laid their crosshairs on that place. A sniper could be waiting for a head to stick up, ready to pull a trigger in an instant.

Greiner found the shady side of a boulder as big as a man's torso. He put his head into the shade and slowly, ever so slowly, raised his head until his eyes could look over. He poked the muzzle of the machine gun over the hill, keeping it in the shade too. Greiner adjusted and dusted the ammunition belt so it could fly through the action clear of grit. He shifted his body so he could lie spread-eagle. He welded the stock of the machine gun to his cheek, the plastic painted in the Dijon-mustard tones of the desert. He picked a group of soldiers below, and trained his gun at their knees. Night Runner would be proud of him. That Night Runner.

Always fire low, the gunny had told him. *When the muzzle rises with the recoil, the slugs will shoot through the target. If the men dive to the ground, they will be lying down in the beaten zone of the bullets.*

Greiner figured he would take out three of the enemy on his first burst—and decided it would be a long burst. He was ready. He confirmed to himself. He was ready to kill. Only then did he report to Swayne in a low voice.

"Spartan Four in position."

SWAYNE HAD ALREADY laid the red beam on a boulder to test it. The spot seemed bright enough but awfully small. Would the men notice it? Would they be able to spot the laser source and open fire, pinning him down in position here?

Swayne had already picked the terrorist honcho. He walked third in file. He carried both a digital telephone and a portable radio. His body language gave him away as the squad leader. He'd slung his rifle over one shoulder, while the men ahead of him carried their rifles at the ready as they walked point. They kept looking for danger, knowing they would be the first ones hit in an ambush, sure would lose the first feet and legs to a land mine. Swayne had known old point men and bold point men. But he'd never met any old, bold point men.

Behind him the men were more alert than their leader. In the rear, the last two men in the file turned, every ten meters or so, keeping watch to their six. He respected their vigilance, and dared not sell them short. They would be tough fighters.

More than any other reason Swayne ID'd the leader because he identified with him. The man stared at the ground as he walked, leaving the problem of safe travel to his men as he worked out problems that he'd have to face later today. He walked with the burden of the mission ahead, the logistics for tomorrow. Like Swayne, he had begun to mentally shape his report to his superiors, to think about next week's payroll, next month's recruiting goals, next year's terrorist target. Lucky for Swayne, he wasn't too worried about what to do if a Force Recon team sprang an ambush in the next few minutes or so.

Swayne splashed the red light on his chest. Nothing. So deep in thought was he that he did not notice it. So Swayne hit him on the bridge of the nose with the beam so bright that—

MUSTAFA HAZZAN ABU Saddiq swatted at his face, at first thinking a hornet had begun to harass him. Odd. His hand had passed through the hornet without feeling its touch. Saddiq heard no sound, felt no breeze of tiny wings. But of course it was no hornet, and he knew it within the next instant, when the fiery color slashed him a second time.

He dove for the ground, flattening among the pebbles, feeling stones dig into his ribs like knuckles. He drew breath to shout a warning. No warning necessary. The men behind him had seen and heard him flop to the ground. They needed no more. Not these battle-hardened veterans of the war against the infidels. They had fought all over Asia, and some of them had been across the waters into Africa and the Philippines. Even their training missions meant fighting with live bullets.

In seconds all ten men lay flat. Ten weapons pointed outward, like the spokes of a huge wheel. Exposed as they were, they could answer any attack from any direction. Nothing happened.

For a moment, Saddiq doubted himself. Had he imagined the spot of light? Or had there really been a hornet? He scanned half the horizon in front of him, a jagged, sloping, mountainous horizon. Nothing. He rolled and twisted, so he could look in the opposite direction. Again, nothing.

His skin prickled. This could embarrass him. One of the top lieutenants to Osama bin Laden lying on a patch of bare ground in the desert, hugging the earth? What would that look like when the stories of these idiots got around?

To make matters worse, the dog—that damned dog—thought it great sport that his party of ten had decided to lie down to roll in the dirt for a collective dust bath. He rejoined the group, moving from man to man, licking faces and sticking his nose into the crotches of their pants. Any other day, Saddiq would find it funny to watch the animal torment battle-hardened veterans. The dog could make them whine as well as its master, because the men knew that to lay an unkind hand on it would earn instant retaliation from Saddiq's own hand. But today was not a day of amusement.

With a grunt for a command, Saddiq got to his feet and ran twenty meters to the next boulder, half-expecting to hear a burst of fire. As he neared the boulders, he heard the noises of his men scrambling behind him. Muttering. Demanding to know what was going on. Asking if he had gone mad. Like all soldiers, grousing.

Saddiq took a monocular from his pack. Zeiss, ten-power, compact, and with a large objective lens that gave him a good field of view and superb detail. He swept the glass over the most dangerous ground, the ridgeline to his northwest. He found nothing out of place and began searching toward the south. Again, nothing.

He heard somebody gripe so loud he could not fail to hear: "Are we taking a break? Or is this a new way to pray?"

trained it himself at one of the chain of camps he'd had the responsibility to manage. Goat. He'd named the animal Goat. He should have left it at camp. The creature was too mild in dispostion, willing to track, but not to attack.

Saddiq felt his throat tighten. He ran faster. It would not do for one of the men to catch up to him and see him with tears in his eyes. The danger was too great that the man would tell the others. Saddiq could never explain the tears were not of fear, but for the dog named Goat.

So any man who saw him weeping would have to die. A loss Saddiq could not afford. For, at his core, he was in high spirits. All those who would die in the next thirty-six hours would be Americans. Reason for celebration.

SWAYNE HAD TO suppress a laugh. Inside, he felt giddy. Not because the terrorists looked so frightened, which they did. They had cleared the area like a cluster of Keystone Kops, the film running at twice normal speed. Leaving the dog.

The dog. It stood in the center of the ambush zone, barking. Not after its men. But on the alert, staring up the hill directly at Swayne and Greiner's position. It likely could not see them. For sure, it had their scent. The goat fur on its back stood up, so much so the animal now had a hump.

It looked away now and then, up the trail after the fleeing men, bewildered that its followers had not responded to his alarm.

Swayne switched off the laser light. He put the crosshairs of his scope between the animal's eyes—or where he guessed the eyes to be. Its hair covered the face with white dreadlocks, and only the black spot of a nose gave a clue that eyes might be two inches higher.

He debated. Then decided to let the dog live. Shooting the animal was problematic. The sound of a rifle shot would burst the bomb that he had planted in the terrorists' minds.

"Don't make a move," Swayne said into his microphone. "If it spots us, it might come looking. If not, it will probably follow its people back home."

"Wilco," said Greiner. Swayne half-smiled in appreciation. The kid was good. Never tempted to elaborate. Never cursing out his enemy or laughing at him at times like this. Unlike Friel, who always stood in the shade of mutiny.

Friel would have—

He wished he were here now. He wouldn't mind his chatter, his smart mouth, his maverick ways. He hoped the kid was doing all right.

BENEATH THE STREETS OF BOSTON
09SEP01—2213 HOURS LOCAL

FRIEL SAW THE trouble coming, but not until he had been left alone with it and vulnerable to it. The last of the late commuters on his car had stepped off onto the platform. They dashed toward their exits, their escalators and stairs, to climb up into the night, rats taking their race back home from the city in briefcases and bags.

Once the commuters had left, he was alone with the three bangers, who most definitely were not out to escape the tunnels. They were waiting for just the right mark at the right moment. Friel could see he was it.

He lay half across two seats, his arms folded on his chest, his eyes closed to a squint, as if drowsy.

He checked the car door. Still open. People still huddled at the funnel of the exit gates, pouring out of the station, squeezing their fat asses through the jaws of the toll gates. One guy's three-ax-handle butt looked like he was smuggling a pair of year-old babies in his pants. Was it just him, or had the entire civilian race gone over to blubber? Every day riding the subway he saw more ten-by asses than a freaking pig farmer.

Through his squint, he saw the three make their move, crossing over the aisle to seats on the opposite side, moving nearer to his spot. He still had time to dive out of the car. The computer voice announced the next stop. The doors creaked. He tensed himself to rush outside. As he did so, he saw the three getting ready to tackle him if he tried. They had pulled this gig before.

No longer the sleeping, helpless man, Friel smiled. He smiled widely. So. They wanted to get him. The way they had gotten others before. He might look disheveled, needing a shave and seeming slow, and slow-witted. He was anything but that. A Force Recon Marine did not turn to jelly in a month. Even a month of hard drinking, washing down a chain of bean burritos with Haig and Haig.

The door swished closed. Friel shook his head. The trap was sprung. Too late for the bangers to escape, even if they wanted to. His smile widened into a grin.

The wild grin triggered a moment's pause in the gang-bangers. Not that it had freaked them out. Just that it didn't seem normal for a mark to be smiling. Here was a guy who knew they'd begun closing in. Yet he did not run.

Could have been anything. Maybe the guy was a subway cop. Or a narc.

Or maybe he was just drunk, the stupid smile not a smile but a gas pain.

Whatever. It had set them back a moment in their thinking.

It gave Friel a moment to consider as well. He could sit up straight. Not act the victim. Not be the victim. They might—*might*—leave him alone.

He studied them through the slits in his vision. Nope. Not that. They were too young to have a good sense for danger, somewhere between thirteen and sixteen. Unlike the adults who had just left the car, these were not pig butts. They were lean, like weasels, their eyes darting in all directions, looking for danger from every quarter of the train and their man, especially their man. They studied him hard and without passion. He and they were insects. They wanted to see if he had any form of defense before they attacked. They waited until the car pulled away from the station. They would wait a moment longer, Friel supposed, until the train sheathed itself in the darkness of the tunnel. After only the lights inside the car lit them up. They would make their move and light him up.

So he moved first.

He stood up. Straight, so they could see he was not a drunk. He brushed off imaginary lint and straightened the creases in his clothing. For the first time in days, he saw how he looked. In the reflection of the window glass. He saw a slob. He smelled his own armpit and grimaced. If he didn't do something about himself, he was going to look like the pig butts off to home and their macaroni dinners. Having beer desserts in front of the boob tube, morons getting off on feeling superior to the weakest-link morons on the show.

Weak. No way for a Force Recon Marine to be.

"What kind of Marine you be? Forci-con?"

Friel frowned. Had he spoken aloud? Because the tallest of the three weasels had just asked the question. He could not know that he was a Marine unless Friel had just spoken his thoughts aloud.

"Force Recon Marine," he corrected.

The three of them began laughing among themselves, chattering in their street language, weaving and bobbing and sharing their secret handshakes as they flashed signs at each other. Making fun of him and getting up their blood all in the same dance ritual. All three wore baggy black denim jeans barely held up by chain-mail belts. Their only visible weapons, but weapons enough, thought Friel. If they started in whaling on him, it wouldn't take long to cut him to ribbons. Their jackets were blue denim, cut short along the waistline and meticulously, fashionably tattered. Their colors showed in the red bandanas tucked into the front of their pants behind their zippers, only a flash of fabric visible between the black denim and their boxer underwear, half-exposed.

Friel had to laugh. Except for the pants falling down, not much had changed since he was a street tough in this very town. He had not been a banger with this gang—he was too Irish for them. He recognized the handshake, the signs, and the colors. At times his group had been allies with them. At times they had fought them.

And now? Although he had stood up to do it, he did not want to fight them again after all. To do so would confirm that he was, after all, a weak link.

He wanted to fight, all right. But not them. He belonged in the Marine Corps. This civilian life, even on medical furlough, did not suit him. He would rather be on some base pulling kitchen duty. Aboard ship walking a post.

Of the more than one hundred times he had been in street fights and ambushes, both as ambusher and ambushee, all of them had seemed to be important. Until he went into the Marine Corps, choosing the uniform in lieu of a jail term.

Then, finally, when he had his first encounter in battle as a Force Recon Marine, every episode of street combat meant nothing. It wasn't the fighting that counted. It was being a strong link on a strong team.

Facing a fight now that he might never get out of, first because he had looked vulnerable, now because he looked belligerent, he realized he wanted to go back to where he belonged. He could only mend his head in uniform.

He realized that the leader of the trio had asked him a question. The banger had begun twitching, a kind of agitated new step to his dance. He didn't like something about Friel. Somehow Friel had dissed him.

Friel wondered if he could bluff his way out of trouble.

"What did you say? I didn't hear you. I was hearing the voices."

The kid was the oldest of the group, sixteen going on twenty-to-life. He stepped forward, strutting, bobbing, always keeping his hands near his belt buckle.

"Say what?"

"Voices. In my head. Some of them are telling me to run away, and I don't want to do that. Some of them are telling me to kill you, and I really don't want to do that."

The kid danced back a step. Off his stride just a little. Friel sized him up. He guessed that he had probably practiced every day, snatching that buckle loose, unsheathing the belt, and lashing out in a single, swift motion.

The kid spat a stream of insults and curses at him, daring Friel either to fight or flee.

Night Runner had told him once about facing down a mountain lion. You could not run from it. Flight triggered a predator's pursuit. Rather, you might stare the animal down. Or you might advance on it. Either way, you must be prepared to fight, but never must you flee.

Friel took a deep breath. He did not advance. Neither did he take his eyes from the weasel's hands. He merely waited.

"You deef?"

Friel cupped one hand to his ear. "Yeah, man, I've been around too much gunfire in the Marine Corps." If they knew he was a trained fighter, they might leave him alone.

The weasel continued to dance, back a step, forward two steps. Friel looked past him to the other bangers. They hung back. That was good. If all three of them got into his face, not just this slimeball, there might be too many hands, too many belts for him to get away unblooded. If he could deal with them one at a time—

He wondered what the captain would do. No, forget the captain. He was an officer. What would Night Runner do to get out of a scrape like this? How did you handle a

freaking mountain lion that just wanted to stand its ground
and talk trash?

SWAYNE STAYED IN position for another twenty
minutes, a full fifteen minutes after the dog ran after its
men. He did not want to move too soon and risk being
seen. If the squad of terrorists came back to check on the
dog, they might spot him. Since there would be no smart
bomb seeking to meet up with the laser spot, though, he
did not want to hang around if the Al Qaeda fighters resumed their original march.

Finally, he crept among the boulders toward the crest
of the ridge, moving along a different route than Greiner's. Once over the ridge, he rested for a few moments
as Greiner moved toward the first of a series of rally
points Swayne had briefed in his mission order. After that,
Swayne move past to the next point as Greiner covered
him. Leapfrogging past each other, the pair settled into a
secondary observation spot by mid-morning.

Where Swayne prepared for the most unpleasant task
of his day so far, the report to his one-eyed boss in the
Force Recon Operational Mission Command Center below ground at Quantico. Every ass-chewing from Colonel
Zavello, big or small, left its scar. No matter whether he
got a crocodile-size butt amputation or a simple leeching.
He never wanted to get into the water with either the
crocodiles or the leeches again.

Butt amputation. Funny. That was one of Friel's terms.

BENEATH THE STREETS OF BOSTON
09SEP01—2221 HOURS LOCAL

FRIEL KNEW HE must do his best to avoid a fight if he had any hope of staying in the Marine Corps. If he hurt one of those kids, they would find a way to make him regret it. Toughs like these knew the law because they had been in contact with it all their young lives. They knew freaking lawyers that would come after his ass to mug him in the courts. He wouldn't have a chance. They were black, he was white. They were young, he was an adult. They were street toughs, but he was a Force Recon Marine—they would say that, with his training, he should be declared a lethal weapon. They would sue him and the Marine Corps. Whether they won or lost, Friel would lose—the Corps would throw his ass out. He had to scam his way out of a fight.

He wished he had stayed sharp during his psycho-pass. The gunny had always tried to tell him to stay in shape. Friel had always thought the chief was, talking the talk of all noncoms. Night Runner—weird, but the chief was the one guy he wanted with him now. Maybe he could get out of this scrape alive and un-jailed. Get back to the team. Join up with Night Runner. Put all the other crap behind him. Maybe even apologize to the gunny.

"What you be looking at, Forci-con Mreen?"

Friel focused his eyes downward to the young man's chest. Staring a dude in the face was as much a sign of aggression on the streets as it was among the animals in the wild.

Friel became aware that his own body looked ready for a fight, body squared, feet wide apart, knees bent, fists balled. He relaxed his hands and shifted his body to the diagonal, letting his shoulders droop, fixing his eyes on the windows of the moving car. He let his body sway with the car's motion. Keeping it cool, going with the flow.

Of course, he could not cower either. That would be seen as a sign of weakness and encourage these shark pups to attack. So Friel watched in the reflection of the glass. Most of all he watched the hands of the one closest to him. The kid's left formed a fist, the thumb hooked into his waistband near his hip. With the right hand, he pointed toward Friel's face with one of those gangster-rap gestures, forearm vertical, wrist cocked, half a fist, with the little finger and forefinger pointing at him, thumb bent like the hammer of a pistol.

Without changing his position, Friel pulled his head away from the pointing fingers, as if yielding. Again, without cowering.

The lead weasel turned his own head toward his mates. They still had not decided whether to take on Friel. There didn't seem to be a reason to—he was unshaven, dressed in a threadbare red-and-blue-squared flannel shirt, the sleeves too short, several buttons missing, the collar rumpled. He wore blue jeans so tattered any mother—even his own—would have thrown them away. He carried his Department of Defense identification card in his shirt pocket, so there was no bulge of a wallet anywhere on his body. He did have cash, six fifty-dollar bills in his right front pocket and the change from another one in his left front. It didn't show. He did not look like a good robbery target. Now, if only he didn't piss them off. Maybe he could get off this train without a fight.

Nope, not to be. The pair in the background tossed their heads slightly. *Go on,* they were telling the lead weasel, *bust him.*

Friel acted on the command as quickly as any of the three, stealing the initiative from them.

The lead weasel's hands shot toward his belt buckle. The one thing that Friel could not let happen. They could not thrash him out of his wits with the three lengths of chain mail that they wore around their waists.

The kid was fast with his hands, but he had left himself open to attack by getting in so tight with Friel. He left himself without room to defend. His hands worked the buckle loose and slid the snake of linked metal from his pants loops.

Friel gained a second by faking the kid out by opening his eyes and giving him a look of terror. The kid fell for it. He had seen it before, likely many times. Friel stepped in, pointing his left arm from shoulder to fingertip. The banger shrieked as Friel's fingertips hit him in the eyes like the fangs of a striking snake.

The kid put his hands to his face, yanking up the stainless steel belt. On the recoil of his strike, Friel yanked the belt from the kid's hands, raking it across one of the thug's cheekbones. His weight on his back foot for a second, Friel lunged forward again, this time bringing up his left leg, striking with his left boot, hitting the banger in the chest, driving him backward into his mug-mates.

They were eager to get Friel but they now had to go over their leader's limp body.

The computer voice announced the next stop. As the train began to slow, the two bangers fell toward Friel, stumbling over their partner, who did not make things easier for them because he writhed on the floor, gasping and wailing, his hands still clenched to his face.

The second attacker swung, but his chain came at Friel in too wide an arc. It lashed itself around the car's chrome pipe on the overhead. Friel grabbed him by the wrist and gave him a short tug, pulling him by, landing a forearm shiver to his temple, sending him to the floor of the car.

The third attacker did bring his belt down on flesh and bone. He struck his leader across the lower back and buttocks, raising more shrieks, adding to the squeal of the train's brakes.

Friel wrapped the chain mail around his right fist. The third banger saw the three pounds of steel headed toward his face. He ducked left. Putting his nose right into the open palm of Friel's empty hand.

Friel felt the bones in the nose give like corn chips crushed in a sock. He kept moving, stepping past the bodies on the floor so they could not tackle or trip him and bring him down. He turned, ready for another attack. None came. The bangers had had enough of him. Each one had his pain to deal with. Friel dropped the chain.

The car doors opened with a rush of air, and Friel stepped out onto the platform. To the knot of commuters gathered there, ready to push past him, he said, "I wouldn't take this car. A bunch of gangbangers are having a war in there."

The riders saw the tangle of three toughs on the floor of the car. The sight of blood and sound of shrieking curses kept them in awe as Friel walked away.

He ducked into a public rest room and ditched the flannel shirt in a trash can. Underneath, the Boston Bruins hockey sweater was in no better shape than the shirt. But at least it was mostly golden in color. Nobody looking for red would pay much attention to him. He turned on a water faucet and wet his hair in the sink. He didn't dry it as much as plaster it to his head with paper towels. The wet look also turned his hair two shades darker. He couldn't help noticing that he was going to need a haircut as soon as he got back to the Corps.

When he walked out of the MTA station, he felt his heart pounding in his chest. He was scared. Not because he might have to put up with an assault beef. But because he did not want any thing to delay him from getting back to Quantico. He did not belong in civilian clothes. He was too dangerous to be left out on the streets. He would rather peel potatoes than civilians.

First chance, he would check back with the hospital. Get a clean bill of health on his head—he could fake sanity well enough. Hell, that's how he got into Force

Recon in the first place. Then get back to duty. As soon as he could, get back to the field with his team.

NORTHWEST AFGHANISTAN
10SEP01—0953 HOURS LOCAL

SWAYNE HAD LEARNED enough about combat reports to know Colonel Zavello's threshold of patience was about to run out. So he spoke into his microphone and bit his lip as he waited for his one-eyed boss to reply.

"This is Eagle One, go."

Swayne reviewed what had happened, consulting his GPS to give updated coordinates to the command center. The personal locator beacons, technical wonders able to transmit on discrete frequencies so a headquarters could identify the units and locations of friendlies, day or night, had been compromised two missions ago. The tekkies were working on modifications that would make them safe to use again. But for now, there was too much danger that enemy artillery and mortars could target signals from the PERLOBEs. As they had in Kosovo.

Of course, the satellite probably had their positions well marked. His report was not wasted. The OMCC would compare the accuracy of the GPS to the satellite. This entire mission was mostly experimental anyhow. He was to make no assumptions but to go by the book, the mission briefing book prepared by scientists, not combat types.

Next, Swayne transmitted the digital imagery from his gun camera, in particular the face of the Al Qaeda leader and his men. Satellite pictures could easily pick up images of men playing cards, reading a hand over a man's shoulder. If it were not too cloudy. Or dusty. Or too bright. But the satellites could not change positions or points of view. Too often, the only view was the bird's-eye view, directly overhead. So Swayne's video pictures, taken low-angle, from the normal man's point of view, did better than just take pictures of the tops of heads. Much better than what a satellite might get, no matter how sharp its eye.

Zavello said, "We're going to shoot you some raw video. The boys you scared off with your little trick back-tracked a bit, a mile or so, then headed off the trail. They disappeared below deck. Looks like a cave entrance that we had not found before. So that's something new we got out of your game of laser tag."

Swayne could not hide a smile. He felt good that the recon had been worth the effort. He'd learned something new, and without firing a shot.

Zavello ordered Swayne and Greiner to begin moving back into Uzbekistan by day.

Swayne thought to protest. In his premission briefing, Zavello warned him not to stay invisible inside Afghanistan, not to give the Taliban Government a clue to his team's presence. "Don't get caught playing with your pud in the Taliban's backyard," Zavello had warned him. Now he wanted them to march across the country in broad daylight?

Zavello said the satellite had cleared him to set off. Analysts could see no Afghans visible within fifty miles of his position.

Swayne shook his head. If the analysts were so clever, how come they did not see where that squad of Afghans had come from in the first place? Why hadn't they given him an identification yet for the man whose picture he had just transmitted? Screw the analysts.

He made a gesture to match his last thought.

"I saw that, mister," Zavello growled. "Now get moving."

A heat wave more intense than even the sun over Afghanistan hit Swayne. Zavello could spy on him in real time using the satellite images. If they could see him make a hand gesture, then nothing was private. Using the head outdoors might be politically incorrect in the new high-tech battlefield. What with women manning the satellite downlink screens.

Swayne called Greiner to his side and made the snipping motion under his chin. They turned off their microphones. Only then did he utter a curse word. Then he got down to business, briefing Greiner on which route they would use to get back to Uzbekistan for tonight's mission, code-named Toy Story.

QUANTICO, VIRGINIA
09SEP01—0631 HOURS LOCAL

THE DAWN ON the East Coast of America found Gunnery Sergeant Robert Night Runner standing in front of his military judge for sentencing. The judge had set an early hour. He wanted to be done with Night Runner and get back to a normal life of dealing with real criminals.

Or so Night Runner's JAG officer told him. "Try not to piss him off, Gunny," the ensign said. "It's none of your business if he doesn't want to send you to the gallows for this. Too bad if he thinks that you might have some worth in the Marine Corps."

Night Runner knew he deserved the sarcasm. He hadn't behaved well. He had no reason to act with disrespect toward such an officer, a man who had worked hard. A man just doing his job. Just trying to get his client off—or at least with a light sentence, now that his client had screwed up the defense for him.

The judge stormed into the courtroom. Night Runner and the two officers present bolted to attention. The slamming of the door, the stomping of the heels, and the robes fluttering behind the judge, like an eagle in the attack, gave notice. He was in no mood to be screwed with.

He did not wait for trial counsel to read the docket number to the court. He growled, "We're gathered here to tend to the matter of sentencing for Gunnery Sergeant Robert Night Runner, who has entered a plea of guilty to the charge of assaulting a subordinate and conduct unbecoming a noncommissioned officer." This he recited from memory, all the while glaring into Night Runner's face, his glittering eyes under rumpled eyebrows adding, *You got a problem with that, Sergeant?*

Night Runner kept his look neutral. He would rather cut off his own face than let it give offense, angering the judge by mistake.

In the next thirty seconds of silence, Night Runner, even with his keen ears, could not hear even the sound of breathing in the courtroom. The judge had not invited anybody to sit down. From the meteors of fury now shooting from his eyes, it was clear he wasn't about to worry over these men's discomfort.

Night Runner did not dare to make eye contact with the judge. He relaxed his jaw so he would not look defiant. He exhaled slowly, letting his posture sag. He wasn't used to asking for favors, let alone mercy. But mercy was just what he wanted. Anything that the judge threw at him, short of forbidding him to go back to Force Recon. He let his eyelids go shut in a full one-second blink. *Anything, Judge, just give me a break.* The near side of a prayer.

"I sentence you to—"

"Your Honor."

Night Runner shuddered. He could not believe that his defense attorney had spoken up. *Interrupt this judge? What was he thinking?*

The same question was on everyone's mind, and every eye in the courtroom except Night Runner's had turned to stare at the ensign.

"I beg the court's indulgence, Your Honor."

Night Runner finally did look up at the judge. His hands were on the bar, his elbows raised level with his shoulders. He looked as if he were ready to leap over the bar and shake the ensign's throat in his teeth.

"May I speak, Your Honor?"

Night Runner had to give the kid credit. He did not betray fear with even a slight tremor in his voice. The kid had guts. No, balls.

The judge lowered his elbows, the moment of danger past. He gave the ensign permission to speak, not with a word, but with the dipping of his head a scant quarter of an inch.

"If it please the court, may I ask permission for the defendant to say a word in his own behalf?"

Night Runner saw in the periphery of his vision that the ensign had turned his head to look at him. He heard him speaking into his right ear: "Perhaps to express his regret and to apologize to the court for his strident behavior over the past few days."

Night Runner blinked again, this time for two seconds. When he opened his eyes, he found himself staring directly into the judge's. Night Runner blinked. No way would he try to outstare this judge.

Something in his bearing took the edge off the judge's wrath.

"Except for the defendant," he said, "everybody be seated. Gunnery Sergeant Night Runner?"

Night Runner had faced dozens of life-and-death situations in his Marine Corps career, and even before on the rez in Montana. He had stood up to a marauding cougar one time in the Flathead National Forest. He had put himself in danger of a grizzly attack. In combat, he had faced artillery, small arms, American ordnance, everything from bombs and napalm to hand grenades and, once, a scimitar, the sword he himself now carried into battle.

He could not remember ever one man being so frightening. This judge had the power to take away his ability to be a warrior. And, he realized, nothing was more important to his heritage, his being.

Night Runner wished he had thought over that guilty plea before—

Everybody in the courtroom stared—at him now, instead of the ensign. They expected him to say something on his own behalf. The ensign should have talked to him about this last night. Public speaking left him in dread. Facing the grizzly had not been more frightening.

The judge cleared his throat and narrowed his eyes. *Get on with it, Gunny.*

So Night Runner spoke. "Your Honor. I thank you for the chance to speak. I thank my defense attorney for his earnest and professional preparation. I wish I had listened to him because he knows this arena, and I do not.

"I wish to thank trial counsel, who has been faithful to his oath and cordial to me as well."

Night Runner felt weary already. For every thought that he expressed, ten thousand rattled off the inside of his skull. He took a deep breath and went right to the point.

"I believe a man, especially a noncommissioned officer in the Marine Corps, should take responsibility. Part of the duty and the essence of honor demands this from us. If we do not act with honor on the home front, how can we expect ourselves to act honorably in combat? I believed that I acted with dishonor on the battlefield by putting a man's life at risk. For this I must be punished. Not only because of the laws of the Armed Forces, but also because of the code of honor of the fighting man. I do not ask for special favors. I do not ask for light punishment. I ask only—if it is within the discretion and willingness of the court—that I would be allowed to return to the unit that I left. To serve with honor. To redeem that which I have lost, the esteem of my fellow Marines, whom I have let down."

Spent, Night Runner visibly slumped. Not even a ten-mile hump with a sixty-pound pack could have drained him more than his brief speech. He felt cold trickles of sweat sliding down his spine beneath his dress blouse.

Beads of hot perspiration had formed across his brow. His pulse raced as he waited for the judge's judgment.

He became aware that the judge had grown uneasy. He saw the man squirm in his chair, toying with a sheet of paper before him. Finally, with a huge sigh, the Navy captain gathered himself.

"Gunnery Sergeant Night Runner."

Night Runner felt a rush of air beside him as his defense attorney stood up.

"It is the judgment of the court—" the judge was reading from the piece of paper, and Night Runner knew that he had come in with a sentence in mind. Nothing Night Runner had said in his plea for mercy had made a mark with the man. Night Runner's behavior during the brief trial was to be repaid in spades.

The judge's voice grew faint, and Night Runner realized it was a roaring of white noise in his ears that dampened his hearing. Already the man had said words that sounded like, "reduced in rank to the grade of staff sergeant, E-6."

Busted one grade. A spasm gripped Runner's gut. Not so much because of the loss of pay he would suffer. But because he might never get back to a Force Recon Team with that kind of disgrace, not—

The judge was not through with him.

". . . forfeiture of one half of base pay for three months."

Night Runner's knees quaked. He didn't care about the money. It was that reduction in rank that was going to kill him. Hell, he never had any place to spend money anyhow. They had stayed in the field for so long, either in training or in combat, the past few years—

". . . restrictions to quarters at your duty station for one year, except to travel back and forth to work assignments and to only those places essential to carrying out normal off-duty functions as necessary, including church, gymnasium or athletic facilities, base exchange, and commissary."

His knees buckled. There it was. Might as well have thrown him in the brig for a year. If the judge confined him to quarters, the effect was the same.

Night Runner stopped breathing. He saw the courtroom tilt, and thought he might fall over in shock. The ensign grabbed his elbow to steady him. The young officer had a strong grip, and the pain on the nerves just above the elbow joint helped Night Runner regain his balance.

He noticed that nobody in the courtroom had moved. The judge wasn't through. The rushing sound came back to his ears.

". . . except that the reduction in rank and forfeiture of pay will be suspended for a period of one year. If the defendant keeps his record clean and exhibits exemplary behavior for that time, the conviction will be set aside, records of it will be removed from his personnel jacket, and all evidence of this proceeding will be destroyed. That is the order of the court."

The judge tapped on the bar with the handle of his gavel, stood up, whirled, and tramped from the courtroom before the grizzled trial counsel could snap to attention.

The ensign had grabbed Night Runner's right hand and was shaking it, making his arm flap. The trial counsel stepped across the midpoint of the room and held out his hand as well.

"Congratulations," the Marine major said. "I doubt if I'll ever see you in the courtroom again. If you had kept your wits about you, we might have settled this outside the courtroom in the first place." The major shook Night Runner's hand, turned on a heel, picked up his briefcase, and left.

The ensign shook his head. "I've never seen that before. You know why the judge was so easy on you?"

The bewildered Night Runner shook his head.

"Guy was a Navy SEAL before going to law school. He understands."

Night Runner studied the young man's face. "Well, that makes one of us. What happened here? How am I going to ever get back to my unit if I have to spend a whole year under house arrest or whatever you want to call it?"

The ensign smiled. "I thought you went to law school."

"I did."

"Then I guess you weren't paying attention the day they taught how to read between the lines of a legal order. It's all in the language. The judge said you were restricted to quarters, all right. You must not have heard all of the exceptions."

"The gym? The commissary? Church?"

"On duty and during operational missions too." The ensign looked at him and ducked his head a little, looking up under his brow. "Get it? If you were on a mission with your Force Recon Team, the house arrest, as you call it, wouldn't apply."

A tiny smile creased Night Runner's face. Justice. It did exist after all. The smile widened until a double set of parentheses bracketed his mouth.

The ensign matched the smile with one as broad. "You're not going to hug me, are you? That's not a very Marine thing."

"No, but I can shake your hand can't I? Sir?" Night Runner did not wait for permission.

He grasped the young, strong hand and shook it until the ensign cried, "Uncle."

SOUTHWEST UZBEKISTAN
10SEP01—1817 HOURS LOCAL

SWAYNE AND GREINER crossed the border into Uzbekistan just as the sun scorched a pocket into one of the mountain ranges to the west.

Swayne felt a moment of relief because he and Greiner could now walk in the shade. They no longer had to deal with their shadows cast ten meters long. All the earth-tone camouflage in the world was useless in late afternoon if a black shadow rippling across the desert pointed right at a soldier.

Although he didn't have to deal with that any longer, he could not relax. With a word of caution to Greiner, he made certain that he would not let down his guard either. For one thing, boundaries were disputed in this part of the world. For another, the many hostile tribes and opium gangs and bandits didn't respect boundaries anyhow. Too many guns had found their way into the region. Far too many.

Two miles inside Uzbekistan, Swayne's nose caught the acrid smoke of cooking fires and the fragrance of roasting meat. He checked his digital topo map to confirm that the Uzbeks detailed to guide them were the most likely source of the fires. When he had satisfied himself, he moved ahead of Greiner so he could be first to look over the camp from a mile away. No telling what might have happened during the day. The Uzbeks might have turned on the Marine security platoon and the civilian scientists for all he knew. Or the fires were from burning bodies after a bandit attack and not so fragrant after all.

One more time, Swayne wished that he had Night Runner along on this mission. It had crossed his mind more than once that if he could not have the gunny back, maybe he did not want to be in Force Recon himself. He had put in his time. He could justify it to himself that three years and a measurable amount of his body weight in scars was enough. The idea of moving around a strange country with a reduced Force Recon team he could deal with. But when you added a reinforced platoon of Uzbeks who looked no different to him than the Al Qaeda squad he had evaded earlier today, the situation turned into a rat screw, to use one of Friel's terms.

Add three Ph.D.s to the equation, and you had nothing but rat screw cubed to improve upon the Friel-ism. He missed both his missing men.

QUANTICO, VIRGINIA
09SEP01—1320 HOURS LOCAL

ZAVELLO HAD BEGUN to feel his arthritis more than ever. It happened every damn time he had to spend his days and nights at the Operational Mission Control Center. When one of his teams was out, he had to be out there with them, at least in spirit—and voice. He barely found time to sleep or eat, let alone exercise to oil the joints. Hell, he would not even have left the OMCC, except that his boss had called him in for a face-to-face.

His boss was a civilian, in rank right up there with the major generals. Except that he was a civilian, Zavello held nothing against him. Today he wasn't talking about operations in and around Afghanistan, wasn't talking about anything to do with Force Recon. The civilian bigwig had been trying to get the colonel to take a different kind of desk job, a paper-caper with no mission time.

Zavello wouldn't have it. He didn't need to be a ROAD officer, retired on active duty. If it weren't for the void under the black patch on his face, he would be trying to weasel his way into the field—even something as innocuous as going along with the Toys R Us team in Uzbekistan with Swayne and his boys—boy. But no, the drippy-nosed, saggy-lipped, slack-jawed, mouth-breathing GS-13-grade civilian wouldn't allow one-eyed colonels on even that kind of candy-ass mission.

Zavello took a shortcut across the grass. Not a Marine thing to do. But he wanted to spit. So he spat on the grass because it was against his principles to spit on a sidewalk.

Zavello dreamed of a regulation that allowed him to kill two people a day, two people who pissed him off. He would even promise to use his power with discretion. Before long, the Marine Corps would be a fit place to live. As long as he could kill anybody he wanted, including people who outranked him, especially civilians who outranked him.

Not that he wouldn't use it on his subordinates too. For instance, the pair who stood at attention before him now, blocking his access to the elevators.

"What the hell do you two bozos want?" he said to Night Runner and Friel.

SOUTHWEST UZBEKISTAN
10SEP01—1822 HOURS LOCAL

AFTER FIVE MINUTES of surveillance, Swayne judged everything normal at the camp. The Uzbeks had gathered in half a dozen groups of three to five men. Each group clustered around a small rabbit-fire, heating water for their pungent tea and preparing to roast game. As part of the agreement to provide guides and security for the American camp, the Uzbeks were given food and bottled water, plus new weapons and ammunition—and, Swayne guessed, a good deal of cash.

Even so, the Uzbeks had gone hunting. They'd brought back a goat of some kind, possibly wild, but maybe not. They had finished skinning it, and had begun butchering the carcass, cutting off chunks of meat and tossing them, one each, to a delegate from each squad. At least three men handled each piece of raw, bloody meat with his bare, dirty hands.

Swayne spent another five minutes checking the security at the camp, the task of the Marine platoon commanded by First Lieutenant Billy Radford. To his mind, the lieutenant had done an excellent job of using the ground to get the best lines of observation and direct fire.

At least one position commanded each of the avenues of approach into the camp.

Swayne switched to the camp frequency and called both Radford and the lieutenant's counterpart within the Uzbek group, a senior leader by the name of Momadou, who went by one name, as if he were a Brazilian soccer star.

Momadou had a habit of looking down his ample nose at Swayne. He was commander of twenty-five men. He knew the territory. He could speak English, whereas Swayne could not speak either his tongue, Uzbek, or Russian. He said outright that he found it notable that Swayne commanded only himself and one enlisted man—three when he was at full strength. Not counting the three scientists.

Swayne let the man have his ego trip. Momadou had earned his chops in fighting against the Soviets before and during the 1980 Afghan war. Let him swagger.

Besides, Swayne had work to do. Now that he had finished inside Afghanistan, his night job was to evaluate a series of experimental weapons and some surveillance gear. He was to give thumbs-up or thumbs-down to the toys developed by the Special Weapons and Operational Development Group, the secret command to which the three Ph.D.s belonged.

They had pulled this kind of mission before, when Friel was a young pup on the team. They had traveled to the jungles of the Philippines to run their trials—Friel had been the first one to call it the Toys R Us mission.

True enough, some of the devices did no better than toys. One disaster had been an odorless mosquito repellent. Soldiers had always bitched about the eye-stinging, oily DEET formula that stunk so bad that special-operations soldiers could not use it. Not only could an enemy detect it from a hundred yards away, it also ruined the sense of smell for the person using it. So scientists had come up with a fragrance only insects could detect, a pheromone that kept mosquitoes at bay.

Trouble was, the SWODG tested the new repellent in marshy areas of North America. On an operational mission against cocaine bandits in Colombia, Force Recon Marines from Team 2121 found themselves swarmed by hordes of giant moths. The insects blocked their vision, their nostrils, and mouths during a firefight. No lives had been lost in that debacle, but from that disaster onward, no weapon went into the field for use until a Force Recon Team had tried it out in conditions as close to combat as possible. In an area of the world where such combat situations were likely to occur. As it turned out, scientists had created a synthetic sexual-attractant pheromone for the jungle moths. From then on, Force Recon Marines worldwide called Team 2121 the Love Bugs. Until the Corps retired the unit number 2121.

That's why the scientists and Swayne and Greiner had come to Uzbekistan. After the barely intrusive recon today, they would operate outside the borders of a hostile country, Afghanistan, run by a hostile puppet government, the Taliban, which in turn was run by Osama bin Laden and his terrorist network.

You didn't get any more realistic than that.

Swayne made his radio call to alert Momadou and Radford of his route back into the camp. Momadou ordered him to flash a red light three times at the nearest outpost. "Did you know where this outpost is located at?" he asked.

Swayne did, although he did not give away anything about his PDA and the topographic map. Nobody but nobody could be allowed to have access to those satellites. He said as much, then added, "Don't let your man signal to me." It wouldn't do for an outpost to be flashing lights to advertise his location to somebody outside the perimeter.

"Of course not that. We are not—how you Marine peoples say?—idiot-assholes."

Radford simply rogered Swayne's report.

QUANTICO, VIRGINIA
09SEP01—1342 HOURS LOCAL

ZAVELLO HAD HEARD enough from Friel and Night
Runner. He had led the two members of Swayne's Force
Recon Team 2400, Team Midnight as they were called,
for the obvious reasons, into an anteroom of the Operational Mission Control Center. Neither of them, although
they had the highest possible security clearances, could
get access into the main control room, called the CAB.
CAB was not an acronym, just a capitalization of *cab,* as
in a truck's cab, where Zavello did all the driving.

They had no need to know about the driving of Force
Recon missions from thousands of miles away. Information inside the room was to stay there. No field Marine
would ever see the secrets or equipment. Drugs or torture
might somehow break the best Marine's intentions never
to betray what went on inside the OMCC.

Zavello snarled at the pair. "What is it you want again?
Are you out of your minds?"

"We want to get back to Captain Swayne," Night Runner said. "Sir, if you can, get us back together as a team."

Zavello snorted. "Don't pull that shit on me, Gunny.
Don't give me that look of innocence either. If I can get
you back together? Of course I can. That's not the question. The question is, am I enough of an idiot asshole to
put you two morons back into combat without any assur-
ance whatsoever that you won't go batshit on me again?"

Friel's jaw dropped. The man was reading his mind.
He had never met Zavello before, hardly ever talked to
him on the radio. Even though he had overheard him biting roasts out of the captain's ass, he could not appreciate
the man until now. Now, he was looking into his eye,
feeling the spray of his voice, getting a whiff of his breath,
vile as a piss tube. If Friel had had Zavello with him on

that subway car with the three bangers, the man could have breathed on them, and they would have jumped through the emergency exits onto the electrified track. The man was as evil as any vampire, and probably could scare off the queen of the screwed.

Zavello had not finished with them yet. "One of you gets his ass court-martialed, and the other gets his head wrung out by the nut-busters. If it was up to me, I'd send both your asses out there and drop you from twenty thousand feet without a parachute. If it was up to you, I'd send two boneheads over there into a sensitive combat area to do a critical combat mission. I could stay back here so the Marine Corps would have somebody's ass available to throw in jail after you two got the country into a war with Afghanistan and the entire Arab world." He gasped for breath after his last sentence.

Then he slapped himself on the forehead so hard, it sounded like a small-caliber gunshot. "Let me think this one over." He whirled on them. "No. You got that? No. No. No."

Each curse word that followed was a blast of putrid air mixed with fumes from his gut into Friel's face. *Easy, Dragon Man,* Friel thought. *I might qualify for a plot at Arlington National Cemetery, but does it have to be tonight?*

SOUTHWEST UZBEKISTAN
10SEP01—1846 HOURS LOCAL

RAFORD'S PLATOON HAD been hard at it during the day, improving the scientific detachment's secure perimeter. They used camouflage netting to hide the site from the sight of Momadou's Uzbeks. Like everything with the Toys R Us detachment, this was not normal camouflage netting. Ordinary netting scattered thermal images to reduce the signature of anything hiding beneath it. This net also scattered electronic omissions. It also had its own circuitry wired into the netting so it could transmit null wavelengths to cancel out stray emissions. The only way to send a signal from inside the netting was to use a directional antenna. The three scientists had set theirs up on its tripod, aiming toward the overhead satellite, shooting its signal like a cannon. Nothing except a receiver on a direct line of sight could steal their transmissions. Swayne wondered when such technology would be available for PERLOBEs.

The tekkie detachment had a weird command structure. In theory, Randy Whitfield supervised the trio. He was no more than a spokesman for them. Probably because he was the one who spoke plain English—the others talked a science dialect of English. Each man—and woman, because there was one in the group—took charge during the running of tests for their own toys. So Swayne never was quite sure of whom he would deal with.

He and Greiner zigzagged their way into the tiny compound through a maze of concertina wire and a tunnel of netting. The entrance had to bend at least twice to prevent any fragment of line-of-sight emissions from escaping from inside. Tangles of wire channeled visitors into open areas. Nobody could sneak into the place. Nobody could slither through that wire in one piece either.

Swayne went right for Whitfield. "Who's up?"

"Bonnie," said Whitfield, flashing his all-American smile. "She's in the back. Come on."

In fact, Whitfield was an all-American, a six-feet-four ball-handling guard from Indiana, trim and athletic. Swayne knew it from his pre-mission briefing. Whitfield had not brought it up on the twenty-hour flight from Charleston, South Carolina, or the ten-hour drive from their landing strip in the interior of Uzbekistan. Swayne gave him points for that. College jocks and Annapolis graduates usually let you know about it within the first three sentences after introductions.

Upon meeting Whitfield for the first time at the C-141, Swayne thought, *Man, don't get lost going out into the bushes to take a leak.* Because any special-ops type would mistake Whitfield for a terrorist. He wore his dark hair full, in large, loose curls. He had thick eyebrows and a beard that crept up his cheekbones to just under his eyes. Artificially whitened teeth flashed beneath a full mustache. Dressed in a khaki safari shirt and cargo pants so large that they billowed like the Uzbeks' pantaloons, he looked more like an intruder than the lead scientist on this mission. Put a turban on him and anyone in the cockpit of an F-16 would rub him out because he looked like an Al Qaeda fighter. Any terrorist would kill him because he looked like he had gone AWOL from one of their training camps.

Bonnie Downes also seemed out of place, too blond, too perky, too hyper. She was short, no more than five feet two, and not petite but compact, more a linebacker than a scientist. Swayne wanted to be friendly with her, except that he couldn't stand to be near her. She talked in a shrill voice, on a frequency that hurt his ears. He thought if Team 2121 had used her voice pitched a little higher and beyond the range of human hearing, they might have had that insect repellant they'd been looking for.

Whitfield led him past Ernesto Ramirez, who stood about six feet tall. In contrast to Downes, he hardly talked. Swayne thought that he must be one helluva scientist to be a scientist at all. He talked in a low voice, and his sentences, although they usually began in English, often ended in Spanish. Too bad Friel wasn't here to ask: *How'd that Bunsen burner get through scientist school?*

Whitfield took Swayne to the back of the tiny scientific compound, where Marines from Radford's platoon had dug out a section of ground like a mortar pit. They'd sunk a circular hole ten feet across and three feet deep in the hardpan. Sandbags stacked four high and two thick circled the pit. Downes directed a pair of Radford's Marines trying to position an oversized mortar tube.

"It has to be vertical, perfectly vertical," she said. The Marines, drenched in sweat, gazed at each other for a moment, then looked away so they would not laugh—or at least she would not catch them laughing. Swayne didn't blame them. Downes's voice was even more high-pitched than usual. She was talking faster than Alvin the Chipmunk. How could anybody take her seriously? Swayne wondered.

She turned toward him, and Swayne saw another strike against her as a serious scientist. She was too pretty. She wore her thick hair chopped close to her head. She had fine eyebrows, natural, not plucked, a straight, regal nose, full, compact lips—like the red wax lips he used to get as a kid around Halloween—and a chiseled chin. She smiled at Swayne, looking not at all like a Ph.D., not at all as if she were about to launch one of the most important, most secret military experiments on this trip.

"Captain Swayne," she said, piercing him with her green eyes. "Are we ready to go?"

He felt as if he were picking her up for a date. "Ready," he said. He couldn't help taking a second, closer look at those eyes. They seemed too green to be real, more like the bright moss in a Northwest forest than any natural eye color. Sure enough, he saw the discs of her colored contact lenses.

She turned to the two Marines, who now stood, both of them with their hands on their hips.

"Perfectly vertical?" she chirped.

As if they were introducing a friend, both Marines swept an open hand toward the tube. *See for yourself, lady.*

Swayne watched her step up to the levels, four of the instruments welded to the side of the tube. She leaned in close to examine the bubbles, one at a time. Swayne caught the two men looking at each other, then toward the darkening sky.

Swayne didn't think much of the XD-11. X for experimental. D for drone. Eleven for who knows what? By its full name, it was the Drone, Unmanned Reconnaissance and Ordnance Delivery Aircraft, DURODA-11. Or as the scientists called it, the Dirty Birdie.

The tube was more a rocket launcher than a mortar tube. At about two hundred millimeters, or eight inches, the smooth bore would take a projectile the diameter of a soccer ball. At four meters long, it looked as if somebody had planted half a telephone pole here in the middle of the moonscape of Uzbekistan. Swayne, like the two Marines, couldn't help looking toward the sky. This was a dubious proposition, this Dirty Birdie. At least for Force Recon Marines. Who was going to carry this into combat for them? Where would anybody find the time in a hot zone to spend an entire day doing prep work and setup. Forget about digging a hole—you couldn't get one deep enough to camouflage it. What were you supposed to do with the tube? Leave it standing for anybody to see from ten miles away?

He already knew the conventional Marine Corps had rejected it as impractical on the modern battlefield. In fact, conventional Marines had contributed to the thing's nickname. After the Dirty Birdie's launch, it left a signature in the air, a plume more than a mile high. Might as well draw an arrowhead at the bottom of the plume and hang a sign at the top: *Shoot artillery here*.

From what Zavello had told him, the threat of counterbattery artillery fire would not deter Bonnie Downes. She had argued, and rightly, that the conventional battlefield wasn't going to mean the conventions of World War II or even Desert Storm anymore. Everybody in the world, including Saddam Hussein, had seen that. The battlefield would involve more special-operations types, not fewer, she said.

Swayne figured she must have connections in high places. Otherwise, how could she force herself and her Dirty Birdie all the way down the throats of the Marine Corps chain of command to this hole in the desert?

Which hole she popped out of now, and stood before Swayne, looking for all the world as if she might give him a friendly punch in the gut.

"Ready, Jack?"

He recoiled from the pain in his ears, as if somebody had poked a needle through his eardrum. "Let's give it a look."

She pushed past him, setting a course for the launch-control room, not much more than a sandbag igloo. He showed Greiner a crooked grin, trying not to let Whitfield see it.

"Stop smirking, Jack," she said without turning around, chipper as ever.

"Who's smirking?"

"You are. Private Greiner, who's smirking?"

Greiner, smiling, looked toward Swayne, who shook his head. "I don't know anything about smirking, ma'am," Greiner said.

"I'm so sure. Randy? Who's smirking?"

"Leave me out of this."

Downes led the way into the domed bunker without even nodding her head. The men behind her practically had to crouch to get inside the cramped, dark space, lit only by red lights to preserve their night vision once they went outside again. She planted herself on a case of rations. In front of her on two other cases of rations was a notebook computer.

"You're cowards to a man," she said. "But what you are about to see is going to wipe those smirks off all your faces."

Swayne doubted it. He liked Bonnie because he liked all women. He could endure Whitfield well enough. Even Ramirez was bearable, mainly because he kept his mouth shut. Now that Swayne had made it out of Afghanistan without creating an international incident, he should have been enjoying himself. The mission was important, but not life-and-death. They would spend no more than a couple of days here, then pack up and head back to the States. He would not even have to face these three alone and tell them whether he liked their toys. He'd make a video report back at Quantico. Later, he would participate in a conference of scientists, including this trio. He would be flanked by Marine officers all singing from the same sheet of music. He would not have to defend himself. Senior officers usually agreed with the man in the field about whether to put one of the toys into the hands of Marines in the field. If Swayne said that any piece of equipment was not worth taking to the next step of development, the Marines would back him up. Usually with their stock rejection remark: "Send it to the Army."

Downes made her pre-launch checks. Swayne, more concerned with security, checked in with Radford and asked him to get one last report from each listening post. He also checked in with the OMCC, to be sure they could see no thermal images of intruders within the surrounding ten miles. Once he was satisfied, he told Downes she could proceed. He pulled a pocket notebook—the paper variety—and a pen and prepared to take notes.

Downes started into her launching sequence, counting down from twenty seconds.

Whitfield cursed. He started patting down his pockets, then fished into one of the cargo compartments of his pants, bringing out small plastic packets. He tossed one each to Swayne and Greiner and began tearing at the wrapping of his own.

The two Force Recon Marines didn't need a whack on the side of the head to realize what lay ahead. They opened their own packets of hard foam earplugs and squeezed the tips of the cylinders into cones before inserting them in their ears.

But before the foam had barely began to expand to plug their ear canals, a wet-towel slap of concussion like that of a cannon firing hit them. The blast lifted Swayne's soft cap and caused a moment of overpressure in the igloo. A flash of white light, as if somebody had stood in the doorway with a strobe light, brightened the interior of the bunker.

Downes cheered at what she saw on her computer screen. Swayne looked at it and then at Greiner. They shrugged at each other. A diagonal line ran from the lower left of the screen to the upper right. A second line began to scroll across the screen on top of the first line. Downes put her face close to the screen, and each time the second line began to drift above the first, she used her computer keys to make adjustments, bringing it back down. Swayne noticed a second, vertical set of lines, which she manipulated as well. He guessed that the original lines indicated a program trajectory. The second set of lines showed the actual flight.

Downes talked to the computer screen. "On course, on trajectory. Passing through five thousand feet. On course, on trajectory. Approaching burnout in ten seconds, nine . . ."

She continued the countdown. "Three, two, one. Flameout." She touched a computer key. "Booster separation. Passing through ten thousand feet."

The line that she had kept nailed to the diagonal began to drift in a slow arc toward the bottom of the screen.

"Wings deployed," she said. The arc leveled off into a horizontal line. "Cruise flight achieved at"—she pointed to a set of numbers at the bottom of the graph—"twenty-four thousand, nine hundred, ninety-six feet." She turned around and flashed a brilliant smile at Swayne. "Not bad, huh? Just four feet off in twenty-five thousand. You want to know what percentage of error that is?"

"No need," he said. "I'm more interested in what the thing can do now that it's up in the air." He pointed at the screen. The line had dipped below the horizontal.

"No problem," she said. "It's just soaring now with no power. See how gradual the altitude loss is? This thing could fly all day powered by a rubber band." She turned toward Swayne, her smile now more of a dare. *Don't contradict me, buster.*

Swayne had thought she looked pretty in the daylight, especially at dusk when the dim light hit her flaws. Now, in the harsh glare of the interior of the bunker, she looked like a gargoyle. Besides, her voice in the tight space had already made his ears begin to throb.

He pointed at the computer screen. "Let's see what it can do."

"I'm game," she said. She turned to the computer, and her fingers flew over the keys. "Engine ignition. Check. Instruments on. Check. Controls activated. Check."

Her fingers danced again, and a new screen came up. This one was a digital topographic map of Uzbekistan and Afghanistan. At the center of the screen, a tiny airplane icon flew as seen from above.

She pointed to a couple of spots in turn and told what they meant. "That's the drone, the Dirty Birdie, of course. The launch site. The track of the craft is this faint dotted line. As you can see, we launched into Uzbekistan, away from our recon target area. The craft is on default auto-pilot right now. I'll take the controls and fly it manually for a minute." Again her fingers rattled the keyboard as if a giant cockroach was running across it. "I've activated the joysticks." She placed the control in her lap and moved to operate the pair of toggle switches. "One for climb and dive. The other for bank and turn. A system of servos automatically puts in the right amount of rudder and adjusts flaps. Now I lock in the course and altitude. The onboard computer takes care of the rest."

She pointed to a zigzag line at the top of the screen. "This is an autopilot course. All I have to do is grab it—" She used the track pad to move the cursor arrow and select the crooked line. She pulled it down onto the screen and put one end of it into the target area. The other end she stretched toward the icon of the flying drone. "I can use preprogrammed courses. Circular. Oval. Linear. Or I can draw one with the pointer."

Swayne leaned over her shoulder. He couldn't help notice how nice she smelled, considering where they were, considering the heat.

Before he could say anything, she said, "You're looking at the spot where the preprogrammed course flies directly into this mountain peak."

"That would put it to a sudden stop. Or else within easy range of a rifleman."

"That's what makes this next feature so outstanding." She used the track pad and moved a segment of the line away from the peak. "Simple as that. Move the course ten miles faster than you can say, 'Move the course ten miles.' "

Swayne made a humming sound in his throat to let her know he was impressed. He was too. But already the XD-11 had failed the test, to his mind. This device was so far outside the Force Recon mission, he was surprised somebody hadn't already scrapped it on paper. Downes must have an uncle in the Department of Defense. *Send it to the Army,* he thought.

Even doing that would require a convoy of trucks. The thing was too heavy, too noisy, too visible. A nice toy for the Army. They could build a base as big as Fort Bragg and fly dozens of them. It would take three infantry and two armored divisions to secure the area. That was the Army. It was what they did.

Meanwhile, Downes explained how to engage the autopilot and capture the preprogrammed flight path. She did it with keystrokes. He saw months of technical training for some MIT graduate. Force Recon Marines, the best fighters in the world, didn't have time for such technical training on top of all the physical, tactical, and mission prep.

Once the drone began flying on a pilot toward its target recon zone, Downes used the time to bore Swayne and Greiner with technical detail. Poor Greiner, thought Swayne. Up before 0300 hours, trekking across the desert all day, staying up now to listen to this scientist brag about a piece of equipment that would never make it into the Marine Corps inventory. Hell, if it grew talons and flew down to pluck Osama bin Laden himself out of the lunar crater of Afghanistan and carry him out to the Indian Ocean to feed him to the fishes, it would be a wonderful thing. The Marine Corps wouldn't be using it at the Force Recon level. The Army? That was another thing.

Downes, talking about drones, began to sound like one herself. She explained that the CIA was already testing an unmanned aircraft called the Predator, which was so huge they might as well have given it a pilot—twenty-seven feet long with a wingspan of forty-eight feet. It did have the capability to take real-time pictures, lock on, and fire Hellcat missiles. It also required an airstrip and a team of scientists to fly and fire it. From a less-than-mobile command center.

Swayne couldn't stop himself from glancing around the interior of the igloo, as if to say: *Do you call this mobile?*

Downes caught him looking around and smiled a wicked smile. He knew that she had set him up. She bent over the computer and unplugged it. Without shutting it off, she folded down the top and picked up the joysticks.

"Follow me," she crowed.

Outside in the dark, Swayne felt the chill of the region's night air. Temperature drops of fifty degrees from day to night were as routine as dust storms and scorpions, famine and pestilence.

Downes turned toward him in the dark and said, "Here."

He held out his hands for the computer. She was going

to let him operate the drone, and he needed to act as if
he cared. Still, he grabbed for the computer as it slid from
her hands well short of his. All he grasped was the cord
of the joysticks, and that pulled out of the back of the
computer as it clattered across the rocks. He squished a
curse between his teeth. When he bent over to retrieve
the computer, he found her boot on it, tapping.

"Watch this," she said. He stepped back as she stood
up on the computer. With both feet.

Now she had his attention. Forget about the drone. Had
she really invented technology tough enough to withstand
the beating this computer had taken? If so, Force Recon
would be first in line for it. His team could seldom take
on successive missions without entirely replacing all their
computerized gear, from GPSs to PDAs, to the miniature
PowerBooks they sometimes carried. Not to mention
night-vision devices and digital gun sights.

Except. If Downes's little stunt blew up in her face,
that drone, probably a multimillion-dollar prototype in a
half-billion-dollar research program, would be flying
around the most unfriendly skies in the world like a ballistic missile. Once it crashed—

"Watch this," said Downes. She picked up the computer, dusted it off roughly, and opened its top. There it
was, the drone's icon, still creeping along its course. Still
at airspeed, still at altitude. She made her fingers fly again.
The drone started into a left-hand turn.

"I'll fly it in a circle and let it recapture the autopilot
course. Impressed?"

Very."

"Too bad your sidekick isn't."

He turned around. Greiner was gone. Swayne ducked
back inside the igloo. Greiner sat upright on a pile of
sandbags, leaning against the side of the bunker, sound
asleep with his eyes wide open. Swayne waved his fingers
in front of the Marine's eyes. Nothing.

Swayne let him rest. He wouldn't need Greiner for

making his decision about the XD-11. No matter how well it performed in its next phase, the reconnaissance, he knew he wouldn't be recommending it.

He wished that he had a full team out here. Then they could get some rest and play with these toys in two-man shifts. A cloud of sadness descended over him. He doubted whether his team would ever be together again

QUANTICO, VIRGINIA
09SEP01—1516 HOURS LOCAL

NIGHT RUNNER AND Friel intercepted Zavello in the passageway outside the OMCC.

Night Runner could see that the colonel was walking with his head and eyes glaring at the deck to avoid eye contact, sending a signal: *Don't screw with me.* Runner made his own body rigid, and Friel snapped to attention as well. They didn't exactly block Zavello's path. They just made it hard for him to get by without a detour or brushing past. For a second Night Runner thought that the one-eyed colonel was going to lower a shoulder like an offensive guard and plant it in his sternum to bowl him over. But Zavello pulled up, his good eye red-rimmed and watery.

"What the hell do you two want?"

"Sir," said Night Runner. "The two Force Recon Marines wish to know if the colonel was able to arrange for them to rejoin their team."

Zavello shook his head, lifting one half of his upper lip into a sneer. "The colonel isn't the moron the two Force Recon Marines are. He's not stupid enough to ask for an aircraft to transport two men halfway around the world to join a mission already in progress, a pissant mission at that."

Both men knew they had better not argue with Zavello. Night Runner merely closed both eyes in an extra-long blink. Friel stared straight ahead.

Zavello started to push past after all. When he held up again, Night Runner felt an inkling of hope.

Zavello growled, "I heard about your court-martial. It's a wonder they didn't throw your ass out of the Marine Corps, lock you up, and throw away the key. Your judge was a friend of mine—until he met you. I've never seen him so mad. When he started talking about you, I thought maybe you had pissed in his combat boots. He tells me I can assign you anywhere—don't get your hopes up. I need another enlisted man to work in the command center. How would the gunny like to carry coffee and push papers around for the rest of his miserable, head-cleaning, deck-swabbing, cigarette-butt-policing, sock-sucking life?"

Night Runner did not answer. He did not need to. His slack expression answered as if he had just heard his death sentence.

"And you," Zavello said to Friel. "Your nutcracker had to get a shrink for himself after peeling your skull. He told me I should get a restraining order. Keep you a thousand meters away from the human race. He said I should put you out of the Corps. Hang a sign on your ass that says shit-for-brains and give you the heave-ho, maybe give you a transfer to the Air Force."

Friel flared his nostrils and widened his eyes. "The Air Force? Sir?"

"But I couldn't do either one of those things. Why would I punish myself by hanging one of you around my neck like a millstone? How could I turn the other one loose on three hundred million civilians, much as I hate civilians? Or even the Air Force, much as I hate the Air Force?"

The Marines were still, except for their eyes. Their hopeful eyes. Which Zavello didn't like.

"Get your greasy eyeballs off of me."

When he was satisfied with their thousand-meter stares, he said, "Besides, I need to make Swayne pay for giving me the finger today. So I'm going to send you both back for retraining in Force Recon. Be ready to report when he gets back."

Both men's chests expanded.

"Wipe those greasy smiles off your faces. Don't get me to thinking that you're in love with me or something."

They sobered up.

"Now, up against the bulkhead and make way," he grumped. After they had slapped the walls with their backs, he passed by. He wore a glimmer of a wry grin on his face, a twinkle in his eye, a string of obscenities leaking from his lips, as cheerful—if that's what it could be called—as he ever became.

Behind him, Night Runner and Friel pumped each other's hands in a four-handed shake.

Zavello called to them over his shoulder, "Don't you let me catch you hugging, girls. Or you'll have a whole new set of problems on your hands. Report to your quarters and stand by. I'll have orders for you by morning."

SOUTHWEST UZBEKISTAN
10SEP01—1902 HOURS LOCAL

SWAYNE HAD BECOME engrossed in the drone's mission. Mainly because Bonnie Downes had handed him the controls. He directed the mission now. He hadn't changed his mind about it being unfit for Force Recon Marines. He had decided that technology as good as this should not be handed off to the Army as he had at first thought. For one thing, there was the indestructible control panel. Downes had told him that the Force Recon team would never have to be responsible for transporting and launching the drone. Somebody could launch it from hundreds of miles away or even from an aircraft platform. The team on the ground could control the drone with the miraculous computer as even he did now. Finding it not so complicated that it would require an MIT degree after all. The

Force Recon team on the ground could take the controls with them into the field. They would have a set of eyes in their hands.

No longer would they have to wait for a priority to get satellite time. No longer would he have to worry about cloud cover blocking the satellite's eye. The drone could fly beneath the clouds to take pictures. No more would he have to keep up commo with the OMCC half a globe away. He smiled to himself. *No Zavello to deal with? Could it be? Nah, some miracles simply could not be.*

Downes showed him how to access other screens. On the thermal imager, a screen of green would reveal radiated heat. Swayne spotted a cluster of such images and pointed them out to Downes.

"Looks like some critters," she said. "Reminds me of antelope we saw during field tests out in Wyoming."

"Do you have to fly down to get a close-up?"

"No, we can zoom in, both optically and digitally." She worked her magic on the keys, and the bright spots grew on the screen until Swayne could clearly identify a herd of nine desert goats, including two rams, one with full-curled horns and the other a juvenile. The thermal discrimination was so fine, he could see the outlines of the eyes and the differing temperatures in the animals' striped color variation.

"I'm going to show off a little bit now," she said. "It will jiggle some, but you'll see." She placed the crosshairs of the screen between the eyes of one animal and tapped three keys. The screen blinked and brought up a full-face view of the animal. Its tongue flipped out of its mouth, lapped its nose, and vanished like a snake down its throat. Then the goat took a step, vanishing from view.

Swayne let out a gush of air. "I'm impressed," he said. He pointed to the altitude readout on screen, now ten thousand feet. "Whoa."

"That kind of quality is routine because of the gyro-stabilized platform," Downes said. "But pictures during the day will blow you away. The resolution is as good as broadcast-quality, high-def digital video taken in the same room. Speaking of broadcast, it can be. Uplinked to the satellite and shot round world."

Swayne was gaining respect for the XD-11 by the minute. He no longer even thought of it as the Dirty Birdie. He started thinking of benefits of the device that he had dismissed earlier. For one, it didn't require an airfield for launch. For the first few seconds of its existence, it was simply a ballistic rocket shot into the atmosphere. Then it sprouted wings and became a glider. It also had a low-powered motor and two rear-end propellers to keep it aloft at night. By day, it rode the thermals and—

"Hey!" He looked over his shoulder. "How do we recover this thing?" he asked.

"We?" Downes smiled down at him. In the dim glow of the screen, he could only see a flash of green reflecting off her teeth. "I'm glad to see *we* care about getting back the drone. *We* have two options. First, we fly it to a safe area—here, for example. Bring it down low and slow. Deploy a parachute, and pick it up."

"The second method?"

"We . . . *wait*—" She was looking past him at the screen. He turned, feeling her move in close to him, pressing against his shoulder with hers, leaning over the thermal-imagery screen.

He saw what she had seen, a string of thermal hits. "More goats?"

"No. Totally different thermal profile. People. Move over. Let me have the controls."

She impressed him by her intensity, all business, focused on reading the images and controlling the drone. He also felt a surge of adrenaline. He should've been as exhausted as Greiner, but he was not. The XD-11 had gotten his blood up. He liked what it could do, especially that it cut out so many layers of intel types. If he had control of such a recon vehicle on the ground, he would never again have to travel blind into a hostile situation.

Downes murmured a curse word.

"What?" He saw that she was zooming out, taking in a larger view. Before she could answer his question, he saw what she had seen, a second set of thermal hits. One group was moving toward the other. "More people?"

"Yes, more people. Tell me, Captain Swayne. Does this look like an ambush situation to you?"

Swayne put his head next to hers and felt the tickle of her hair against his cheek.

"Let me see a close-up of the static group." He counted ten thermal images, arranged like a backward 7.

He dragged his finger across the screen and through the top leg of the 7. "Is this a trail?"

"See the faint image?" she jabbered. "The temperature differential between smooth ground and the surrounding area would indicate—"

"When I ask you the time, don't tell me how to build a clock," he said. "Trail or not?"

"Trail," she said. "No need to get snippy—"

"Don't take it personal. Yes, that looks like an ambush. Classic L-shape. But it could also be a simple meeting of two groups of terrorists. One group just lying in position, waiting for the other group to assemble at a rally point. Can you give me a close-up on some of the faces in this static group?"

"You bet I can." She acted like a puppy eager to please now that he had established that this was not a contest. Now she could strut the XD-11's stuff. "I'm going to drop down to five thousand feet and stand off about three miles. That will give me a low-angle view."

He put a hand on her forearm and squeezed. "Please, no extra explanation. We're not in a test anymore. We're actual now." She reminded him of Friel, only worse because of the shrill voice, although he would never tell her that. If she had ever found out he had compared her to a man now on psycho-pass, she might hunt him down later, even years later.

He watched her work the controls with no wasted motion, no extra effort. The drone lost five thousand feet of altitude in only seconds.

"How did you do that? I've never seen in aircraft dump so much altitude so quickly and level off." He heard her chuckle.

"The bird has retractable wings. I fold them back, and it drops like a bomb. Then, gradually, I extend the wings again, and it levels off. Just by slowing down, I pick up the extra three miles—sorry, I'm getting chatty again."

So chatty Swayne was biting holes in his tongue. He watched as she set up the drone in an orbit east of the spot where the ten images lay in wait. She then aimed the camera lens by selecting the icon of a human eye and dragging it from the drone on a straight line to the group of men. When she released the icon, the screen revealed two men lying side by side, one of them talking into a handheld radio. He was pointing at something.

"Pull back a little. Can you see what he is looking at?"

"No. But I see another guy—here—" She pointed to the image on the screen and Swayne saw what she was looking at. "A spotting scope."

Swayne's mind went to work on the situation. He factored in everything that he had seen and all that he might deduce. Worst case for the group of nine trekking across the desert, they were trekking into an ambush. He sorted through the intelligence reports, both friendly and enemy, that he had been privy to in his exchange of reports with the OMCC earlier that night. No reported Taliban forces within a hundred miles. Surely there were no other American forces operating in this area—no, Zavello would never have cleared this mission if it might conflict with another unit.

The other possibilities? Maybe a gang of drug smugglers? The Taliban, in their only act of civility so far re-

corded in their short history, had banned the production
of opium poppies. That drove the business underground.
Taliban forces might just be out to enforce the law. More
likely, they were going to rob the smugglers. At a minimum, demand a toll for traveling the trail and try them
for smuggling drugs. First the toll, then the death sentence.

As he worked through his mental gymnastics, Downes
shifted the camera lens from one terrorist to another. By
the third one, Swayne recognized that this was the same
group he and Greiner had encountered earlier that afternoon. He noticed they had left their dog home tonight.
Which increased the likelihood that they expected trouble,
that they knew a group would be passing by, that they
intended to use force at a minimum, to wipe out the group
as a maximum. They didn't want a pesky dog's bark to
give them away.

Swayne turned on his radio transmitter, made contact
with the OMCC, and asked if intelligence sources had yet
identified any of the faces he had transmitted that morning
from the satellite. Zavello came on, less gruff than usual,
and told him the man's name was Abu Saddiq. He gave
some of the terrorist's bio, and promised to downlink a
full dossier within the hour. Swayne already knew the
name. He was a second-level Al Qaeda leader, below only
Osama bin Laden himself. Had Swayne known, he might
have asked permission to take the man out earlier that day.
Since that ship had already sunk, he kept his mouth shut.

Then, acting out of character, Zavello gave him a brief
update on Night Runner and Friel. "The bad news is,"
Zavello muttered, "when you get back, you're going to
have to take them onto your team."

Stunned that Zavello would let down his stern policy
against chatter on a tactical net, and relieved at the news
he would get his team whole again, Swayne felt like
shouting.

He said, "Roger, Spartan One out."

"The bad news is good news?" Downes asked.

"Very."

Downes didn't pry. "If you want, I could take a closer peek at the other group. I can get them almost head-on."

"Go ahead."

As the lens moved in on the group, Swayne judged from the first two images in the marching file that he had been right. Bandits or smugglers. The pair carried Kalashnikov rifles—in this region of the world, who didn't? There was no uniformity to their gear, no tactical order to their march. Just a group on a night hike across the desert. *Coming from where?* he wondered. *And what were they smuggling?*

"Can this thing backtrack along their trail?"

Downes hummed to herself. "Never had that question before. Let's look. Is it okay to explain what I'm doing?"

"Go ahead."

"I'm tweaking the thermal differentials. It's like increasing the contrast controls on a television set. The blacks would become blacker, the whites whiter. In this case the hots become brighter, the colds become darker. The idea is to isolate only the trail. If there were any differences caused by just a warming of the footsteps—I'll be damned."

"I see it, the trail is coming out of the background."

"I never dreamed," she said. "It was just a hunch. I guess I'm brilliant, wouldn't you say?" Since she was talking to herself, Swayne did not bother to answer. He was more interested in her science now. She began zooming out. Nothing was left on the screen but a faint fog of the trail that diminished in brightness the farther away it got from the marching spots, now just pinpoints of bright light on the screen. She touched the spot where it faded to black.

"Hmmmm," she said. "I can backtrack them about ten miles. Then the temperature peters out. It's late enough so that not even the ambient warmth from the sun is left as a differential."

"Can you put down a map overlay, so I can tell where it is?"

"Sure—wait. Look here."

He saw what she had pointed out on the screen almost as soon as she had said it. A hot spot. Very likely the place a group had spent some time waiting until dark. Possibly even a—

"Campfire. Right here," she said, her voice climbing an octave higher. "They probably had supper, then crossed the border after dark. This is Uzbekistan, about twenty miles southwest of here. Then they marched into Afghanistan."

Swayne examined several other, larger hot spots around the campsite. He asked her about the odd, figure-eight shapes.

"Parked vehicles, probably. They're gone," she said, although he could see it for himself.

One more piece of the puzzle fell into place. Somebody had dropped off the group, but nobody was waiting, expecting them to come back tonight. So, where were they going?

"Shit-oh-dear."

"What?" he said, not wanting to hear her answer, because he already knew it would be bad news—in the time that he had known her, she had not used any but the mildest epithets.

Downes had began zooming on one of the hot spots, one that Swayne had assumed was one of the vehicle parking places. It was not. Before she had even finished enlarging images on the screen, he could see individual bodies visible amid the mass of green. Mass indeed. At first glance, he counted twenty dead, the bodies stacked like cordwood, head-to-toe, two deep. A fog covered the image on screen.

She explained it even before he asked.

"It's a shallow grave. No more than a few inches of dirt thrown over the bodies. We're looking at their body heat burning its way through the covering. By tomorrow morning it won't be visible from the satellite. In a few hours, after the bodies cool, you won't be able to see a thing."

Swayne kept silent. Not because he wasn't listening to her. He was. His mind had already leaped ahead to consider why so many people had been killed. Had it been the group marching through the desert? If so, who took their vehicles?

"Take me back and give me a closer look at the group marching."

She zoomed out to pick up the group on screen. After adjusting the contrast controls, she began closing in on the group. At the same time, she turned the drone. "I'll put the bird into a tight racetrack pattern," she said. "That will keep it out of hearing range. Notice how the lens stays on target as the craft turns."

He looked at her in the dark. Somebody had killed twenty people and laid them in a mass grave. This was no longer a technical test. Time to forget about showing off the XD-11's stuff.

She sensed his dismay. "Sorry, I'll keep my mouth shut."

But she did not. "Well, dear me," she said in the next second. "Would you look at that."

He did, recognizing the face, even before Downes said, "It's a blessed woman."

Blessed, hell, he thought. "That's Nina Chase."

"You know her?"

NORTHWEST AFGHANISTAN
10SEP01—1849 HOURS LOCAL

NINA CHASE STUMBLED along, remembering one other infamous night trek across the desert. No, she decided, she would not think about that. That was a bad experience with a bad guy. This time it would be different.

For one thing she was not traveling with Saddam Hussein's right-hand terrorist. This time, she was in better hands.

Brian Carnes knew what he was doing. She could tell that from the moment they met. He was professional, thorough. He reminded her of somebody else married to his job—Jack Swayne. Besides, like Swayne, he was a looker. Tall, dark complexion, strong jaw. When he smiled, she could see every tooth in his head. Just looking at it made her want to laugh with him. She wouldn't mind a laugh now and then. The only thing she didn't like about Mr. Carnes was his hairstyle. Slicked back and wet-looking, even in the desert. He still hadn't noticed that the wet look had vanished. Oh, and his eyes. She didn't like his eyes, all buggy, like some cartoon character ogling her. Oilcan Harry came to mind.

Anyhow, she was going to get a scoop on the rest of the world of the journalism, both print and broadcast. Carnes was so adamant that he would not tell who he worked for that he could only work for one organization, the CIA. She had asked him directly when they had first met this afternoon.

"I can't answer a question like that, and you know it," he said, a wink in his voice as well as from one of his bulging eyes.

She answered his big smile. She liked his looks, and in her previous life, had not minded playing games with a man. She could hardly even dredge up a smile for any man anymore. She had aged a lot in the last year as she recovered from her wounds. The gunshot wounds and broken bones were the easy part of healing. The things inside her head—they were another story. Practically losing her life, being dragged across Kosovo, being left for dead in a mass-murder scene that she could not erase from her mind, even with half a bottle of vodka every night to help her drift off to sleep.

After that, she had vowed to avoid the dangerous assignments. She couldn't blame her network. They had given her every beat she asked for. First Capitol Hill. A more boring venue she could not invent. Once politics had seemed so exciting to her, and she had reveled in it. Now, boring—in the aftermath of excessively exciting Kosovo, she supposed.

So she tried law and order. Even went through training at the FBI Academy at Quantico. She had talked her way onto a serial-killer task force. Tracking killers was not the heart-pounding, breathless business you saw at the movies. Tracking killers was a matter of processing information. Inputting data. Spitting out tables and lists. Endless footwork, phone calls, and follow-ups. A lot like investigative journalism. Boring.

Only the stars shed light on this part of the world right now. The men in front of her walked as if they had headlights guiding them. She felt like a blind person. Suddenly the serial-killer task force did not seem so bad.

She had layered up with fleece and wool and more wool. Still, she was cold. Not as cold as she was that night on the forest floor, lying among piles of bodies. But since then, she'd had a lower tolerance for night temperatures. The Afghanistan night was as cold as it could possibly be without raining, without soaking her to the skin.

This might not be a big story, but at least it was a change of pace, one that did not seem likely to get her killed. At a minimum, Carnes promised to show her an abandoned Al Qaeda cave complex. Back in the world, the caves had reached mythical proportions. The Russians had been defeated in 1980 by hordes of Afghan fighters pouring out of caves from all over the country. For all anybody knew, for every inch of earth surface in Afghanistan there was a mile of underground tunnels. All of Afghanistan just an ant farm, the Taliban living aboveground feeding off its own people. Al Qaeda pulling the strings from below ground, from a network that stretched to all parts of the globe and to every terrorist cell on the planet. For all she knew, Al Qaeda never even had to surface. The terrorists could pack a bomb from Afghanistan to Washington, D.C., through one of their tunnels, come up through a sewer line to a given toilet bowl. They could plant a bomb right in the ass of Senator Jamison Swayne, Jack Swayne's grandfather, a man so old and so sour he wouldn't even know until it exploded.

Of course, Al Qaeda and the Taliban were Greek to most Americans. No doubt she would have to invent words that would make people in the United States sit up and take note. Nobody cared what happened in Afghanistan. Face it, she was just on a boring training mission. Newspapers even had a term for it: Afghanistanism. When the editorial writers needed to fill some space, they could always express their indignation at the political circumstances in Afghanistan. Hell, put a globe down in front of John Q. and tell him either to find Afghanistan or a ten-pound booger, and the first thing he'd do is stick two fingers and a thumb up his nose.

Even so, what made her think she was so smart? She was the one out here in the vast wasteland, smuggling forty pounds of clothes across the faceless desert on a night so black that it made no difference to her whether she walked with her eyes open or closed.

She must have been out of her mind. Volunteering to go into a country where the Taliban only put a woman on a pedestal when they wanted to whip her. What the hell had she been thinking? She came out here to do what? Arrive at night, spend the next day in a cave, and walk back out in the dark? Was that really a smart thing to do?

Oh, well, she thought, do it and get it over with. Maybe she could find the energy to talk high, loud, and breathlessly about her experience. Like Geraldo. He was always able to make something out of nothing. Why couldn't she? It was what Americana had come to: watching Geraldo and fornicating.

She thought about it for another five drunken steps in the dark. Until something stabbed her in the leg. Either some kind of thorny desert vegetation. Or a venomous snake.

Probably just a bush, she thought. Her life had become too boring for the other.

Southwest Uzbekistan
10Sep01—1851 hours local

Seeing the face of Nina Chase struck Swayne with a whole spectrum of thoughts and feelings. As Downes found each of the other faces among the marchers, Swayne cranked new data into his estimate of the situation. The massacre back at the border had to have happened after Nina left. It did not look as if she was walking as a captive—nobody guarded her, no gag or blindfold.

He saw another American face in the group, a guy in his thirties dressed in khaki pants and a U.S. military field jacket camouflaged in desert tones. He might have been another newsman. Except that he carried a Kalashnikov semiautomatic with a telescoping stock instead of a camera or sound gear.

The others were Arabs who walked with ease of men who had grown up in the desert.

So this group might not know about the killings. Swayne asked Downes to pull back on her field of view so he could get the big picture. He didn't like what he saw. A pair of men at the front of the marching file walked shoulder to shoulder. As they walked, they inclined their heads toward each other, talking as if they did not want anybody else to hear them. Every now and then, one of the men would point toward the horizon. The other would either agree, or point to a different spot on the horizon. Both pointed in the general direction of the ambush.

Swayne now felt sure of the ambush. Everybody else in the group kept plodding forward without any concern about what might be on the horizon less than a mile away. Everybody else walked as if the march might not be over for hours yet.

Except for the man at the tail end of the column. He acted skittish, hanging back from the group, allowing the gap to grow between himself and the main body.

To Swayne's mind, he and the two up front knew about the ambush. They acted nervous because they wanted to avoid it.

So, half a dozen people were to die in an ambush, one an American television reporter, the other an American—possibly CIA, possibly a Delta Force soldier, although that was less likely. As far as Swayne knew, Delta Force did not operate in groups smaller than two, rarely less than four.

Swayne had no idea who the other four people were, but it was a good guess that they were guides that Nina or the CIA had hired, maybe Uzbeks.

"What?" Downes asked.

Swayne realized he must have been muttering to himself. "Nothing."

"Yes, something," she said. "I just heard you say something about somebody getting killed."

"Oh. Maybe. There's not a damned thing anybody can do about it."

In the dim glow of her computer screen, he saw her teeth shining. She was grinning at him.

"Wanna bet?" she asked.

"Hold all bets, dammit. Swayne, turn on your ears."

Downes turned to her computer, where the voice had originated. "Who the heck—?"

Swayne put a hand to her mouth. He didn't need to ask who it was and didn't want her spouting off. He recog-

nized the voice transmitting on her computer. Zavello. He
didn't sound too happy. Swayne switched on his radio and
pulled down his radio mike boom, adjusting it until he
could kiss it with his lips pursed.

"Eagle One, this is Spartan One, over."

"This is Eagle One. Don't interfere with anything happening on the ground, got that?"

"This is Spartan One. You realize the group is about to
be ambushed?" Swayne wondered how long they had
been paying attention. Maybe they had not seen the group
lying in the reverse-7 formation. Zavello probably didn't
realize that at least three of the Arabs in the marching file
were in on the ambush.

"Leave it alone."

"Spartan One, wilco, over."

"Out."

Swayne's wilco was universal military terminology that
stood for *I understand my orders and will comply.* Hollywood films about military communications were a joke
among the Marines. When a superior officer commanded
a Marine to do something, it was by definition an order.
Every Marine understood that it would be redundant, if
not a sign of insecurity, for an officer to say, *That's an
order*, or even more ridiculous, *That's a direct order*. Marines didn't give or get indirect orders. All orders were
direct, and orders were orders.

QUANTICO, VIRGINIA
10SEP01—0855 HOURS LOCAL

ORDERS. THE ONE thing Zavello hated about his job was
taking orders from civilians below the rank of Secretary
of Defense. It did not matter to him whether their civilian
rank was equivalent to a major general or even higher. If
he didn't get his orders directly from the chain of command, that is, somewhere along the direct line from the

President to the Secretary of Defense to the Chairman of
the Joint Chiefs of Staff to the Commandant of the Marine
Corps, then Zavello didn't want to hear it. But he *had*
heard it. Directly from one of the assistant directors of
Central Intelligence. *Leave it alone,* the man had said. So
that was exactly what he had relayed to Swayne in the
field.

Zavello had been on duty in the OMCC to monitor
activities of another Force Recon team in the Philippines.
Instead of an operational reconnaissance mission, that had
turned into a rescue. Two of the four members of the team
had injured themselves rappelling through the jungle canopy in the freakiest of freak accidents. While shooting
down the rope from the fuselage of a helicopter, one of
the Marines had stirred up a nest of hornets. They had
stung him more than a dozen times, once in the eye, and
he had lost consciousness and fallen, all in a matter of
seconds. He had landed on top of one of his mates, already on the ground. The injury report was a disaster, with
broken ribs, possible broken back, concussion, and a compound fracture of a collarbone, which had snapped, one
broken end of the bone spearing the Marine in his own
neck.

Once Zavello was satisfied that the men were aboard a
rescue helicopter and their medical conditions stabilized,
he turned his attention to Swayne's toy party in the Middle East.

By then, things were getting interesting, and he began
to immerse himself into the situation. He had been privy
to intelligence coming out of Afghanistan for weeks.
Something was up, but nobody knew what. Now he was
getting the chance to look at some actual Al Qaeda troops
on the ground.

His curiosity turned to anger when he recognized a
CNN correspondent, Nina Chase, tripping through the
dunes. Then to alarm when he recognized Brian Carnes,

a CIA operative who, like most of those CIA numb-nuts, was out there freelancing it.

Defense had clearly staked out that area for testing and reconnaissance. He had been the one to put in the request to reserve the ground and the airspace above it.

Zavello ordered a download of the thermal images from the drone. Before sending them to the CIA and making his phone call, he made a double check of the zone that he had reserved. After he had finished, he was sure. The CIA guy didn't belong there. Somebody at Central Intelligence needed to take a bite out of his ass. Zavello bared his own teeth, like cones in the killer whale's mouth. As if to do the biting himself.

Then Zavello began to put together the ambush situation. The CIA was going to lose somebody if they didn't act quickly.

Using the government's closed-circuit, firewall-protected, encrypted e-network, Zavello shot the image to the CIA and picked up the horn to the assistant director on duty.

The man told him, *Leave it alone*.

So Zavello took a seat in the OMCC to watch events unfold. With a wet one-eyed glare over each shoulder, he drove away the crowd of rubberneckers that had gathered around his monitor.

He had access to the thermal satellite picture. It gave a good overall view of the area, like a football coach's clipboard with Xs and Os. He liked the XD-11's view better. Not just because he had access to better pictures than Central Intelligence. The low-angle and high-resolution pictures, even in the infrared mode, gave him a more realistic look. He felt that might even be lying on his stomach, a pair of night-vision binoculars glued to his eye—and patch—watching the action in the chilly air. This drone was something else. Since the Marine Corps would not allow him to go to the field, the Dirty Birdie could bring the field to him. He wondered what it would take to install a gun camera and a 20-mm to the aircraft. *Think about it, Karl,* he told himself. *What would it be like to pop a cap on one of Osama bin Laden's ragheads from halfway around the world?*

He saw the agent slap at his pants pocket and begin to dig. He came up with a digital telephone. The CIA duty officer was giving him a buzz: *Hey, shit-for-brains, start thinking up your famous last words.*

Zavello wished he could eavesdrop on the phone conversation. He wondered what it would take for the toy store to develop some long-range audio for its drone.

NORTHWEST AFGHANISTAN
10SEP01—1830 HOURS LOCAL

WHEN CARNES SLAPPED at his leg, Nina had to laugh. She could hear the digital telephone vibrating against some coins in his pocket. One of the two Arabs walking directly ahead of them turned his head to grunt at the noise. Carnes wasn't making a great impression on his guides. *Some spook.*

Good, she thought. Let him take some heat for a while. For the first hour of their march, the rancid Arabs had been bitching to Carnes that she was making too much noise. But by the time they had walked about ten miles, they were less concerned about her than running their little iron-man marathon across the desert at night. Men over here weren't very much different from men anyplace else. Men here—

Suddenly her news senses kicked in. The tone in Carnes's voice had changed. Somebody was chewing him out. His voice sounded tense.

"Don't whine, Brian," she said. "It's so unbecoming."

He hissed at her to be quiet. In turn, the two Arabs did the same to him. Carnes said a few words in their language, and the group came to a halt. Then he moved away from the trail until she could no longer distinguish his words.

In a minute he was back. "We've got a problem," he said.

She could tell by the tremble in his voice that it was a serious problem, but she said, "Keep your voice down. You never know when somebody you don't suspect can speak your language." She remembered all too clearly a terrorist who had played dumb about speaking English, letting her call him every name but decency, nearly getting herself killed by pissing him off.

Carnes huddled close to her ear and whispered, "I'm supposed to meet somebody out here to get some vital intel. My agency—organization—didn't know I was operating solo. But we've been picked up on satellite, and somebody recognized me—what are you doing with your hair?"

"Nothing." She nearly laughed aloud. She realized she had begun primping her hair for the satellite camera without thinking about it. Too long in the news business, she thought. "So what? You're in trouble with your bosses because somebody recognized you?"

"No—well, yes. I'm not exactly supposed to be out here. But we have other problems that are worse."

"There's something worse than marching across the desert at night, breaking your leg in every badger hole—?"

"Shut up, Nina. The people watching us through that eye in the sky say we're walking into an ambush. About a half mile ahead."

Her heart kicked her in the chest. *Ambush?* Hadn't she already lived that scene in her life? In a different Mideast country that didn't look a bit different from this one? She wasn't about to go through that again. "Ambush? Well, forget that. Let's go back."

"It's not that easy."

"Of course it is. You flip a U-turn and haul ass. Pretty

soon you're back where you came from. Simple as that."

"Look, I'm supposed to meet some people tonight."

"Not to be obvious about it, but isn't that what an ambush is? Meeting somebody?"

He found her forearm in the dark and patted her to reassure her. "Look, from twenty miles up in the sky, one group of people waiting for another group might look like an ambush. That doesn't mean that's what's happening. We should go ahead. When we get close, I'll leave the main group behind and send out a scout. That makes sense, doesn't it?"

"I thought you were going to show me a cave complex. So I could take some pictures. I don't remember you saying anything about meeting anybody." She couldn't suppress the edge in her voice. She didn't like it when people played games with her. In the desert at night in a country as hostile as this to women and civilization in general.

"I'm sorry. I couldn't tell you about the meeting. I'm supposed to pick up—"

"I know. Some vital information. Right?"

"Keep your voice down."

"Want vital?" she said, not caring who heard her. "I'll give you vital. My butt. Where my butt is concerned, I think it's vital that I get to know when somebody is laying for us in the desert, don't you?"

He gripped her arm more tightly now. No longer reassuring, but threatening. "Nina. Please. If you want, I can send you back with a guide, maybe two. No more than that. I couldn't spare anybody in case something did go wrong—"

"Something will go wrong, Brian. Something going wrong is one of the definitions of an ambush."

"Nina!"

"You're hurting my arm, Brian. Let loose."

She sensed some movement nearby. She smelled the rancid odor of men who lived in circumstances where they might not shower more than once or twice a year. A soft voice spoke to them from nearby.

The CIA men answered it. "He wants to know what's wrong."

"Tell him you're an asshole. That's what's wrong."

Carnes spoke in their language again, and Nina could hear him biting off the words. His anger was apparent in any language.

"I told them you turned an ankle. Suppose you stay here. I'll leave a man to guard you—"

She snorted. "Now I'm down to one man?"

"Make up your mind. I must have been out of my mind to bring a—newsperson out here on a sensitive mission."

Amazing, thought Nina. Amazing what the darkness could do for her intuition. She didn't have to read the CIA man's face to tell that he was lying. "You knew exactly what you were doing, you sonofabitch. You thought you were going to get some intelligence that might make you a hero. But you would never be able to tell anybody about it. So you told me that you were coming out here to look at some caves. Perfectly innocent. Then you run into somebody who gives you the information, quite by accident, a convenient coincidence that he is at the same caves you were going out to take pretty pictures of. So the story about the heroic CIA man gets into the press. Suddenly you're a freaking public hero."

He let it lie where she had thrown it. She waited, and the silence in the darkness told her that she had nailed his motives. By now he'd started turning the color purple. Partly in anger, partly in embarrassment. Busted.

He sputtered, about to make denials and excuses, she knew. She cut him off. "Too late, Brian. What you are speaks so loudly, I can't hear what you're saying."

He turned his head to spit. He never looked back in her direction, as if it were too embarrassing, even in the dark. "What's it going to be?" he asked, a note of resignation in his voice.

"Go on. Don't leave anybody with me. I'll wait here alone."

"Have it your way."

He didn't say it, but she heard it there in the tone: *Have it your way, bitch*.

SOUTHWEST UZBEKISTAN
10SEP01—1910 HOURS LOCAL

SWAYNE WATCHED IN disbelief. For two reasons. First that the main party would leave Nina alone in the desert. Second that the American who had just answered his digital cell phone, probably a CIA operative, had huddled with his Arab force—minus the one who had dropped off the trail of the formation. Then the entire group set off, to Swayne's dismay, directly for the ambush. *Maybe the guy knows something,* Swayne thought.

While Nina had been talking to the American, practically cheek to cheek, Zavello had called him to alert him that Night Runner and Friel would be dispatched to the region as quickly as possible, their airplane charged to the CIA. Which meant their job would be to rescue the SOB about to get his tail caught in a blender.

Swayne could never figure Zavello. One minute you hated the guy, the next you wanted to hug him. He could toss a Marine's emotions around like the heavy seas—or a woman. Somehow, the mess that his Force Recon Team had become during and after their last mission was going to be made right. *Night Runner and Friel traveling together?* That news alone told him that things were on the mend. He had worried that they might never be able to work together again.

Elated as he was, the situation on the scientific computer screen might well unravel before he or any of his team could influence the action. He put his joy on hold. No matter how fast they traveled, and Zavello had said they would be coming by VIP craft, they could not get here in less than fourteen hours. He did the math. Tomorrow morning at the earliest.

Meanwhile, the seven men had resumed their march toward the ambush. Nina moved off the trail and nestled into a fold in the desert floor.

Meanwhile, the straggler unmasked himself as a bad actor. After falling back from the group, he struck off on the diagonal. Swayne could now see that he had begun running, trying to talk into a handheld radio as he bypassed the group. He ran on a circular course that would take him in the general direction of the ambush site, where he might even join in the attack.

Swayne would not allow himself to believe that an innocent meeting was about to take place. The behavior of the trail man alone warned of trouble. The pair at the front of the file were now as tight as copulating snakes, constantly whispering into each other's ears, taking turns talking into their radio.

Again, he wondered what he could do about it. This time he kept his words to himself and leaned over Downes's shoulder to whisper.

She nodded and pushed herself away from the keyboard. As they walked away from the computer far enough so their voices would not be picked up by his microphone, Swayne checked his own radio mike to be sure it was off.

When he was satisfied nobody could overhear, he said, "Will the drone be all right?"

"Perfectly," she said. "I put it on autopilot."

"Tell me about your ace up the sleeve."

"Beg your pardon?"

"You led me to believe you might be able to do something about the situation out there—you wanted to bet on it."

"Oh, that. Right. You wouldn't want to bet against me."

She began to tell him how she could influence the action in the desert more than ten miles away. As usual, she turned it into a scientific lecture, but Swayne stifled his impatience. Now was not the time to alienate her.

After she had finished, he asked her to round up Whit-field and Ramirez while he went to collect Greiner and Radford, the leader of the Marine security platoon. Once he had them formed, he kept his briefing short. He and Greiner were going to infiltrate Afghanistan once more. To put themselves into a position when they could help out the Americans—if there would be any Americans alive to help by the time the rest of his team arrived from the States.

The others were eager to help. Radford offered to take his platoon along. The offer tempted Swayne. Radford ran a tight ship. His noncoms had Gulf War experience, and his men looked to be tough and disciplined. But Swayne refused the offer.

"I don't have the authority to change your mission," he said. "Even if I did have the authority, I don't know that I would. Somebody has to stay here and help secure this sensitive equipment—and scientists. Momadou could be trouble." Swayne had seen a lean and eager look about the Uzbek leader. "He may not know what is going on inside our little science lab. He does know that if it takes a platoon of Marines to secure it, he could sell it on the international black market for a lot of rubles. No, you can't go."

Radford dared not argue. He looked crestfallen, but he had his orders—as directly as if Swayne had said: *That's a direct order, Lieutenant.*

"There is something you could do to help, though," Swayne said. Radford brightened. "Hand me your map." Swayne rotated it to orient it to the ground. He traced his route to the border of Afghanistan. "Take a squad and recon this approach. Identify the best ground to defend. In case somebody tries to follow us across the border when we come back."

Whitfield and Ramirez offered to position some of their scientific toys along the route. "If it would help? It would be, like, an expedient test. It would give the lieutenant's men a reason to be out there."

Swayne liked the idea and said so.

Downes gave him a handheld screen. "It's a kind of PDA that can download images from the drone. It has a radio built in. You can—" She bit off the words, holding up the palms of both hands. "Well, you know what you can do with a radio."

In less than ten minutes, he and Greiner were under way. He had briefed Radford about doubling the watch. He had no overt reason not to trust Momadou, but he warned Radford to be wary. The lieutenant smiled weakly. "I think I've already been getting a bad vibe from the guy. I should not have even suggested leaving these people alone with him."

Swayne led him off his own hook. "I'm impressed that you would want to go out with us. You ought to look into Force Recon training."

ALTHOUGH THE NIGHT had chilled to below freezing, Swayne's clothing was drenched with sweat after humping the first mile at double time. They walked using their stereoscopic night-vision goggles, which gave them depth perception enough even to run in the dark. Using the latest in Starlight technology, the goggles not only converted ambient light into 20-20 resolution. They also processed color. Images at night did not reflect color as brilliantly as under the sun. So the picture was like that of a well-colorized black-and-white feature film.

Swayne couldn't help shaking his head. Color was certainly a great advancement, but out here in the desert, day or night, the only colors were 256 shades of brown.

Swayne kept telling himself that he had done the right thing in going back into Taliban land with light packs, carrying most of their extra weight in ammunition, some high-energy food, and two canteens of water each.

They had at least twenty miles to cover. Conventional soldiers planned to make two and a half miles an hour under weapons and field packs. Marines could sustain three miles an hour for about six miles. Force Recon Marines traveling relatively lightly, as they were, might make four miles an hour for two hours. They could possibly do better by jogging. The distance was so great, it would not be worth it. He did not want to arrive spent, so he planned on fourteen hours, hoping to arrive at the same time as Friel and Night Runner.

Naturally, Swayne was interested in Nina Chase. More interested than he should have been. They were lovers, and had been for years. Somehow they had kept the secret both from the news media and the Marine Corps. They had crossed paths before, while she was on assignments that took her to the same places he had gone on missions. So he could have found any number of personal excuses to go out there and pull her out of danger.

But Zavello was another matter. He would never have authorized a rescue mission for somebody from the press. *Journalist* was just another word for *enemy*. If Al Qaeda wanted to kill a journalist sticking her nose into military matters, well, that was merely a side bennie.

No, Zavello was interested in the other American. Because Zavello wouldn't talk about it—and made such a point about his inability to talk about it—Swayne knew for sure that the guy was CIA. He must be important. Because Zavello had never found anything better to say about agency men than he did about the press.

Swayne thought he could make some educated guesses about why Zavello let him and Greiner go back into Afghanistan, once Swayne suggested his plan. If there were trouble, nobody was likely to be willing to risk American aircraft getting shot down by American Stinger missiles that had been supplied to the Taliban more than twenty years earlier. A couple of soldiers on foot were another matter. The government only had to deny their existence. They could be from anywhere, remnants of the Soviet special forces, the Spetznatz, now soldiers of fortune making mischief around the world. Or Israelis, whom all Arabs named as villains in everything from drought to flu to suicide charges going off prematurely in terrorist bomb factories.

The United States Government could plausibly deny the existence of Swayne and Greiner. All their families would ever know was that they died in a training accident, their bodies burned beyond recognition or lost at sea.

Swayne didn't worry much about that. Those questions he had settled in his own mind a long time ago. Those were the questions you answered for yourself before joining Force Recon Marines. If you couldn't deal with that up front, there was no reason to go through the grueling training and lethal missions like the one this had turned into.

Lethal, he hoped, for the Taliban and Al Qaeda fighters out there in the night. But not, he hoped, for Nina Chase.

It both excited and worried him that he would be seeing her again. Excited because it had been a while. Worried because—

No, he was not going to worry about anything happening to Nina Chase. It would be his job to see to that.

QUANTICO, VIRGINIA
10SEP01—0910 HOURS LOCAL

NIGHT RUNNER AND Friel settled into their life of luxury aboard the Lear 25D VIP jet craft, called the "pocket rocket" because of its airspeed of five hundred miles an hour, more than eighty percent of the speed of sound. They had strapped their gear and weapons into the empty seat at the back of the craft across from them. Besides the pilot, copilot, and flight engineer, they had the craft to themselves. The flight engineer was a woman in her mid-twenties, an Air Force staff sergeant who looked like a starlet but behaved with the humility of the novice nuns Friel had met growing up Catholic in Boston. The combination had such a powerful sensual effect on him, Friel couldn't look at her. Too worried that she might trigger one of his psychotic episodes—or worse, that she might read his unclean thoughts about her. He hadn't been to confession since—well, for six purgatories and three hells ago. She'd already stoked up enough unclean thoughts for a penance two Lents long. Hell, the priest would kick a hole in the confessional door just hearing Friel's thoughts about her.

She offered them food and drinks. Both men hesitated at first. Then, of course, they realized they had plenty of time to digest at least two meals before arriving over Afghanistan. The liquor tempted Friel, but he refused it without even looking at Night Runner to see if he should. Again with the drugs. The nut-busters had warned him against drinking while taking them.

After steaks and baked potatoes swimming in a robust mushroom gravy the color of dark chocolate—Friel had two of each—Night Runner reclined his luxury seat and raised the footrest. Against his natural instincts he ate the heavy meal, then let it lull him into narcolepsy. He would rather sleep on the carpet, but could not act in a way that would create any doubt about his fitness to go back to Force Recon. So he draped a blanket over his shoulders and bunched one thin pillow under his ear. Before trying to sleep, he glanced across the passageway to see Friel staring at him.

"I can't sleep," Friel said. "It's still day."

Night Runner knew Friel had not even tried, but he also knew that bringing it up this way was more than a case of insomnia. Night Runner sat erect in his seat, putting down the footrest. "Do you want to talk, Henry?"

Friel nodded. "I don't know what to say, though.

Chief—I mean, Gunny—I'm not good at sharing."

"When have you ever known me to be good at it?" Night Runner shook his head as he felt the anvil of sadness on his chest. He decided to face it. "Look what I did to you on our last mission instead of talking about it."

"It wasn't your fault, Gunny." Friel leaned forward, resting his elbows on his knees. "It was my fault for acting like a shithead—"

Night Runner put up a hand like a traffic cop. "Understand this, Henry. Yes, you acted like a shit. But I should have handled it. I treated you badly—terribly. I deserved what I got."

"No, it wasn't worth a court-martial. I just don't think—" Friel couldn't find the words, although he was pressing his fists against his temples, as if to force thoughts out of his brain.

Night Runner shook his head. "Henry, I don't want to stop you from talking about this if you want to. For myself, I have heard enough, seen enough, said enough. We don't always get do-overs. So forget the things you did to Greiner. I'll get over what I did to you—no, no need to forgive me again. Just know this, young man. Greiner does not hold a grudge against you. The captain and I— I haven't talked to him lately, but I'm sure I can speak for him on this—both of us want to put this team back together. First we lost Gunny Potts, and the very next mission Perfect went down. We haven't been right for a long time. But we can start healing. By putting the bad things behind us."

Friel looked surprised. "You mean we don't have to talk about this? The cap is not going to—"

"No," Night Runner said. "I'll brief him on everything. If he wants to ask you questions, he will. But I don't think so. You should make your peace with Greiner and let it go. He's a good kid, Henry. He won't hold a grudge. He wants to be a part of a good team. Which is what we were once. Which is what we can be again. Starting on this mission."

Friel's face took on an unfamiliar aspect. A smile. "You think? You really think?"

"Depend on it, Henry. We're Marines. We can prove ourselves right by doing right. That is what I intend to do. I don't think we have to talk about this like a bunch of ladies in group therapy. Do you?"

"Shit, no." Friel buried his fist into his pillow.

Night Runner done with his second speech in as many days, leaned forward and held out his hand. Friel took it eagerly. For the second time in less than two days, they engaged in a hearty four-handed shake.

Friel, still smiling, threw back his seat, raising the footrest. He pulled a blanket over him and adjusted the pillow with a few more punches, falling asleep even before Night Runner had adjusted his own seat. Inside, Night Runner felt that same smile that he saw on Friel's face. He felt it in his heart. For the first time in months, he saw hope that the team could begin to operate the way it was supposed to operate. There was nothing he would like better than to mold his band of Marines into fighters as deadly as himself. All the talking had wearied him. But before letting himself drift off to sleep, he spoke the prayers of the warrior to the heavens outside his window, hoping the air screaming past would carry his words from his spirit to theirs.

He had a fairly good idea of what his ancestors looked like as they prepared for battle. He had seen enough Remington and Russell paintings in his lifetime. He had studied them in detail, knowing that both artists tried to remain true to his culture.

He wondered. From their heaven in the Cypress Hills of Saskatchewan, were they watching him now as he rode into battle? What would they think of a Blackfeet warrior, descendant of Heavy Runner himself, shrieking through the air like a lance at six hundred miles an hour?

NORTHWEST AFGHANISTAN
10SEP01—1906 HOURS LOCAL

SADDIQ CHECKED HIS watch. Time had slowed down,
as it always did any time he waited for a battle to begin.
Since the moment his battle had become overdue, more
than an hour ago, time had stood still.

Yes, he had been in touch by radio. By two radios, in
fact. Redundancy, the Americans called it. The Americans
had trained him well. He had attended the best military
schools—not only the tactical ones like the Ranger
School, but also the strategic ones like the Command and
General Staff College at Fort Leavenworth and the Naval
War College at Newport, Rhode Island.

He went to America in the uniform of an Egyptian officer, carrying the dossier of royal lineage. Something that
his mentor, Osama bin Laden, had arranged. Bin Laden
could arrange anything. Rather, money, usually American
dollars, could arrange anything. All it took was somebody
who knew where to place the money where its effect
could be most felt. This was what made Saddiq a genius.
Like bin Laden, he could walk into a room wearing a
smile, handing out handshakes and a quiet word of en-
couragement. All the while looking for the person most
eager to feel the color of money, most able to use it to
good effect.

Redundancy. Within the column marching in his direction, he had placed two sets of spies. The first pair did
not have a brain between them, but together they were at
least functional. He kept in touch with them by one radio.
His backup agent nearly had nearly a full brain of his own,
although he had a history of being inept in the field. Saddiq kept in touch with him by a second radio, on a separate channel. He could talk to one, then another—or both
at the same time by putting both radios to his mouth at
the same time. They fed him information enough that he

could lie on the sand with his eyes closed and see the picture of their progress across the desert landscape.

Now that things had began moving again, he could open his eyes and find them in the spotting scope that Osama bin Laden provided him, the Starlight technology capable of seeing a full kilometer's distance.

Saddiq was not happy with what he saw. The pair in front of the column—Uzbeks paid by his men—practically ran across the landscape toward him. They feared sharing the ambush with the American. Somehow, they had gotten the notion that it would be better to run toward men waiting for them in the dark with loaded rifles, rocket-propelled grenades, machine guns, and a protective belt of antipersonnel land mines.

He did not care if they died. He expected casualties anytime the shooting began. He did care that they might imperil the attack by springing the ambush too early. He worried that a stray bullet might kill the American agent before Saddiq could find out how much he knew. Clearly, he knew something. He had made inquiries at Mazar-e Sharif. Boldly, in the marketplace. Now Saddiq wanted to make some inquiries of his own, secretly, in the desert caves, where a man's screams could not be heard for a hundred meters, let alone a hundred miles.

Saddiq had intended to snatch the man from Mazar-e Sharif days ago. It would have been so much more convenient to take him to his private villa—again a gift from Osama. He had hidden, soundproof rooms in the villa—along with secret escape tunnels, a standard architectural feature of all bin Laden houses. In his hidden chambers he had extracted secrets from even the most hardened fighters of the damned Northern Alliance. Already he had done so, reducing a veteran warlord with a glorious record of fighting against the Soviets to a blubbering, hysterical schoolgirl.

The American agent had bolted from the town in the west of Afghanistan, returning to Afghanistan through

Uzbekistan to recruit guides and fighters for a raid on a cave complex not far inside Afghanistan from the Uzbek border.

The more he moved, and the faster he traveled, the greater Saddiq's interest in the American, who called himself O'Brien.

Saddiq had his own operatives everywhere in the region, including Uzbekistan. So it was an easy matter to drop some hints about a major action against the Americans in their own homeland. Using Islamic martyrs, which the Americans wrongly called suicide attackers. He had used all the right words and even his own name. The mention of Saddiq had finally attracted the American, whose real name was Carnes.

Others of bin Laden's lieutenants had chastised Saddiq for letting on about an attack against America. Not bin Laden himself. He thought it a brilliant strategy. They might learn whether the Americans had any true intelligence about an actual attack. They might be able to plant some false details, such as a fake time or place.

Still basking in the glow of bin Laden's gentle, admiring smile, he was about to deliver the American. He planned to take video pictures to show Osama the American's report in his own words, as he gave it. Tonight he had cut off the CIA man's retreat. He had trapped the American in the desert. The Uzbek fighting force had not fought hard in the surprise attack at the border by another of his units—they would have run away if that had been an option. Now that the American was well inside Afghanistan, well away from the disputed border, there was no way that other Uzbeks could save him with regular forces, even if they were somehow to muster the courage. The American belonged to Saddiq.

He spoke into his radio, and when he had their attention, he told the pair of half-wits in front of his position to stop running toward the ambush. Out of breath, they told him that they had stopped, that they were waiting for the American and his bodyguards to catch up. Saddiq could see for himself that they had not slowed down at all.

So he told them they were running through a minefield. The two raised dust clouds as they skidded to a stop. Both gasping for breath, neither daring to breathe.

When he was satisfied that he finally had them under control, he left them standing about three hundred meters away from the killing zone. They would stay glued to their last footsteps until he told them to move.

Next, he began to look for the American. He caught a flash in the night-vision scope. The dimmest of night's light had gleamed off bare skin. A forehead bounced into sight from a fold in the earth where the trail, a well-worn vehicle track, dipped into a wadi. The dry creek bed was so broad and so shallow, it might not even be visible during the day. The man's full face came into view. Yes, the American had taken over the lead. About four hundred meters away. Still too far to spring the ambush. As others walked out of the earth, he looked for the woman. She might make a nice diversion. He could not see her. He wondered, *Has something gone wrong?*

"What about the woman?" he snarled into the radio tuned to that held by the two men standing like statues in the open. They did not know. He changed frequencies and asked the same question of his other man. He did not know anything about the woman. True, she had gone into the desert—he could confirm that. He had followed the plan, so he was no longer able to keep track of her.

"I dropped far behind," the man reported. "Now I am bypassing the group. I have not seen her in the last hour."

Saddiq complimented him and asked, "Do you need directions?"

Out of breath, the man insisted he did not, expressing enough pique to show he resented the idea that he could be lost, yet with enough restraint to avoid giving insult himself.

Saddiq did not reply. Yes, the man had bypassed the marching column. He had also bypassed the ambush squad. If he kept going, he would bypass all of Afghanistan, perhaps finishing his journey in Pakistan. Let him, he thought.

Saddiq selected yet another radio channel to talk to the officers who would be responsible for the ambush. "Try not to kill our two statues," he said. "If it happens, it happens. Take careful aim and use your ammunition with thrift. Do not kill the American. Do not kill the woman, if she appears." He paused, letting them acknowledge his orders, rechecking the formation as it marched toward him. He confirmed to them the woman had vanished.

He worried that somehow she might have turned back toward Uzbekistan, that she might escape. He wondered what she knew from the CIA man. She might be CIA as well. That worried him.

He told his men. "As soon as the American is under our control, we will have to search for the woman. It is essential."

NORTHWEST AFGHANISTAN
10SEP01—1957 HOURS LOCAL

SWAYNE CALLED A halt an hour into their march. More than taking a rest break, he needed to check the screen of Downes's handheld computer, the one linked into the drone's camera. He bit his lip, knowing that he and Greiner were not going to be able to do much tonight to influence that situation. He saw that Nina had begun creeping away from the trail, walking with her arms out front, as if she were blind. Good, he thought. She might escape the Al Qaeda fighters in the dark. Now, if only she wouldn't travel too far. Her course would take her into the heart of Afghanistan. If Al Qaeda didn't kill her, a fall in the mountains might.

He spoke into the onboard microphone of Downes's PDA. He asked her to focus the camera's lens to a larger field of view, so he could see what was going on with the ambush force and the marching column.

That didn't look great either. Except that the lone man who had been walking trail had wandered into the interior of Afghanistan, taking him out of play. The ambushing force had laid their weapons on the American's line of march. He thought it odd that the two Uzbeks who had run off ahead of the column now stood in place not far from the killing zone. Why would they stop nearly in the cross fire of the legs of the layout?

He asked Downes to check over the ambush formation one more time in close-up to see if he had missed anything. He wondered if part of the ambushing force was on the payroll of the CIA, about to turn their weapons on the people setting the trap.

Another pass showed no change. If anything, the ambush men were more intent on Carnes's group. Swayne saw that they had night-vision devices. Modern ones too, which meant a well-bankrolled group. Not too many organizations had that kind of money, but Al Qaeda was one. The other was the Taliban, the fanatic religious government that had drained Afghanistan, keeping the people poor, spending most of their money on weapons, and making global mischief.

Finally, on a swing back toward the marching column, he saw that the American had his digital telephone plastered to his ear. Finally, he had come to a stop. Finally, he dropped to one knee behind a cluster of boulders, keeping the rocks between him and the ambush site. Finally.

Although they had stopped for less than a minute, Swayne murmured to Greiner through his radio mike, telling him to take the lead. Greiner, who had been sitting so he could watch their back trail, turned and shuffled into a position where he could watch for a moment in the direction they were going to head out. He adjusted the heads-up display inside his night-vision goggles, the one that showed him the preset course to take. Once he was satisfied that the area was clear, he got under way.

Swayne smiled. Greiner was a good kid. You never had to tell him anything twice. He had that great disposition, never feeling the need to argue or resist. Always interested in doing the right thing for the team.

The team. He stood up and found his pace behind Greiner, keeping about thirty meters back. Now, more than ever, it was important to stay dispersed. That tired Marine saying, *One hand grenade will get you all,* sounded more ominous now that there were only the two of them.

NORTHWEST AFGHANISTAN
10SEP01—1958 HOURS LOCAL

CARNES GOT AN earful from his CIA boss. His troops had looked at the tidbits Carnes had given them. They had weighed the credibility of his sources. That much checked out. They had begun to compare Carnes's report of possible mischief in America by Al Qaeda. They had bounced vague questions off allied spook agencies and gotten vague answers in return. They had looked at voice traffic. They had seen increases in cell calls from countries like Afghanistan, Iran, and Iraq. They may have found something of value in the coded content of those calls, but the translations were in progress. They did see a sharp spike in the number of calls. And a shift in times of calls to the middle of the night tipped analysts to trouble. Some calls tested by voice-stress analysis showed anxiety between the Arabic callers. VSA machines could isolate stress in a human voice no matter what the language or who the speaker.

His people at the CIA told Carnes that many key indicators were up, especially high-stress calls from likely areas of terrorist activity—Yemen and West Germany.

Yet analysts could find no specific warnings to cite. Something might be up, but nobody in the spy agency could identify what or where the terrorists might strike.

The new evidence confirmed an attack to Carnes. The agency wanted him to back off, to cut his losses. If he could avoid a firefight, they said, he might still escape.

Carnes told them what they wanted to hear. "I'm pulling the plug on this one." He could hear the relief in the voice at the other end.

Still, he did not move. He kept running his options. There had to be a way for him to turn the tables on Saddiq—the agency had somehow gotten pictures of Saddiq in real time. He was among those lying prone in the ambush. How that overhead satellite could identify him from the back of his head, Carnes did not know. But what he did know was that Saddiq would be the ultimate prize, next to snatching Osama bin Laden himself. Saddiq would know about any attack on America. He would know all bin Laden's hiding places. Capturing Saddiq would be like snatching Joseph Goebbels out of Germany in 1939.

And the bastard is only a quarter of a mile away!

Carnes decided it might be worth it to take a risk, hell, any risk short of outright suicide.

The agency had told him he faced ten Al Qaeda fighters. He also knew that he had lost three of the Uzbeks to the other side.

Carnes called together his four men and told them of an ambush set by four men—lying about the numbers. They would be frantic enough about even odds. Forget about a nearly three-to-one disadvantage.

He briefed on his plan for a hasty retreat. Two of the men would run back down the trail to the wadi. The other three would support them by fire, covering their retreat. The three left behind would then run for the edge of the wadi too. They would exfiltrate to Uzbekistan, picking up the woman along the way.

"What could be more simple than that?" he asked.

The Uzbeks didn't care about simple. They grunted in relief at turning away from an ambush zone.

The group had two night-vision devices among them, small handheld monoculars with a range of a little more than a hundred meters. The CIA was paranoid about losing high-tech devices to thieves, either enemy or friend. So paranoid that the agency would issue second-rate equipment to its own men.

Carnes divided the group into two teams and allotted one monocular to each team. He made sure that a good marksman was in each group.

"No shooting unless they shoot at you," he said. "Now, group one, get moving."

As their footsteps crunched out of his hearing, he turned toward the ambush and set his Kalashnikov to automatic. It amazed him to see two men standing in the open barely one hundred meters away. His two Uzbek deserters. What the hell were they doing? There they stood, in the open. Maybe they had not betrayed him. Maybe they were waiting for him to catch up.

Why hadn't Saddiq and his ambush troops opened up by now? Why hadn't they reacted at all to the two Uzbeks? He decided to force the issue. He cut loose with a burst, fully half a magazine, firing over the heads of the two men who had been in his group.

Not far enough over their heads, he saw. Although one of the men dived to the ground and began crawling toward cover, the other's head snapped like a disco dancer's, but just once. The man fell over, dead before he pitched into the sand.

"We're under attack," Carnes shouted to his two guides. "Only ten meters away." He emptied the rest of a clip into the darkness nearby. The other men could not see a thing because there was nothing. But like any men believing they were under fire, they shot back.

He ordered them toward the wadi. "Move! Now!" he

shouted in their language. "We don't have much time. We have to leave now. Go! Go! Go!"

The two men needed no urging. They took off into the night at his first word. He waited for the ambush to respond.

No sooner did he wonder about it than the shooting began. "What took you so long, Saddiq, you bastard?" he muttered.

He tried to imagine what was going on up at the ambush site. Nothing could be worse than an ambush sprung by its targets.

Even so, the group had done a good job of laying their own weapons on this pile of boulders once he and his men had began shooting. Bullets snapped overhead and sang off the rocks. They slapped into the sand all around. Somewhere behind him, one of the Uzbeks cried out that a bullet had hit him in the back. Too bad, thought Carnes. He really had hoped they might escape, pick up the woman, and keep going. He doubted the Uzbeks would stop for any woman, let alone an American Christian babe with an attitude as vile as Nina Chase's.

Northwest Afghanistan
10Sep01—2028 hours local

Saddiq knew something had gone wrong, even before the firing began. First the American had hidden suddenly and without provocation. Then he had called together his Uzbek guides. Somehow he knew what was going on. Probably from the American satellites. Saddiq thought about yesterday's experience with the laser spot in the desert. He wondered if there might now be just such a spot on him now. He could not resist turning over to see if a spot of red covering his back would now be painting his belly. He could not help feeling relief to see nothing but darkness on his chest.

Seconds later, he was not so surprised to see the Uzbeks running away. The ambush had failed. Still, Saddiq had not survived in his line of work for as long as he did without seeing many failures. And without being very cautious. He did not respond to the running men, although one of his team leaders with a night-vision scope alerted him and asked for permission either to open fire or to take up a pursuit.

"No," Saddiq said. "Wait."

It surprised him when the American began shooting, killing one of his own Uzbeks. He could not help admiring an act so ruthless. Perplexed, Saddiq gave the order to fire. Not because he felt a need to defend himself. Rather, he wanted to find out what was going on. When the group behind the boulder began shooting into the dirt in front of their position, he was confused again. Was the American so much an amateur that he would shoot at the shadows? Or was he so clever that he wanted to look like an amateur? If so, what was he up to?

Saddiq decided to take no chances. He called his most trusted lieutenant on the radio. A reinforced company of more than two hundred men lay in wait less than fifty miles away, inside a temporary network of caves, out of sight of the American satellite's eye.

The men hidden there were his best fighters besides those with him tonight, fierce, smart, and able to remain organized even in the dark. They could handle the fighting against a mere handful of Uzbeks and the American. They were fresh and spoiling for a fight. In the worst case, his ambushing soldiers might only pin down their enemy, unable to put a decisive conclusion to the fight. By the morning light, he could surround the American with his two hundred day fighters and force a surrender. If the woman was not with Carnes, his troops would search every square meter of the desert until they picked her up.

He ordered his fighters to muster and begin moving within the hour. Then he ordered his fighters out of their ambush positions to outflank and capture the American agent.

NORTHWEST AFGHANISTAN
10SEP01—2032 HOURS LOCAL

CARNES PEEKED AROUND the cover of the nest of boulders and surveyed the landscape with his night-vision monocular. He could see two groups of men on the move, four or five in each squad. Both squads slithered down from their ambush setting, skirting the area directly to his front. That might mean there were mines in the area. Or they were worried about the Uzbek from his party that he had not shot. At any rate they would be coming for him. Since they no longer had the advantage of deliberate, aimed fire, now it was time for him to un-ass this spot. No reason to be coy about it. He got to his feet and sprinted toward the wadi.

As he approached the slope where he would find cover, he began calling out his name and the names of the Uzbeks. He didn't want them shooting him by accident, but when he felt the ground falling away from his feet, he knew they'd already un-assed the area. By staying behind the boulders, he'd let them believe that he had been hit. He did not expect them to wait more than a minute or so in the wadi.

He put up his night-vision monocular and checked the area for footprints. Three sets. And a pair of drag marks. He followed the drag marks to a lump about fifty feet away. They had carried their wounded man that far. Until they realized that he was dead. Then they dropped him and set off to save themselves, heading toward their native land.

He continued running alongside the drag marks and beyond the body of the fallen Uzbek. Then, when he came alongside a pile of boulders, he leaped from the trail onto the rocks. After getting the lay of the land along the wadi, he took off on a line perpendicular to the original trail, trying to get clear of the track the Al Qaeda fighters would follow after the Uzbeks. They would follow, of that he was sure. If they wanted him bad enough to set an ambush, they would go after him.

Once he found a good vantage point about a hundred meters away from the trail, he searched for a spot to lie low. A spot where he could wait, ready to spring an ambush of his own.

NORTHWEST AFGHANISTAN
10SEP01—1939 HOURS LOCAL

SWAYNE WATCHED EVENTS unfold on the handheld PDA. He had to admire the CIA guy for his cool thinking. He had remained behind the boulders, allowing his men to take off. Only after the firing had stopped did he bug out. Then, instead of getting into a footrace with the Al Qaeda fighters, he hid out. If Saddiq's men did not have trackers in his group, the guy would survive the night. Tomorrow he might slip out of Afghanistan on his own. Not a good strategy for making friends with the Uzbeks, but certainly his best chance for survival.

A scratch of static in his ear took his mind off the situation with the CIA operative.

"Captain Swayne, stand by for a refreshed view on your screen," the high-pitched voice of Bonnie Downes said. Swayne saw Greiner shaking his head a few feet away, where he had set up security. Coming from the tiny speaker of the PDA, Downes's voice was even more shrill than in person. Swayne turned off the speaker, wishing he had an earpiece. He wondered how far her voice carried in the chill night air.

A new view washed down the screen, and Swayne saw that she had zoomed out to allow coverage of about a hundred-mile square. One corner of the view had begun to glow green. It would take too long to count the individual thermal hits. He estimated more than 150. Saddiq had called out the reserves. They must have been hiding underground in one of those fabled cave complexes as big as the lost city of Atlantis. The extra-hot spots meant trucks.

He asked Downes to zoom in, and surveyed the rest of the picture. The group of five men had left the ambush zone, swinging in an arc to the south toward the spot where the CIA guy had opened fire. Another group of four had circled down from the north. They were about to join up at the pile of boulders where the American and the Uzbeks had hidden out. Swayne picked out the American's hiding spot. He saw the fallen body near the ambush killing zone, already cooling in temperatures now below freezing. He watched the three surviving Uzbeks, who had strung out along the track, half-jogging. As fast as they ran, the Al Qaeda fighters, all nine of them, kept gaining. They knew the ground. They were going to catch up. They would be disappointed. The American had fooled them. They were moving too fast, not tracking, but simply following the primitive roadway.

He found the spot where Nina had hidden out. Neither she nor the American were likely to know it, but they were less than a hundred meters apart. She had stumbled into a narrow gully, one in which part of the wall had fallen away, leaving an undercut. The overhead satellite would not be able to pick her out, but the low-angle drone could glimpse her briefly on one part of its orbit. She would be safe for now.

So he asked Downes for a tight focus on Saddiq. The Al Qaeda leader had not left his position above the ambush site. Downes obliged Swayne's request to search in the area around Saddiq. Unless he had bodyguards in a nearby cave, the man was all alone in the desert nearly twenty miles inside Afghanistan. What a prize he was too. Next to Osama—

Of course!

That's what the CIA agent was up to. He wanted to pick off Saddiq. Swayne envied the CIA man. He wished he had thought of it first. Not that it mattered. He was still miles away, with miles to go.

As he watched, Saddiq stood up and dusted off his clothes. In no hurry, he started down the slope, following the path that one of his teams had taken, being careful only to stay in their footsteps—and Swayne knew for sure that a minefield was nearby.

Swayne wished he could stay tuned, so he could see events unfold. He wondered whether the CIA man could handle Saddiq physically, now that he had outsmarted him.

He and Greiner had to hurry if they were to help the CIA man. He gave Greiner the order to saddle up. This time he led out. At a faster pace even than before.

NORTHWEST AFGHANISTAN
10SEP01—2047 HOURS LOCAL

CARNES CHECKED HIS watch at the first sight of Saddiq's men in the wadi. It had taken them less than ten minutes to organize and give chase to the Uzbeks. He gave them a nod of approval for the way they crested the edge of the wadi. They had spread out on a line about thirty meters on each side of the trail. When they came over the slope all at once, they all had weapons at the ready. The Al Qaeda fighters had made themselves virtually impossible to ambush by a smaller force.

Nobody walked on the trail itself until they had cleared the embankment. Through his monocular, he spotted two night scopes working the bottom of the depression. On a signal invisible to him, the men returned to the trail so they could travel faster. They took off at a run after the Uzbeks, keeping an interval of about fifteen feet. That was about the killing radius of a hand grenade. Once again, he gave them a tip of the CIA hat.

He was glad to see that Saddiq was not in the group. Carnes might have been tempted to spring an ambush on the entire Al Qaeda group. That would mean pure suicide, the way the soldiers had dispersed.

If only he could sneak up on Saddiq. Trouble was, he did not know where to look for him. The Al Qaeda leader had likely returned to his bat cave. By now he was sipping at his tea inside some warm, dry cave.

Carnes checked his watch again. Too late. He could not make it to Uzbekistan tonight. Best he put some distance between this spot and himself, find a place to hide before sunrise, some kind of rabbit hole to sleep away the day. Then slip back into Uzbekistan tomorrow night.

Once he had his plan, his first impulse was to jump to his feet and get moving. His training stint with Delta Force rapped him on the skull, telling him to scope out the landscape first. Using his night-vision device, he studied the horizon where he supposed the Uzbeks and Al Qaeda pursuers to be. All clear for as far as he could see. Just to stay on the safe side, he checked the trail at the closest edge of the wadi, where Saddiq would come, if he had decided to follow up on his team. Again, all clear. He made it to his hands and knees before he felt his digital telephone vibrating in his pants pockets, startling him nearly out of his wits. He had to laugh at himself for thinking that he had been attacked by some desert animal, that maybe some kind of Mideast rattlesnake had crawled into his pocket. He knelt, sitting back on his heels, and answered the phone.

A frantic voice yelped at him.

"What? Slow down and speak up," he said.

"Look out behind you, Carnes. Look out behind you."

He tensed his muscles. As a second rap hit him on the

skull, this one not figurative. This one sent shooting stars
through his head. He toppled. The earth rose up to slap
him in the face. His final waking concern was not that
some Al Qaeda scout had crept up on him, but that he
was going to smother with his nose and mouth pressed
into the bosom of Afghanistan.

NORTHWEST AFGHANISTAN
10SEP01—2052 HOURS LOCAL

SADDIQ SLIPPED THE nylon loops over the wrists of his
CIA captive and pulled the straps tight. Ever since he had
seen these throwaway handcuffs on the American television program *Cops,* he had wanted to use them. In fact,
he had carried them around four months now without the
chance. Here, for the first time, he would get to use them
on a CIA man. Praise Allah. Once his man was secure,
he rolled him over so he would not suffocate with his face
pressed into the sand.

Then he carefully patted him down for weapons besides
the Kalashnikov, finding two pistols, one on the belt in
his holster, a 9-mm, and the other a small-caliber pistol
strapped to his ankle. His belt buckle formed the handle
of a three-inch broad-bladed, double-edged knife. A bayonet was in a sheath on his belt. A tanto two-edged military dagger came out of his boot.

Finding that many weapons on such a cursory search
made Saddiq nervous. So he patted down the man again,
removing everything from his pockets. He found a pen
that pulled apart to become an ice pick, something that
he had seldom seen in his own country. Inside the hem
of his trousers was sewn a knife of some sort of composite
material of plastic and graphite.

He found the digital telephone, of course. He decided
not to answer its vibrating signal. Instead, he threw it
away, half-expecting it to blow up when it hit the ground.

Then he lay back, resting his head on his captive, looking up at the sky. Somewhere up there, the spy satellite orbited, looking down on him. Of this he was positive. No doubt, the telephone vibrating was to give the CIA man a warning of Saddiq's approach. It had come too late. He knew the obscene finger gesture of the Western cultures. He signaled to the satellite, one finger extended from the fist of each hand.

EVENT SCENARIO 21

SWAYNE HAD SEEN the entire sequence unfold on the screen of the PDA. Not a minute ago, Zavello had called him, telling him to stop in place to observe. Zavello had told him that the CIA had tried to get through to their man, but too late.

"Looks like you get a new mission," Zavello grumped.

Swayne had half-expected the agent to be killed, that he would have to turn back. Now he'd have to move faster than ever. He said, "Eagle One, this is Spartan One, I've seen enough. We have to get moving."

Zavello didn't even bother to acknowledge. Swayne didn't blame him. Swayne had never been on such a mission. From the very beginning, he was little more than a spectator. The closest he had come to influencing the action was the shining of his laser beam on Saddiq to fake him out. Ever since then, he had watched the battle take

place as if he were at the movies. Nothing he had done
had made any difference. He had contributed nothing. He
and Greiner were as worthless as *Survivor* contestants running across the desert, wearing themselves out with no
chance of getting into a fight for hours. Meantime, one of
the world's most wanted men had pulled off a stunt that
would elevate him to superhero status in the terrorist
world. Single-handedly, he had seized a CIA man who
had no business in Afghanistan. If the terrorist's luck held,
he would stumble across Nina Chase by morning so that
he could do a standup interview in the desert, film at
eleven.

NORTHWEST AFGHANISTAN
10SEP01—2112 HOURS LOCAL

NINA CHASE AWAKENED to the sound of gunfire in the
distance. She knew gunfire. She had been in it, had been
its target. She had been shot at and missed more times
than John Wayne, shot at and hit more times than the
average Vietnam vet.

The gunshots told her that she had awakened from one
nightmare to another. What surprised her was that she had
fallen asleep at all. She had crawled into the space under
the overhang, a spot scraped out by some kind of animal.
Not a desert bear, she hoped. She had never seen desert
bears on the Discovery Channel. That did not mean they
didn't exist. Did it? She put her mind to believing that it
had been some kind of cow or buffalo or antelope. She
didn't ask whether those kinds of things existed. In her
mind they did. Enough said. She pressed her back up
against the wall of the overhang. The depression fit her
hips and shoulders. She wasn't exactly comfortable, but
she wasn't terribly uncomfortable either. It certainly
wasn't warm, but it wasn't freezing. She decided that the

spot was sheltered from the wind, which only made it seem warm.

She had no idea how she might get out of this pickle. She only knew that nothing was going to happen tonight, at least nothing that she was going to do. Maybe tomorrow, after the sun came up. She would find the trail and head back toward Uzbekistan. Easy enough to say. But because she did not have the first clue which direction to take, getting back was problematic.

Somehow, while she was mingling prayers with promises never to go on anything resembling a military mission again, she had fallen asleep. She had dreamt about the gunfire. Then she had awakened and heard the reality of it, a seamless transition from dream to nightmare. Somewhere out there, things were exploding—faint flashes of light found their way into her hideout. The battle could be taking place deeper inside Afghanistan or back toward Uzbekistan. She had no clue. All she knew was she wasn't going anywhere. She lay there a long time. When the next nightmare came, she wasn't aware whether she was awake or asleep.

SADDIQ RESTED WITH his eyes closed. When the gunfire began, he knew well enough what was happening without opening his eyes. He knew his men would finish off the four Uzbeks, if they did not surrender first. Those who yielded, he would question later. They would relinquish any intelligence information of value. Then they would die. Meanwhile, he would stay here, out of harm's way, waiting for his fighters to make their report. He wanted to hear about the woman. Now that he had the CIA man in hand, he wanted that woman. She must not escape.

SWAYNE, NOW THAT he knew the situation on the ground, was more desperate than ever, did not stop anymore for rest breaks or to check the images sent by the XD-11. He had arrived at that point in every military mission where excitement gives way to drudgery. Slogging time. He put his body on automatic pilot, one foot ahead of the other. His mind he kept engaged. He did not entertain hopeful thoughts. That was for rookies. He did not pray. That was for men more spiritual than he. He did not daydream, that was for the foolhardy.

He kept running the events through his head, considering how every variable might play out in relation to every other variable.

Saddiq had taken the CIA man. Not good.

Zavello reported that Saddiq's ambush squad, from the way they fought a hand-picked group of his top fighters, had engaged the fleeing Uzbeks. Already one of the Uzbeks had died. Another lay wounded. Zavello told him that the two survivors had gone into a hot debate, clearly arguing whether to surrender. If they had been from one of the many Afghan tribes, the fighting would have stopped already. In Afghanistan, as in much of the natural world, ritual fighting was more commonplace than actual bloodshed. Although the region's tribes worked at war, played at war, and stayed at war, they tried to keep their combats less than lethal—too much killing would mean too few young men to perpetuate the tribes. Groups surrendered to each other rather than submit to annihilation. Alliances always shifted. Power stayed in balance.

But the Uzbeks could not give up. They could not ask for quarter because they were outsiders in this hostile country. Either they would die fighting. Or they would die, perhaps even more painfully, in captivity, not long after the white flag had come down.

Swayne knew that situation was going to play out on its own, with the likely outcome the death of the Uzbeks.

As to Nina, she had hidden herself away. Saddiq would not let her get away. He would search under every grain of sand in the desert, trying to find her. That would buy Swayne, Greiner, and the rest of his team some time.

The rest of his team. Zavello had kept him up to date.

Night Runner and Friel were going to land inside Tajikistan, at the only airfield in the southern part of the country capable of handling jet aircraft. They would transfer
to a C-141 Starlifter, sitting hot on the runway. The aircraft would scream to thirty thousand feet. They would
jump, falling practically at the speed of sound until they
got to an altitude where it was safe to open a series of
ever-larger parachutes to slow down gradually. Then they
would hit the ground where Swayne told them to land.

Because of the fluid situation, he wasn't yet sure where
that would be. Because he and Greiner wouldn't get to
the action themselves until about the same time, he
wouldn't be able to give the coordinates until after Night
Runner and Friel were airborne from Tajikistan.

Then there was Saddiq's cavalry to consider. Zavello's
analysts have given him a count by now. A convoy of ten
trucks carrying more than two hundred Al Qaeda soldiers
was on the march toward Saddiq. Zavello estimated they
would arrive a couple hours after Swayne and his team
were to be reunited. That didn't give him much time to
operate and evacuate the area.

So many factors, so little certainty.

Yet, of all the things that kept intruding upon Swayne's
calculations, the most intense was joy. No matter how
frustrating this mission, no matter how helpless he felt.
No matter how tired he'd become. No matter how exhausted he would be later today.

More than anything else, he could barely stifle a shout
of happiness that his team was going to be back in action
together. He would never let the group split up again. Not
if he could prevent it.

ONCE THE FIRING had finally stopped, Saddiq checked his
radio to make sure he had tuned it to the proper frequency.
He would give his men ten minutes. In only five minutes,
he got his first report. Three of the Uzbeks had died in
the fighting. One wounded man would survive for ques-

tioning. Of Saddiq's nine men who went after the Uzbeks, two had been killed and two more wounded, one seriously.

Saddiq grimaced. The night had cost him four good men, his best. Too high a price for just four dead Uzbeks—there would be five before the day was out. He thanked Allah for delivering the CIA man to him. With the CIA man, he did not think the cost excessive.

He felt the American stirring under his head. Excellent timing, with sunrise just a few hours away. The CIA agent would be fully alert by then and subdued by his headache. Saddiq had enough men to begin a search for the woman. If they had not found her by mid-morning, the two hundred would be available to scour the land. By noon, he would have his answers. He would know what the CIA man knew. He would have had ample time to spend with the woman, learning anything she had to tell him, enjoying any pleasures she had to give him.

He gave his orders to leave his two wounded fighters in place with a radio. Saddiq would send medics and a litter crew to pick them up. He told the other five to return to the wadi, to move at quick-pace, and meet with him on the trail in half an hour. He said that he had captured a prisoner. The image of modesty, he did not elaborate. He knew they would marvel that he had sneaked up and overpowered the CIA man at night without firing a shot. Saddiq smiled. He would not tell them about the CIA man's moment of carelessness that made his surprise attack so easy.

NINA CHASE LAY still and afraid. Something had gone wrong. The night had gone quiet. The shooting had stopped. *What next?* she wondered.

The answer, she found, was paralysis. After being wedged into her space for so long, the left side of her body had gone numb. She struggled to sit up, feeling the same pains shooting across her back that she had felt every morning since that day in Kosovo when she had been shot, six times in different spots between her knees and her nose, and left for dead.

She struggled to turn her body and lie down again on her other side. She even tried going to sleep again, but everything was wrong. The air had frosted. The ground seemed harder on this side than the other, and the depression did not fit her hips as before. Her heart raced. She couldn't even force her eyes to stay closed. They fluttered like butterfly wings, and she found herself staring into the darkness. There would be no rest. Maybe she should just get up and start walking. But which direction? Wasn't it better to hide out? Immobilized, both by fear and the inability to decide, she lay staring at the bank of dirt just six feet away, trying to make out some detail. She could only be certain of one thing: Sleep would not come again. Not this night.

SWAYNE AND GREINER pulled up just five kilometers from where Saddiq held the CIA man captive. They still had an hour to go before getting into the action. Zavello gave him an instant replay of the terrorist lying on his back flipping the finger at the satellite. Zavello wanted Saddiq. Badly. He took the man's gestures personally. If he could, he would answer the gestures personally. Barring that, he made Swayne responsible for his response.

He also gave Swayne a review of the scenario on the ground ahead of him. He told him the status of Saddiq's men, who were already ten minutes into their march back toward the position where the CIA man lay. Swayne learned that the convoy of reinforcements had dropped two of the ten trucks, one because of a flat tire, the other due to either smoke or steam pouring from beneath the hood. That meant twenty soldiers would be delayed an hour. Another twenty would probably not make it into the action at all. Not the kind of numbers that would make any difference, Swayne thought.

For one thing, he and Greiner were soaked through with sweat from the effort. He knew that the kid would never let up. He also knew that he'd not had enough sleep in the last day to be fit for a fight. Their willing spirit would succumb to fatigued flesh soon enough. Cold as it was, they couldn't even afford to rest for long. The night chill would sap the last of their warmth and render them useless.

On the bright side, his own numbers would double within two hours. Night Runner and Friel were aboard the C-141, already at cruising altitude headed toward his general area, flying too high even to be heard. He already knew that his firepower would be more than doubled. Night Runner had armed himself with the BRAT machine gun, and Friel carried his Blowpipe, the 20-mm sniper rifle that fired explosive rounds.

That was more than enough armament to handle Saddiq's immediate force, whittled already by the night's action. The men would also soon suffer their after-combat crash. That would work to the Spartans' advantage. The Al Qaeda fighters had used up a good deal of ammunition in their hours-long firefights, first against the American, then against the stubborn Uzbeks. If only Swayne could interdict that truck convoy.

He asked Zavello to authorize a bombing mission on the trucks.

"That's already in the works," Zavello said.

By the tone in his voice, Swayne knew that Zavello was merely going through the drill. A bombing mission on an Arab nation wasn't the kind of thing that would fly without everybody getting a chop on it. The State Department would demand to know why a Force Recon unit was inside the country in the first place against public American foreign policy. Since soldiers were already on the ground, how come State didn't have command of it and any other special-operations missions? Forget that the United States did not have diplomatic relations with Afghanistan. State always wanted a piece of the action.

Surely the CIA would weigh in on the side of any action that would pull one of their agent's asses out of the fire. But any decision would have to go all the way to the top of the chain of command. The politicos would have their say. They'd staff it to death. The President's decision, even under the best of circumstances, might take a week. Any delay longer than four or five hours was as good as a no.

Swayne knew he was not defenseless. Downes had offered to help with her drone, making clear more than once during the night that she still stood by. Swayne wanted to use her help, but not until the absolute best moment.

His immediate problem was twofold. First he had to pick his spot for landing Night Runner and Friel. Second, he still had two miles to cover to get himself and Greiner into the action.

He tried a direct call to his men in the aircraft. He held his breath until a familiar voice sounded in his ear.

"Spartan One, this is Two, over."

Night Runner. Once again, a shout tried to jump out of Swayne's chest. He fought it down and answered, giving Night Runner coordinates for a spot to land. He told him to check in at least five minutes before the jump, in case he needed to change the drop zone.

"Wilco," Night Runner said.

Swayne had been all business, even though he did not feel as flat as he kept his voice. Before signing off he said, "It's good to have you back. Both of you."

Night Runner rogered. Friel, who had always had a habit of butting into a radio conversation, came on to say, "Nobody's more happy than us, Cap."

Swayne had never been so glad to have Friel using his tactical radio for chitchat.

"If you ladies are done with your little tea party, we've got a mission to pull off," Zavello said, growling into Swayne's ear. Swayne knew that it was just Zavello trying to be Zavello, but he could hear no Zavello-like venom in the old man's voice. Zavello had lost his nasty edge. Sometime, Swayne thought, when he wanted to cut the colonel to his core, he would mention how soft he had sounded on the radio. On second thought, maybe he would wait until after Zavello had retired. Maybe even until after he had died and gone to Marine Corps colonel heaven, which was hell.

Swayne and Greiner had both finished one canteen and tapped into their second. Canteens for special-operations soldiers had changed a lot in the years since World War II. Sometime in the sixties the conventional forces had gone from metal to hard plastic, keeping the same shape and quart size. That had left the spoke troops wanting, because they could not afford to have water sloshing around as they tried to move with stealth. Canteens were smaller now, so Force Recon troops could carry them for better weight distribution. They were made of a soft plastic, camouflaged and crushable. After drinking part of his water, a man could squeeze out the air before fastening the lid. When he moved out again, the only sloshing would be in his belly.

Greiner and Swayne changed batteries in their night-vision goggles, surveyed the desert around them for signs of enemy forces that they had overlooked, and took off at a fast walk. No more breaks. This time, they would stay in motion until it was time to close with their enemy and engage him. Another stop and they might drop off into the never-never land of sleep. If that happened, their sweaty bodies might freeze.

Swayne had memorized the topography. He had picked his approach so they could keep to the terrain shade, avoiding high ground and staying away from line-of-sight and direct-fire weapons. They traveled on an arc over the last two miles. He chose a route that would put them into a position along the trail, not far from the pile of boulders where the American CIA man and the Uzbeks had turned back from the ambush.

Swayne itched to get it on with Saddiq. For days he'd been a spectator to events in Afghanistan, viewing the action from afar. But he kept to his pace, slogging, slogging. He dared not push too fast now. He had to save some energy for the fight. He switched on his body's autopilot. His mind he put to work reviewing the battlefield once more.

An hour and a half later, as he wished for action, things began to happen at once.

Night Runner made his call to say he and Friel were five minutes from their jump zone.

Zavello butted in to say that Nina Chase had left her hiding place.

Swayne turned on Downes's PDA, and her high-pitched voice sounded even more excited than normal.

"Your terrorist is leaving the CIA guy all tied up," she said. "Here's the picture."

Swayne split his attention between what he was looking at on screen and what he needed to tell Night Runner and Friel about their jump. The image of Nina Chase wandered into Swayne's calculations. Literally. She had stumbled out of her gully into the open, barely a hundred meters from where Saddiq strode toward his men.

Night Runner came on the radio to remind him that two minutes had passed.

Swayne told him, "Change your drop zone." He hated to sound so tentative. "I want you to land no closer than two hundred meters to the east of the CIA man." Swayne bit his lip. He also hated taking risks with his men's lives. They would be vulnerable at only two hundred meters from the American. No, he reassured himself, he had read the terrain. A gentle ridge, more a swell of land than a prominence, lay on that side of the wadi. They could approach their landing with only a brief exposure while under canopy.

Although he surely understood the dangers, Night Runner responded without hesitation. "This is Two, wilco."

Swayne briefed his team quickly—and it felt good to brief all four of them for a change—on the mission. As usual, using the five-paragraph-field-order format.

The situation, enemy and friendly. They understood it well enough without elaboration. Night Runner's handheld computer would have the satellite imagery of the objective area. He would have studied the terrain and weather as well.

The mission. He gave it to them as several phases. First, to recover the CIA agent without injury. Second, to capture Saddiq for interrogation, killing as many of his soldiers as possible. Third, the team would rescue Nina Chase. Swayne hesitated a second, waiting for Zavello to contradict him on that third point, perhaps to say that anybody from the press ought to be left for dead. When Zavello kept quiet, Swayne went on to the third paragraph of his order.

Execution. Simple enough. Friel and Night Runner would land to the east, ditch their canopies, and move directly to the high ground overlooking the wadi, finding firing positions from which to attack. Swayne and Greiner would take up similar positions from the oblique, taking on Saddiq's force from the rear or flank, depending on how Saddiq positioned his men in the next twenty minutes.

The administration and logistics. This paragraph of the order also needed no elaboration. Swayne would have liked to have had transportation on call, say, a helicopter to lift them all out after taking on this force. That was not going to happen. They would have to hump their way out of Afghanistan at double time.

Command and signal. As usual, radios and night-vision devices would let them communicate. The drone would keep them updated on the enemy disposition.

Swayne was happy with his plan. It was simple. He had

good numbers. He had the element of surprise, always a bonus.

He also had the good sense to realize that every airtight plan is capable of blowing up in your face the moment somebody fired the first shot.

Sometimes even before.

NINA CHASE COULDN'T be sure how long ago the gunfire had ceased. Worse, she couldn't even be sure of the direction of the battle. The walls of her hiding place played tricks on her ears.

So, she thought, she should move out into the open and try to get her bearings. If she heard men talking, she could always sneak back into the gully. She would give it a half hour, an hour tops. With any luck, she might see or hear men moving by on their way from the gunfight. If so, she would let them get out of hearing, then find the trail and start walking in the opposite direction. Once the sun came up, she could decide whether she was going in the right direction, maybe by finding her own footprints from the night before. If things got too scary, she could always hide out for the day. Start moving again at night. She did remember that the sun had gone down to her right along the trail they'd used to come into Afghanistan. To her right hand and a little behind her. So if she put tonight's sunset to her left front, she should be all right. By next morning, she should be inside Uzbekistan.

The trucks would be waiting for her there. If not, she could find a road and keep walking away from Afghanistan. Always away from Afghanistan.

After she had run this through her mind, she felt confident. That was all she had to do. Never mind that there didn't seem to be a dime's worth of difference between Afghanistan and Uzbekistan. She might never know which country she was in. Once before, she had walked the deserts of Iran. She tried to think of a difference between this place and that. When she could not come up with one, she decided not to think about that either.

She checked her watch and found that she had been waiting nearly twenty minutes without hearing a sound. It must be safe by now, she thought. Maybe she should walk in a large circle, trying to find the trail.

Of all things, she realized, she was able to see better in the dark than she had been last night. She checked the sky. No, it did not seem any lighter. Yet she could see where she was going. This was not going to be so hard after all.

She took three steps and felt her leg drop into a hole. She couldn't help crying out as her butt hit the ground. Her left leg jackknifed under her, as her right shot straight down some kind of manhole in the middle of the desert.

It had to be the burrow of some kind of man-eating animal—make that woman-eating. She visualized the burrow full of snakes. Or spiders. Or both. And desert bears. Or badgers. She struggled to pull herself out without breaking the leg off at the knee, and struggled even harder to keep herself from crying out.

Her journey to Uzbekistan had begun and ended after only three steps. Finally, she could not get free of the hole. She let out a curse. A single word, hushed. Four letters clipped off between her tongue and her soft palate. Barely a spoken word at all, but seconds later, answered by gunfire.

In no time at all, she preferred her badger hole. She wrenched her body around and slipped her left leg into the desert bear's den beside her right. If she could have, she would have crawled straight down into a nest of spiders. She would have crawled straight to hell. As it was, the damned hole only swallowed her up to her chest. When she bent her knees, they hit against one side of the burrow. Her butt pressed against the opposite side. As the bullets spattered the ground around her, she began digging wildly, trying to make a divot in which to hide her head, burrowing as if she were a badger herself.

• • •

SADDIQ HAD BEEN standing alongside the trail, waiting for his men in plain sight. He did not want to surprise them, to have them start shooting at him if he cleared his throat. Better to stay in the open. They had a Starlight scope with them. They would be checking the trail. They would see him and call to him on radio. They would—

He heard the cry. Then the shots. He flattened on the ground. He dared not speak out, for fear that it might be more Uzbeks that he had not accounted for. Instead he talked into his radio set to the frequency of his pursuit squad.

"We are being attacked from the east," his man reported.

"By whom?" Saddiq wanted to know.

"By one man. No, I see her in the scope. It is a woman instead."

"Stopped firing, you fools," Saddiq ordered.

He did not particularly care whether his men killed the woman. He was more concerned that she had not gotten away. That was a relief. The idea that these men would be shooting to the east frightened him. The CIA man lay out there somewhere in that direction too. He had left him in the open, never thinking that his own men might kill him.

The gunfire had not stopped. Even among the most disciplined troops, once any shooting began, it was hard to shut it off. Only shouting would do. So he shouted. The names he called them over the radio would soon get his point across.

He watched the last of the tracers striking the earth, which bent them toward the sky. Such a waste of ammunition.

NIGHT RUNNER AND Friel had barely opened their final canopy, the flying wing that they would use to maneuver to the ground from three hundred feet, when the firing began. The two gave their report at the same instant: "We've been spotted."

Friel added, "Taking fire, taking fire."

Night Runner could not believe that somebody had spotted them. Who kept watch on the sky for a pair of falling bodies from thirty thousand feet? They had streaked toward the ground like cold meteors. Two tiny drag shoots deployed at ten thousand feet to keep them under control. Then a third chute to slow them down to a manageable speed at one thousand feet, and the final wing, which deployed close to ground. Such a low opening of their wing would have been far too dangerous without the three-dimensional view through their night-vision goggles. They could not have been visible for more than a couple of seconds when the shooting began.

"Returning fire," Night Runner said. Which was not going to be as easy to do as it was to say. His choices were to continue falling, guiding his wing. Or to set his flight controls, align into the wind, unclip his BRAT machine gun and the hundred-round belt, and put down some suppression.

Night Runner checked the desert floor to find the source of the gunfire. That was easy enough, all he had to do was look toward the muzzle flashes. The flashes washed out his night-vision goggles. He could not get a fix on exactly what was going on. It seemed to be one group shooting from the center of the wadi, maybe half-a-dozen men. He also saw tracers coming up from almost directly below. Tracers without muzzle flashes. For a moment, he was stumped. Then he realized what was happening.

As SOON AS he heard Night Runner give the go-ahead for suppression, Friel was on it. When bullets snapped by him, and tracers sparked all around, he did not need to be told twice.

His Blowpipe was attached to his rigging with a single strap, counterbalanced so that he could bring it up and cradle it in the crooks of both arms as he guided his wing to the ground. The second his feet touched, he could keep the gun from hitting the ground. Or from doing something squirrelly. Like twisting so that it hit butt-first, so that he landed on it, jamming the muzzle in places that he did not want to jam a 20-mm barrel.

When the firing began, and before the gunny gave him clearance to return fire, Friel had already shifted the Blow-pipe to one hand. With the first tracers shooting by his feet, he threw up the gun, which he had kept hot. He did not need to aim, because he was using a 20-mm with an explosive head, set to airburst. Like a miniature artillery shell, it would sense when it was at a preset altitude above the ground and go off, throwing shrapnel. It might not kill anybody going off at fifty feet, but he would make most boneheads and ragheads duck for cover.

He aimed at center of mass of the shooters and squeezed off a single round, still wondering why the chief had not started spraying the ground with his BRAT.

As soon as he had touched off a round, Night Runner told him to hold his fire.

"No shoot, no shoot. Hold fire, Henry."

Too late. There was no getting back the explosive round.

Friel did not have time to wonder why Night Runner had changed his mind. The ground rose up to meet him. Far too quickly. He cradled the Blowpipe and reached for his steering handles to pull some air into the canopy, try-ing to stall out before he crashed.

He saw the muzzle blasts disappearing behind a black line of the horizon.

"Hit the brakes," Night Runner called out in warning.

Too late. Friel had already hit the ground. Hard. The muzzle flashes he saw this time were in his head. He tried to curse, but could not get out the words between his teeth—somebody had welded his mouth shut. For a mo-ment it frightened him that he could not breathe—

somebody had punched him in the gut, taking his breath away. Somebody else held his head underwater, making him choke, trying to drown him. He opened his eyes, but could not see past the fireworks. Then everything went black.

SWAYNE HAD HAD barely time enough to hope that his mission wouldn't go to hell so soon after his hasty operations order. But at the same moment as the hope came the hell.

First the gunfire. From the sound of it, Kalashnikov rifles of the Al Qaeda fighters. Then Night Runner's alarm sounded because they were taking fire while still under canopy, the paratrooper's worst nightmare. Swayne had looked to the east in time to see Friel getting off a round from his 20-mm. Then his and Night Runner's flying wings had disappeared beyond the horizon. Much too quickly, Swayne had thought, when he heard in his headset the sound of the two men hitting the ground much too hard. Friel cried out in pain. Swayne hope that he would speak up, even to bitch. Since the only sound was little more than a gurgling moan, Swayne knew that one of them had been hurt. Since the tactical frequency remained quiet, it was probably Friel.

Swayne and Greiner still hadn't gotten close enough to participate in the fighting. Or anything else. He could only hope that Night Runner would be able to defend for a few minutes more. Until Swayne and Greiner could get to higher ground and at least cause a diversion. If he attacked Saddiq from two directions at once, he might turn the battle's momentum, even with his small force.

"Spartan One, this is Two. We're down. Three is out of action. Hard landing."

Friel had indeed been hurt. "Status?"

"Out cold, bloody nose, possible broken jaw. He'll survive, if I can bring him out of it. He won't be eating any steaks for a while. The twenty-mill is a combat loss."

As usual, Night Runner got everything of importance out in the fewest number of words. "This is Spartan One, stand by." Swayne turned on Downes's PDA. He needed an overhead look, and hoped she had kept the action in the field of view. The screen flickered and came to light. Swayne stopped walking and dropped to one knee as Greiner took up security duty, orienting toward the spot where Saddiq's troops had opened fire.

Swayne interpreted the thermal images on his screen at a glance. Saddiq had split his group. He and another of his terrorists were sprinting toward the prone body of the CIA agent. Three other men were running toward the east—Friel's 20-mm had taken out one of the terrorists. Shrapnel to the eyes, apparently. He lay writhing on the ground, covering his face with both hands. Swayne could see that Night Runner had turned Friel on his side so he would not choke on his own blood. Then Night Runner ran toward the high ground, carrying his machine gun at port arms. He would be able to look down into the wadi and defend himself before the Al Qaeda fighters could get within a hundred meters of him. Swayne breathed a sigh of relief. He had chosen his landing zone well after all. By putting Friel and Night Runner close to the high ground, he had given them an advantage.

Then again, if he hadn't put them so close, they might have escaped detection.

Almost as if reading his mind, Night Runner spoke up, reporting between breaths as he ran: "They were not. Shooting at us. They were shooting at the. Woman. Nina. Chase. We were getting. Stray fire."

A good report. Swayne now knew that the terrorists must be confused. Out of nowhere an explosive round—the Blowpipe had no muzzle blast, because the round itself was self-propelled. A blast of compressed gas shot it out of the muzzle, and it did not ignite until well clear of the firer's position. For all Saddiq knew, somebody was shooting mortars at him. For all he knew, that was a marker or round for a smart bomb yet to be delivered from a Stealth bomber from only God knows where.

Once Swayne saw that Night Runner had reached a commanding firing position, he breathed a sigh of relief. He saw that the terrorists were not keeping to cover, did not seem to be aware that anybody was on the ground to the east. He also noted that none of the Al Qaeda fighters was carrying a Starlight scope. He checked back at the spot from which all the shooting had come. Two scopes lay on the ground. The terrorists had dropped them, probably because either shrapnel or the flash had disabled them. So far, the only good news of the night.

Three men had grabbed Nina Chase. They were so bold as to use a flashlight. Swayne had to laugh. The Al Qaeda fighters thought they were in danger from a stealthy bombing.

He could see what they were up to. They were going to take their two prisoners, the American journalist and the CIA agent, and get away from ground zero as quickly as they could.

If only it were an air attack. They might survive that. Swayne saw Night Runner running downslope toward the three men who were both fighting over Nina Chase and roughing her up. Now and then one of them would look toward the sky, as if they might see a laser-guided bomb before it struck them.

They might as well have been looking for bombs. Because they were about to be annihilated. Night Runner carried his machine gun in his left hand. In his right, he held that curved toad-sticker of his, the one he had taken from a Bedouin fighter so many missions ago that Swayne could not count.

NIGHT RUNNER SIZED up the situation in an instant. He was in a good defensive position. That would not help the woman. It would not be safe to use a machine gun at this range. Even if he picked off one or two of the men, the third might kill her for spite.

So he had taken his deadly sword and taken off down-slope, running carefully, swiftly. Silently.

For one of the few times in the field, he relied on his technology more than his senses. He had spent too much time in garrison since the last mission. Sleeping in the BEQ. Spending his days in courtrooms and offices. Under house arrest. He had not spent enough time in the puri-fication rites of his people, making himself worthy. He had not maintained his normal training regimen. In short, he did not trust himself. So he let his night-vision goggles do his seeing for him. He used his speed rather than stealth. He wanted to get to the men while they were still preying on the woman, while they were still making her cry out and curse. While they were still breathing hard, hearing only their own heartbeats, instead of his footsteps.

SWAYNE FELT GRATEFUL for his luck. Even with Friel out of the action, the three Al Qaeda fighters would be no match for Night Runner, who now had closed to within fifty meters, sprinting through the darkness.

Swayne and Greiner had to run almost at top speed if they hoped to intercept Saddiq.

Even as he ran, Swayne kept calculating. He and Grei-ner would have to catch their breaths in order to pull off a surprise attack at close quarters. He had to make allow-ances in case he or Greiner stumbled and fell. He did not want the noise to betray them.

So, as he ran, he referred to his mental map of the area. He picked a spot where the trail dipped across a gully. He and Greiner had worked up such a sweat, they would smell ripe. He did not want to be detected the way that Night Runner had found and killed so many of their en-emy on earlier missions.

Finally, he was sure. They could be in position for a few minutes before Saddiq came by with his prisoner. He allowed himself a smile in the dark. Things were going to work out, after all.

ONCE NINA CHASE realized that the men were not going to kill her on the spot, she gave up begging for her life. Instead she ran through her lexicon of obscenities toward the three men tugging at her hair, arms, and clothing. She couldn't tell whether they were searching her for weapons or just plain groping—yes, she could tell. They were groping. One man stood in front of her, breathing on her face, trying to kiss her, his breath as foul as a corpse's. Both his hands clutched at her breasts as if he were trying to play a pinball machine. Behind her a second man worked at pulling down her pants. Perhaps he had never known a woman to wear pants. Otherwise he would know that, unlike men, women who did wear trousers cinched them tightly around the waist. Nobody could jerk off her clothing without unfastening her belt.

The third Al Qaeda gangster turned Al Qaeda gang rapist was off to the side, groping her both front and back. They weren't talking. Their breathing was ragged. Clearly they hadn't had any sex for a while, and they were in danger of having it in their own pants before they could get into hers. She reached out and grabbed the beard of the man before her, one fistful of cheek hair in each hand. He started to scream, letting go of her breasts to slug her. She braced for a punch in the mouth that did not come. Instead, the man bent over backward to let her alone. The second man dropped his flashlight. Behind her the third man kept trying to yank her pants down over her ample hips. Then he too gave up.

The flashlight rolled in the dirt, and Nina thought she was having another of her waking nightmares.

The man in front of her, the man whose beard she still grasped, had broken in half. At her feet, the flashlight was not all that had fallen to the ground. An arm, its hand still holding the flashlight, had fallen off the second man. He began shrieking, holding his squirting stump at the elbow with his left hand. Then, infected with instant leprosy, his head fell off. The screaming stopped, and all she heard was a rushing of air from the severed neck of the fallen body.

The man playing at her pants somehow suddenly realized that things had gone badly. He let loose of her and pushed her away. Still on his knees, he reached for his rifle and began to raise the muzzle, bringing it to bear on her. Even in the faint glow of the flashlight she could see the murderous intent in his eyes—he fully intended to kill her, clearly thinking she was to blame for the death of his companions. Then leprosy struck him too as his face slid off his skull. He keeled over, the bloody, faceless front of his head landing in the sand next to the flashlight, his blood oozing outward onto the blotting surface of the desert floor. The front half of his face landing so it looked up to the sky, as if somebody had buried him at the beach.

"Shit," she whispered.

A soft voice at her shoulder answered. "Ms. Chase?"

She folded her arms across her shoulders, lowered her head, and closed her eyes, waiting for some of her own body parts to fall off.

"I'm Gunnery Sergeant Robert Night Runner, USMC. Captain Jack Swayne asked me to pull you out of this little scrape. Would you come with me, please?"

AT FIRST NIGHT Runner had thought it a good tactic to crash into the entire group of four, bowling them all over, including Nina Chase. It was a way to separate them from her, sort them out from most dangerous to least, and take on the men in order.

But as he drew within ten meters, he saw that a violent crash would be overkill. Rather than risk hurting her, perhaps breaking a rib or straining a knee, he stopped just ten feet away. Keeping his eyes on the Al Qaeda fighters, he lowered his machine gun, resting the muzzle on a stone, keeping the working parts out of the sand.

He would strike violently after all, but with precision. In a step, he was behind the man molesting her from the front. She held him at arm's length. Which gave Night Runner room for a wide swing like that of a scythe.

He aimed the blade a few inches above the belt line, so any pistols or knives clipped to the man's waist would not chip his blade. The blade entered from the back, at the bottom two ribs. It sliced through his body, loosing jets of gas and fluids, snicker-snacking through his backbone. The man's body broke in half.

Seeing the collapse of his partner, the man with the flashlight pulled away. Night Runner's second blow was a downward stroke. It took the terrorist's right arm at the elbow. Clutching the flashlight, it fell away.

The man turned, favoring his right side, exposing the left side of his neck. Night Runner took his head off.

The third man went for his rifle. Somehow, he was blaming the woman for the deaths of his two comrades. He was going to shoot her. By then Night Runner's blade had began its next stroke. He knew how to wield his weapon. Striking the man straight-on might well have done the job—the weight of the blade hitting him on the frontal part of his skull would have knocked him out. But even its keen edge would not cut through the wraps of his turban with such a blow. So Night Runner used the curve of the blade, striking and slicing in the same motion. He had thrown nylon scarves into the air. Hitting the cloth flush with the blade barely nicked it. But a slicing stroke could sever a scarf. More than once, he had made two scarves of one.

He used that stroke to take off the man's face, cutting the turban fabric cleanly. The blade sliced from the middle of the skull to the jaw. The man's head split like a firm, green melon. The momentum of the stroke carried through the Al Qaeda fighter's forearm and into the stock of his Kalashnikov rifle, where it stuck.

Night Runner wondered what Allah would have to say to the three men when they came face-to-face with their deity, their last act an attempt to molest an infidel woman.

Runner jerked the blade free of the rifle stock so he could be ready for a fourth attacker, if one came. He dropped to one knee, looking a full 360 degrees. In the distance he saw that Saddiq and his soldier had snatched up the CIA man. They had tired of dragging him from the wadi back toward the trail. After only ten meters, they found the going too difficult. Saddiq took out a knife, and Night Runner grabbed for his machine gun. He would have to decide quickly. If the man tried to kill the American, Night Runner would have to risk the shot. But Saddiq meant his captive no harm. He cut the ankle straps and prodded the American to stumble ahead under his own power.

Night Runner sighed. He had the woman, and Saddiq had set out for the spot where the captain was to be.

"Ms. Chase?" he said in a gentle voice, so he would not startle her.

"I'm Gunnery Sergeant Robert Night Runner, USMC. Captain Jack Swayne asked me to pull you out of this little scrape. Would you come with me, please?"

SWAYNE HEARD NIGHT Runner's words to Nina in the earpiece of his radio receiver. He hoped they would reassure her as much as it did him. For Night Runner had spoken to him as well as Nina, telling him that he had pulled off his part of the mission. He would now collect the woman and go back to tend to Friel.

Already Swayne could see three figures, their heads bobbing up and down as they climbed the slope of the wadi and came into view.

At the spot he had chosen, where the trail dropped sharply to cross a six-foot gully, the two terrorists would be preoccupied with their prisoner. They might push him down one slope, but they would certainly have to help him get up the other side.

Swayne had approached on a roundabout path so he would not leave any footprints or scuff marks within easy view of the trail. He and Greiner lay prone, one to each side of the path. Their bellies pressed against the earth not six feet from the edge of the gully that the terrorists would have to cross with their captive. Greiner tried to hide himself behind a shrub the size of a basketball. Swayne had less than that, but with the minutes left to him, he stacked a couple of flat stones. He watched through his night-vision goggles from the side of his tiny wall of Afghanistan.

Saddiq hurried, but he had not abandoned common military sense. He sent his aide walking ahead about five meters, while he stayed behind the CIA man, hanging onto a meter-long strand of rope tied to his captive's belt.

Because he knew that things always went wrong, no matter how well executed the mission, Swayne dared to speak.

"Keep a bead on the near guy," he murmured to Greiner. "In case they decide to use a flashlight or Starlight, take him. I'll take the other one. Head shots only."

In answer, Greiner tapped his teeth twice, sounding like two small-arms gunshots in Swayne's headset.

NIGHT RUNNER GRIPPED Nina Chase's hand as he led her out of the wadi, over the ridge, and back toward Friel. His concern for Friel made him rush, but he would not relax his guard. He did not cross the high ground at the same spot he had used when he went after the Al Qaeda fighters minutes ago.

He found Friel sitting up, conscious, cradling his face in the palms of both hands.

He heard Friel try to talk to him, but his words were mushy, strained through broken teeth. He recognized the number of syllables as his name. *Gunny Night Runner?*

Friel was asking. The words came out as mush.

"It's me, Henry."

Friel tried to tell him his jaw was broken.

Night Runner reached out to touch his man's shoulder. "No talking, Henry. We can't distract the captain."

Friel gurgled something with all the syllables of "Affirmative," and shut off his mike.

Night Runner shut his own transmitter off—leaving the receiver on—and asked Nina Chase to sit by Friel. "Keep an eye on him, please. Don't let him go anywhere." He gave her a water bottle and patted down Friel's day pack, finding some high-energy snack bars. He gave them to her. "He won't be needing these." Through his night goggles, he could already see that Friel's jaw was swollen. Blood still oozed from between his lips and trickled down his nose.

"Ms. Chase, I'm going to see if the captain needs any help." He took Friel's radio transceiver from his pocket and peeled the microphone from Friel's head. He fitted it to her head. Taking her hand, he showed her the switches.

In his night-vision goggles, he saw her grimace and hold up her hands, stained with Friel's blood.

He had no time for that. "I've set this to listen-only. If you need to talk to the captain or me, use this switch to turn it on and speak into the microphone. That's all there is to it. I'll be back in a few."

She murmured her dubious thanks. There was nobody to hear it. Night Runner had vanished so quickly and so soundlessly that she had to sweep one arm through the black air to be sure that he was gone. Amazing. She could still fill feel his touch on her hands from showing her the buttons. Yet he was gone. She wiped her hands dry in the sand.

SADDIQ'S MAN FOUND the edge of the gully in the dark, felt with his hands to confirm it, then jogged back to where Saddiq waited. The two came forward in file, their prisoner between them. They stood Carnes at the brink of the gully, and Saddiq kicked the agent's feet from under him, making him sit down hard at the edge. Together he and his man lowered the CIA officer into the gully, about five feet deep. Without letting go of him, the two Al Qaeda men slid down the slope.

Swayne held his breath as the three heads disappeared for a second below his line of sight—he realized he should have kept one of the PDA screens on to watch the dead space. If anything was going to go wrong because of that little lapse in attention to detail, the whole mission could go south.

He counted the seconds, not relying on his heartbeat, because it had started to race. He tensed, ready to roll clear. He should have been watching, dammit, he should have been watching. If they had been spotted—

No! The CIA man shot into view and fell forward, falling to his chest. His face bounced off the ground. They had thrown him up over the edge. Now they pushed his lower body onto the flat ground, never releasing his ankles.

Swayne relaxed. As long as he could see their hands.

Two heads came up, two sets of hands still clinging to the CIA operative's feet. Swayne looked to his left and saw Greiner glance at him. He nodded.

The two Force Recon Marines lunged at the same time. Swayne went into a crouch and dove toward Saddiq, swinging the butt of his rifle toward the terrorist's face. Saddiq had hoisted himself to where he held himself by his rib cage resting at the edge of the gully. Swayne's rifle butt caught him flush on the face with a satisfying, solid blow.

Swayne called out, "We're Americans, Carnes. Stay down." The last thing he wanted was for the CIA agent to try to lend a hand. Or worse, to try to fight them.

•   •   •

GREINER HAD REVERSED his rifle and struck his man with a blow called the butt thrust, an overhand jab with his rifle stock. Two things went wrong. First, his man flinched. Second, the rifle butt struck something soft. Greiner realized it was the Al Qaeda fighter's turban, which cushioned the impact.

Even so, the blow was enough to knock Saddiq's side-kick over backward into the gully. He landed hard and cried out, but neither the butt stroke nor the fall was enough to disable him.

By the time Greiner could turn his rifle again, the Al Qaeda fighter had begun shooting, spraying bullets everywhere, including the lip of the gully.

Greiner knew he had blown his task—he should have fixed his bayonet and used that. Still, he was not so embarrassed that he would stick his head over the edge of the gully where the man expected him to. He dove to his left, rolled once, and belly-crawled forward quickly.

But not quickly enough.

He couldn't believe his eyes. The man had disappeared. Greiner looked right, then left. At a bend in the ravine, he saw a flash of movement, an elbow and an ankle turning the corner at a full run. Of all things, one of Friel's expressions came to mind. The man in full flight was all asshole and elbows. Greiner's first inclination was to jump down and give chase.

A soft voice told him, "Don't do it, Grinder. Stay up top."

Greiner gained his feet and turned to follow the Al Qaeda fighter, keeping to the top of the ravine, just as the voice had told him. But after only two steps, he caught another movement from where the man had disappeared. It looked at first like a trick of the eye. On second look, it seemed to be a shiny stick. But at last, Greiner finally recognized the stainless-steel bayonet of the Kalashnikov rifle, unhinged, waiting for somebody stupid to run down the ravine and impale himself on it. Or to get shot. Or both.

Greiner said, "Thanks, Gunny. But where are you?"

"In the ravine. Lower your rifle."

Reluctantly, Greiner did as Night Runner told him. He crouched low, seeking cover at the edge of the gully. As he watched, the bayonet tipped toward the ground. A figure stepped out. Night Runner. In his left hand he carried the Kalashnikov. In his right, that scimitar of his, the red on the blade the only spot of color in Greiner's goggles.

SWAYNE HAD HIS hands full. Not so much with Saddiq, but with the CIA man. Saddiq lay on his back, hot brass from his sidekick littering his face. He was clearly out cold—otherwise, he could not have lain still for the burns from the brass. Swayne would take no chances, of course. He produced three nylon tie straps from his day pack, all the while keeping his rifle trained on the Al Qaeda leader. But as he took a step toward the man, a blur came in from the left of his field of vision.

"Carnes, you bastard," said Swayne.

The CIA man, his hands still bound behind him, had slid into the ravine, landing next to Saddiq.

"Are you out of your mind?" Carnes shouted at Swayne. "If you killed this guy, we'll never get any intelligence out of him."

"He's far from dead."

"Who are you?" Carnes said. "Who the hell are you?"

"You're in no position to be demanding anything. But I'm Captain Jack Swayne, U.S. Marine Corps. Force Recon Marine Team 2400 is saving your ass and taking you and a top Al Qaeda lieutenant out of Afghanistan. Got that?"

"Look here, Saddiq is my prisoner. The CIA owns him, and the CIA has precedence over the Marine Corps in Afghanistan."

Swayne had to laugh. "Your prisoner? Would you like

me to show you an instant replay of the satellite pictures from the last hour?" He didn't have to say anything else. The color resolution in his night-vision goggles showed a sudden flush glowing on Carnes's face.

"You know," Carnes said, "even though I did have the man exactly where I wanted him, if you never repeated what I just said, it would spare me a lot of grief."

"Forget about it. Turn around so I can get you out of those cuffs." Carnes offered his hands, and Swayne cut the connecting band loose with his boot knife.

Carnes faced him and took the knife offered by Swayne. But before cutting off the wristbands, he held out a hand. "Brian Carnes," he said. "Thanks, Jack Swayne." He put a hand to the back of his head and winced. "Guy implanted a golf ball in my skull."

"You all right?"

"Mild concussion. Feels like a migraine, but I'll be fine. What next, Captain?"

Swayne was glad for the pleasantries to be over. He told Carnes about Saddiq's cavalry, barreling down on their position in trucks and in numbers. He told him to disarm Saddiq and arm himself with as many weapons as he could find on the terrorist. "Maybe you can find something to secure him. I don't want him getting away, and I don't want us getting into a brawl with him."

"Will do," Carnes said.

The agent had put himself under Swayne's command. The bastard acted as if he just loved taking orders from a Marine Corps officer. Which put Swayne on guard. He had known CIA people before. They were the gods of secret ops. Never would they take orders from an outsider, except to gain an edge. More likely, the man's first re-action after they had tackled Saddiq—to insist that the terrorist was his prisoner—showed his true colors. He was up to something.

But Swayne didn't have time to play politics. Greiner reported that he had set up security. He sounded meek for having lost Saddiq's sidekick. The kid had to learn. Sometimes things went wrong. It did no good to beat yourself up.

Night Runner, always the pro, reported too. He had collected the injured Friel and the woman and would be joining up soon.

As Swayne made contact with the OMCC, he allowed himself a moment's thought about Nina. Not so much Nina for Nina's sake, but because the CIA operative had never mentioned her name. He had spent an entire day with her, leaving her behind in the dark alone. Clearly, he had not given her another thought. He had Saddiq in his grasp. No woman could be worth more. That would be why he was so polite to Swayne. He was going to try to sweet-talk the Marines into giving up their prisoner to him. Swayne allowed himself a cynical grin in the dark. Probably for reasons of national security, he surmised wryly.

He gave Zavello the briefest of reports, because the colonel had access to live pictures from both the overhead satellite and the XD-11 drone. He already knew what had gone on—in fact, he had access to more graphic detail than Swayne on the scene. Once more, Swayne gave thanks that the colonel was not the type of officer who had to micromanage. The technology available now gave armchair commandos far more ways to meddle than even during the Vietnam War, when battalion commanders directed squad tactics from choppers a thousand feet above the jungle.

Since Zavello didn't mention it, Swayne brought up his earlier request for air support.

"This is Eagle One, negative, no word yet. You're going to have to manage on your own," Zavello growled. His tone said more than his words. Zavello was pissed. The higher-ups had stiffed him so far.

Bad as the news was from Zavello, Swayne felt his heart leap when Night Runner led the staggering Friel and stumbling Nina Chase out of the wadi toward the gully. In minutes, for the first time in months, he had his team together again. He had to admit Nina had never looked better to him, even as a mere image in his night-vision goggles.

As she neared the gully, he crossed to the other side. She cocked her head, unsure whether the figure before her could be the man Night Runner said had come for her. "Jack? Is that you?"

"Nina. Long time no see."

She ran to him and hit him with her head, almost before he could lift his night-vision goggles. They kissed in the dark, long and wet. It seemed bizarre to him. To be in the desert, knowing that a convoy of trucks bore down on them, filled with nearly two hundred soldiers eager to get to him and his men. Yet there he was, smooching a television reporter. He remembered the satellite and drone, both taking pictures. He pushed her away, even as he felt her stiffen.

"Have you seen a CIA guy by the name of Carnes?" she asked.

He turned his head toward his right shoulder. "He's back there."

She stepped around Swayne and would have plunged into the gully, if he had not hauled her back. "Whoa, are you trying to kill yourself."

"No, dammit, I'm going to kill *him*."

"Not tonight. I need him." He looked past her and adjusted his night-vision goggles. He saw that Night Runner had patched up Friel, using a chin strap of the bad-ass duct tape to hold Friel's jaw in place. One wrap of the space-age tape would fix it to the top of his head. Swayne had seen the tape used for everything from subduing prisoners to fixing aircraft skin. It was going to take some doing to get the tape off Friel.

For now, that was the least of Swayne's worries. He had studied the latest satellite pictures of the convoy and saw the situation was dire. The trucks continued to roll, headlights blazing into the night, nothing at all tactical about their approach.

Swayne and his ragtag detachment were nearly twenty miles from Uzbekistan, and the night would give way to dawn in less than two hours. At the speed they were traveling, the trucks would arrive sooner than he had first figured. They would need every minute of darkness to gain themselves even the most remote chance of escape.

To get to the nearest point of the border with Uzbekistan, Swayne's group would have to cross a barren plain and perhaps get into the rugged terrain where the trucks could not follow. But even once they got into the hills, his group might be too tired to run from soldiers who were relatively fresh.

He helped Night Runner get Nina and Friel across the gully. He and Night Runner exchanged firm handshakes.

Swayne set up Friel as a lookout, and asked Nina to keep an eye on Saddiq while he called a council with Night Runner. As an afterthought, he included Carnes. The CIA man seemed eager enough to get away from Nina, who looked as if she might still lash out at him.

"The best I have is a tentative plan," Swayne said. "We start moving toward Uzbekistan, get clear of this area— we have to assume that Saddiq gave radio instructions on where he might be found. So, they'll come here"—he looked at his watch—"in a couple hours. We'll have to hide out by day. Get moving again at night." He halfway expected an argument from the CIA man, because he sensed how eager Carnes was to get Saddiq out of Afghanistan and into interrogation.

"Sounds good to me," Carnes said. "You're calling the shots."

Such easy agreement made Swayne even more wary, but he knew he had no reason to mistrust the man. At least no concrete reason. Except that he wasn't all that pleased with his own plan—there was one helluva lot of potential trouble to keep them from hiding out by day and traveling at night. Namely, that two hundred Al Qaeda fighters would be looking for them. They might have some fighting to do.

Night Runner had not reacted. He wanted to clear the area, but Swayne knew the gunny didn't like his plan any more than he did.

"Runner?"

"I have a thought."

"Please."

"They will expect us to run toward Uzbekistan. Lacking any instructions from him"—he tossed a nod in Saddiq's direction—"they will follow the trail."

Swayne nodded, keeping his mouth shut. When Carnes inhaled, as if to respond, Swayne touched him on the elbow, and the man kept his silence too.

Night Runner offered, "If you'd consider an alternative idea?"

"Let's hear it," Carnes said.

Ignoring the CIA man, Night Runner looked to Swayne, who gave him the go-ahead with another nod. Night Runner laid it out.

When he had finished, Carnes said, "Brilliant. You ever thought about joining Central Intelligence?"

Night Runner gave him a blank stare. "No. I haven't. Why would I?"

Swayne marveled at the CIA man's arrogance. Only the CIA had brilliant people? Once again, Swayne bit back his anger, letting his elation have the day. His team was complete again. Impaired, yes, what with Friel's injury. But now, with Night Runner returned and chipping in ideas, the brains of the outfit had more than doubled. Swayne did not allow himself much time to revel in his joy. They had to get moving.

Night Runner took point, and Swayne felt his chest

swelling yet again. Finally, more than the electronic eyes and ears he had depended upon so far in this mission, he had the almost supernatural senses of Night Runner out in front of his team. And those animal instincts.

Swayne marched second in column, to provide support by fire and to give another set of eyes to the front. Then came Nina.

Swayne cut two luminous strips of tape from a roll in his backpack and attached them as vertical strips—like captain's bars—to the back of his cap. All she had to do was follow those strips through the night. He told her to stay close enough so that she could always tell that there were two distinct strips. If she fell back too far, he explained, the strips would meld into one glowing spot. Before they struck out, he smothered the white beam of his penlight with his cap, recharging the glow in the strips.

After Nina, came Saddiq. Carnes had decided that he would tie a strand of rope to Saddiq's neck and let Nina lead the terrorist on a tether about ten feet long. Swayne saw her giving the terrorist a vampire smile. The irony of a Western woman leading an Al Qaeda bigwig on a tether was not lost on anybody.

Carnes followed Saddiq, holding on to a shorter length of rope fastened to the terrorist leader's wrists, bound with nylon tie straps. Friel and Greiner brought up the rear. They traveled together because Swayne did not want to risk having Friel lose consciousness and fall out.

Swayne gave the transceiver and headset to Carnes because Friel could not use it anymore. Besides, Greiner could do the talking for both of them if they stayed together.

Friel refused to give up his night-vision goggles. He wanted to be able to see. Just because he could not talk did not mean that he could not fight. Swayne could see the earnest request in Friel's pained eyes. He was not going to suggest in any way that Friel was still not the best shot in the outfit. He believed it too. If he did not, he would not have curtailed the team's fighting ability just to spare Friel's feelings.

Night Runner had left Friel's damaged 20-mm buried in the sand with two timed charges on it. So Friel carried the Kalashnikov taken from Saddiq's sidekick, its bayonet still extended. They had barely started out when the explosion sounded behind them, blowing the 20-mm and its ammo in place.

GREINER FELT SORRY for Friel. True, the man had given him nothing but grief since he had joined the Force Recon team. But something had changed in the Friel he had known inside Iran. He was not the mean-spirited, nasty bastard who had ridiculed him and even hit him. Sure, Friel had been hurt in the hard landing. And, yes, Greiner could see excruciating pain in those eyes. He could only imagine how much it hurt to have a broken jaw. Just to inhale the frigid night air across exposed nerve endings in his shattered teeth must have been a torture. Beyond that, Friel's body language had changed. He was still cocky, but it wasn't that in-your-face brand of better-than-thou. Friel no longer seemed to have the need to elevate himself by putting down Greiner. As they set out on their march together, Friel had hit him with a light forearm shiver to the chest. Again, different. Not a blow, but a handshake, a greeting of fellow warriors.

Greiner glanced at his former nemesis through the night-vision goggles. He seemed to be some kind of alien, shiny tape wrapping his head beneath the hat. Round, puffy cheeks. A bloody, seeping hole for a mouth. The night-vision goggles like protruding robot eyes.

Friel groaned, as if he had tried to manage a smile for Greiner. Behind the goggles, he might have winked, but Greiner could not see it. So Friel twitched his head. Greiner took it as a wink, a sign of friendship. He would have hit Friel back, but he was afraid of hurting him.

The captain had explained the mission, of course. He

had given Greiner and the others the chance to ask questions. As usual, Greiner kept his mouth shut. He knew exactly what was going on and why. He was glad that he only had to follow orders, instead of giving them. No matter how long he stayed in Force Recon, he doubted that he would ever want to be in a position to dream up a plan like the one he had just heard. He didn't know whether he would ever have the ability to tell his men something like that. Instead of trying to get away from a convoy of nearly two hundred Al Qaeda fighters, they were going to march right down the pike toward the enemy convoy, going deeper inside Afghanistan instead of getting out.

SWAYNE COULD TELL that sunrise was approaching, not because he could see any better in his night-vision goggles. Rather, because Night Runner had taken off his and stowed them in their carrying case on his belt. He marveled again that the Blackfeet warrior's senses exceeded those of normal people. Night Runner was in a class with dogs that could hear high-pitched sounds beyond human hearing, elephants that could communicate in tones beneath the range of humans, and eagles that had ten-power binocular vision.

Nobody in his right mind would consider an operation that risked five men and a woman trapped behind an enemy force of two hundred. Unless, Swayne thought, he had the likes of Night Runner and his team to execute it.

NIGHT RUNNER HAD grown uneasy during the hour-long march. He could not help being resentful that the reunion of the Spartans was marred by having to deal with outsiders. The CIA man he could have endured, arrogant though he was. At least he was able-bodied, and willing to endure hardships for the sake of a mission. The woman, though, held them back, and Saddiq was even worse, stumbling along, literally dragging his feet. Night Runner had looked back to see the CIA agent hit the terrorist leader in the kidneys to prod him forward. Saddiq had picked up the pace for a while after getting hit, but soon slowed again. As time passed, the blows became frequent and gratuitous. Night Runner hated terrorism. He would kill a terrorist in combat without hesitation, and with no sorrow. Beating on a prisoner was another matter. He didn't care for torturing people, terrorist or not. No matter how you looked at it, cruelty was cruelty, terrorism by another name.

He did not call the captain's attention to it. He would have had to use the radio, and Carnes had plugged into that. Or he would've needed a huddle, which might have made the CIA agent suspicious.

No, he decided it was better to have the information and not let on that he knew. He vowed to keep an eye on Carnes for the rest of this mission.

Besides, Carnes was the least of their problems. The twilight would come now in less than half an hour. Then they would have to clear the road, the dusty track they now traveled on. Trouble was, they had not gone as far as he thought they needed to find the best ground for hiding and setting up a defense. He consulted his PDA, and confirmed they would not make it as far as he wanted to go. So he selected a secondary site barely a hundred meters down the road ahead. That would give his team plenty of time to hide. He would need a while to cover their trail.

He found the spot and motioned his group to follow. He went well off the road before he stopped—he did not want them to mill around on the roadway, leaving footprints. After a word to the captain—and to Carnes, who literally stuck his head into the conversation—about defending the ground, Night Runner removed his pack. He traded his machine gun with Friel so he could carry a lighter weapon, the Soviet-made rifle. He left his pack behind, carrying only two tools that he had developed three missions ago. Built into his pack, the pieces he assembled looked like a whisk broom and a dustpan the shape of an oversized lollipop.

Working toward the side of the road where his team had walked onto the desert, he started brushing the tracks away beginning at a good one hundred feet from the road. Within twenty feet of the road, he finished up on the brushing by fanning the dust to remove bristle marks, blending the track into the surrounding landscape.

After that, he smoothed out their trail on the dirt track that passed for a road, carefully brushing and fanning for about fifty feet. Then he worked more quickly, using the brush only. Finally, when he had cleaned up the road, the sky had begun to brighten too much for him to remain in the open much longer. He knew he would never be able to remove all the footprints all the way back to the site where they had captured Saddiq anyhow.

But he could create a diversion that would fool all but the most meticulous tracker. He stopped brushing, and walked over the tracks his group had made. After traveling about fifty meters, he decided it would be enough. So he began walking backward to the spot where he had removed the tracks. He continued walking backward, turning into the desert, continuing toward a depression in the ground. Once the tracks had disappeared from the sight of the road, he reversed himself and walked back to the road again. This he repeated twice more, leaving the impression that six people had walked out of the desert onto the road. He walked backward one last time into the depression and allowed himself a moment to reflect.

He imagined himself as a truck driver, a platoon leader or squad leader sitting in the right-hand seat, riding shotgun in the lead vehicle. He closed his eyes. He saw the headlights cutting into the dark—no, it would be daylight. He warped the image and ran the mental videotape again, this time lighted by the sun.

Driving across the desert track at maybe sixty kilome-

ters an hour. The lower light of morning casts long shadows. Suddenly a set of tracks, perhaps a squad strong, appears from the desert and continues down the road. The leader orders the driver to stop. The convoy stops and bunches up. The squad leader jumps out and walks back to where the tracks turn onto the road. He sees perhaps a half-dozen boot prints. He walks back toward the front of the truck to confirm the direction of travel. He surmises that the squad was going toward Saddiq's last known position.

He dashes to his truck and orders the driver to move out. Quickly.

Night Runner nodded. It could happen. It would work fine unless the Al Qaeda unit had a tracker with Runner's skill. Even if they did have a tracker, it would have to do. The blowtorch of another Afghan sunrise had began to cut its way through the horizon. He turned and ran toward the high ground, keeping his route irregular so that an alert set of eyes traveling on the road could not see a pattern to the tracks. If he saw them at all, they would look like an animal wandering. He spoke his name into the radio before rejoining the group, so they would not be startled. He materialized in their midst without anybody seeing him, despite the warning.

Night Runner briefed Swayne and asked about the defensive position. It didn't take long for Swayne to give it to him. So few people, and so little to work with. Greiner had laid his machine gun along the primary avenue of approach. In the worst-case scenario, the convoy would stop, dismount its soldiers, and attack the position, which was a safe quarter mile from the road. There was no way to flank their hillside without crossing in the open—at least within range of their small arms.

Friel had taken the best firing position on the highest ground, which afforded him a place to lie down to rest. A domino arrangement of flat rocks the size of mattresses had toppled there. They gave him some shade. He lay on his belly, his face turned, fluids draining from his mouth, nose, and eyes.

They carried narcotics in their individual aid kits, but as Night Runner went to tell Friel to keep the BRAT, he didn't mention the pain. Friel had already refused drugs last night. With a fight ahead of them, he wouldn't do anything to diminish his eyesight or reaction time any more than the injury had already done.

Nina Chase sat at the rear of the position, leaning up against a stone the size of a pool table. She glared straight ahead, and Night Runner assumed that she had only one thing on her mind yet.

Which reminded him: "Where's Carnes?"

SWAYNE HAD FOUND a spot in full sunlight, a place to sit where he could cool down from the night march without chilling to the bone. He turned to point to the spot where he had left Carnes and Saddiq. "Gone. Come on." His joints aching, he got to his feet to look for the CIA man.

Carnes had suggested they both blindfold the terrorist leader and tape his mouth shut, so he could not betray them. "Tape his ankles too," Swayne had said. "We don't want him running down the hill, attracting attention when that convoy goes by."

The CIA operative had praised Swayne. Swayne had felt his jaws tighten at the sugar-sweet tone, but had held his tongue. "Just hog-tie him, so he can't get in the way. When the convoy comes, we'll leave Nina—Ms. Chase— to watch him. I'll need you and your gun if we get into a fight."

Carnes had agreed. Again, to an excess.

Swayne had turned to other matters, gun positions and fields of fire. Now Carnes—and Saddiq—had gone. With all the aches and pains of the march just finished, Swayne did not need the aggravation of the CIA agent besides.

"Gunny, come with me," he said. He strode out of the position, feeling a burn rise in his skin. He did not want to leave his team. *His team*—he had to keep reminding himself, he had *his team*. The CIA man, if he did anything to upset the integrity of his re-formed Force Recon Team, would have to pay. He wondered if Zavello would let him bring the man back dead.

Night Runner pointed. Swayne saw a scuff mark on the stone. Swayne looked behind the pile of rocks. Beneath an overhang, he found Carnes hunched over Saddiq.

"What the hell are you doing, man?" he barked. Carnes stood up, tossing something aside, grasping for the Kalashnikov that Saddiq had originally carried. Swayne's own rifle twitched in his direction. Carnes's shoulders drooped, then shrugged. Swayne pointed his rifle in turn at the prisoner, at Carnes, at the needle. Carnes was nervous.

"Nothing going on," he said. "I wanted a better place to hold my—our captive. Out of the line of fire. I'm just making sure he's immobilized—"

Night Runner had moved around and walked downslope a few steps. He picked up a syringe and showed it to Swayne.

"With drugs? What the hell are you thinking? You didn't just kill him with something?"

Carnes laughed, not in humor but snidely. "Why would I do that? I need information from this asshole."

"What then? Some kind of truth serum?"

The CIA man grew agitated. "You've been watching too many movies."

Night Runner took a step to put himself behind Carnes.

Carnes said, "Look, we don't use a truth serum anymore. That's obsolete, old hat, Hollywood stuff. Anyhow, it didn't work all that well. We use behavior-modification drugs now. Psychotropics, they call them. Trust serum, if you want to give it a name."

"You're not to torture him," Swayne said, then looked skyward. Suddenly, it was not lost on him that Carnes had taken his man to a spot where the eyes of the overhead

satellite could not see. Suddenly, Swayne was glad that
he had not revealed anything about the XD-11 drone. He
hoped Bonnie Downes had not fallen asleep at the switch,
that she was getting this exchange on tape.

Carnes saw Swayne look at the sky and tried another
tack. "Swayne, we don't need to use torture. All we have
to do is inject this yes-man stuff and start up a conversation. Look, this guy has information. Something big is
coming down. This has national security implications
written all over it. The Al Qaeda is going to hit America."

"You think you can get him to tell the truth? What if
he lies to you? What if he says a truck bomb is going off
in the Holland Tunnel? Even if he were telling the truth,
what could you do about it? You think anybody back
home is going to shut down a roadway that big? On his
word? Or even yours?"

"I don't know about shutting down anything back in
the world," Carnes said, clipping each syllable. "I can't
control that. All I can do is get information out of this
guy, right here, right now. I get the information"—he
pointed at the boom mike of his tactical radio—"I call it
in. Then it becomes somebody else's problem."

"For now, it's my problem. The Marines have rules
about how to treat prisoners," Swayne said. "This guy
belongs to the Marine Corps. It's all on tape. From last
night—"

"By the authority invested in me by the President of
the United States as a CIA officer, I'm taking over control
of this man. It is no longer your responsibility," Carnes
said. "What I do with him is my responsibility. I take it
fully. Now butt out."

"Captain," Greiner called over the headset. Swayne
knew he would not speak up without a tactical reason.

"Go ahead."

"I got a visual on the convoy, maybe three miles and
rolling fast."

"Roger, be right there," he said into his mike. To Carnes, he added, "This man doesn't belong to me. He belongs to the United States Marine Corps. He's not mine to give up."

Carnes straightened. "Call it in."

"What?"

"Call it in, Captain Swayne. Let your superiors talk to my superiors. If you think it is not my decision or your decision, let the higher-ups make it."

"Both of you back off," came a voice both loud and startling into their headsets. Zavello. "I have the entire story just from listening to you two ladies gossip about it. Now both of you put your peckers back into your pants and get back to the firing line."

Swayne obeyed at once. Carnes caught up to him in several quick strides. "Nothing personal, Swayne. This guy is a big fish. For the good of the country—"

"Listen, there's nothing personal to it and never was. I don't care about the big fish. Or even the intelligence he can give you. What I care about is getting this little coffee klatch the hell out of Afghanistan. Now you have poked him with a needle and filled him with drugs. You're right about one thing. He is a big fish. A two-hundred-pound fish in a stupor. A fish we have to drag around like a white whale."

As he said it, Swayne looked into the CIA man's eyes. He saw a confession in the abashed look. Carnes had never intended to drag Saddiq around. He was going to get his all-important information, information which weighed nothing at all, information that he could carry around in his head, and leave the two-hundred-pound gutted fish behind to rot in the Afghanistan sun.

"You bastard," Swayne said, adjusting his radio mike so his words would be heard, both here and in Washington. "You want to pump Saddiq dry of intel and then kill him? You do it on the CIA's watch, not on mine. The Marine Corps is not going to be a party to it."

The CIA man's gaze darted left and right, looking for

wiggle room, a way to escape the trap Swayne had just set.

"Kill him? What the hell are you talking about?" Carnes actually puffed out his chest in righteous indignation. "We have to protect him at all times. He's in our custody, and our job is to bring him to justice. Don't you forget it."

Swayne smiled. The CIA man had gone on the record now too.

Night Runner turned to Swayne and snipped two fingers under his chin. They both turned off their radio mikes.

"Did you get it on your gun-cam?" Runner asked.

"Every bit of it."

SWAYNE HAD NOT done any actual praying for a long time. But as the first of the trucks came into view, long after its column of dust had betrayed its presence, he entertained some hopeful thoughts that verged on prayer. Everybody in his group had orders. Nobody was to move. Nobody was to breathe or sneeze hard enough to raise dust that might betray them. Nobody except Swayne was to pick up his head to look outside the position until the truck convoy had long passed. No movement. No glare or glitter. No noise, no dust, no talking, no coughing, no potty call, no nothing.

Swayne did not even permit himself to use binoculars. He dared not risk a reflection that might betray them. Lying beneath line of sight, he asked Night Runner to check him out to be sure there would be no forgotten clip or buckle to give him away. At the last, before looking up, he dried his face in the crook of his uniform so there would be no sweat to sparkle, impossible as that would be to be seen at a quarter of a mile. Nevertheless—

Slowly he raised his head, keeping himself and his background in shadow, just to be sure that no vehicle pulled out of column, surprising them.

Eight trucks rolled by. The drivers kept a good interval. Each truck remained at the rear edge of the dust plume ahead. A gentle crosswind cleared the road. Swayne ran the numbers in his head. The convoy, about a half mile long, cleared their position in a minute and a half. Twenty miles an hour or so. They'd be at the wadi, four miles away, in twelve minutes.

Swayne watched as the trucks hit the spot where Night Runner's fake footprints came out of the desert. The lead truck slowed, then stopped. He saw a man jump down. He bent over the tracks, ran ahead of the truck a distance of fifty feet, then carved huge hoops in the air with one hand. The truck drove ahead, picked him up, and the convoy expanded like an accordion.

Swayne caught Runner's eye, and they traded smiles. The Al Qaeda fighters now thought that a squad had walked out of the desert toward the wadi. Perhaps a band of thugs that might threaten Saddiq's group further. The trucks would keep rolling now until they arrived at the scene of last night's fighting. They would obliterate the tracks in the roadway, all the tracks, including those showing the direction Swayne's group had taken.

Indeed, a crackle of static sounded in the captured radio. Carnes brought it out and stared at it. Swayne could tell by the urgent tone in the voice that the man wanted to talk to Saddiq's wounded men, the pair left alive after the battle with the Uzbeks. No doubt wanting to know if they'd been attacked by any new groups. Swayne waited for Carnes to translate.

"The cavalry in the trucks," the CIA man said. "They want to know if another group has come by to attack them. They don't know any more than last night. Except now they know to be more scared."

The tone in the radio speaker changed. Swayne recognized the phrases from before.

"They're trying to raise Saddiq again," said Carnes. "I

gotta hand it to you, Jack. You're little plan is driving them bug-nuts."

Swayne winked at Night Runner, giving the gunny credit—Carnes already had forgotten where credit was due.

Swayne then consulted his PDA to check the status of the roadway fore and aft of the convoy. Nothing had changed. Eighty kilometers back, the truck that had broken down with engine problems still stood next to the roadway. The Al Qaeda fighters who had been riding inside had set up a perimeter and were taking turns napping. Just thirty kilometers back of the convoy, the tenth truck, which had been delayed by a flat to one of its inside dual tires, was plowing the dusty track, trying to catch up. In half an hour, it too would pass. Then Swayne could relax. The Al Qaeda force, unable to locate Saddiq among the dead bodies in the wadi, would assume that the Uzbeks had captured him.

To Swayne's mind, that left them only three options, in the absence of instructions from Saddiq. One, search the area of the wadi. Two, continue along the track toward Uzbekistan, hoping to catch up with the force that had kidnapped Saddiq. Three, return to the interior of Afghanistan. Swayne allowed himself a moment to bask in the confidence that came from knowing his team had outfoxed his enemy. Because he had the satellite eye in the sky and the XD-11 drone as a backup, he would know which option the Al Qaeda troops had taken. Then, after nightfall, he and his group could take their time, spend all night if they wished, getting back to Uzbekistan, crossing at a place—anyplace—where the Al Qaeda wasn't.

Swayne ran all the contingencies through his head once more. He felt safe, even daring to feel cocky. As his adrenaline began to ebb, his body, which he had pushed on the all-night march, began to crash. He assigned Night

Runner first watch and gave the second watch to Carnes. He figured he might have all of four hours to catch up on his sleep. More than enough to restore himself.

He ate a packet of nut-raisin mix and washed it down with the last of his water. He let his eyes go shut. He ran down one final checklist and, finding no chinks in his defense, let his mind go shut.

He thought he might have been asleep for hours when he heard Alvin the Chipmunk chirping at him from the script of some cartoon. He awoke, astonished that he had closed his eyes only five minutes ago. He felt a stab of disappointment that Downes had not been a dream after all. As he tried to get his bearings in the midst of all her chatter, he realized that she was insisting he check the screen on his PDA.

What he saw slapped him awake in an instant.

That damned dog! Saddiq's pet, the animal that looked like a goat, had jumped from one of the trucks deployed at the wadi. His handler dragged the animal on its leash, trying to direct it toward the body farm where Night Runner had harvested parts of the three Al Qaeda fighters.

The huge dog, easily 120 pounds, had set its mind— most likely directed by its nose—to tracking in the opposite direction. Toward the road. Not the road to Uzbekistan either. Instead, the path Swayne and his little group had taken.

For now, the Al Qaeda handler fought the animal. Sooner or later, perhaps after he tired, he would come to his senses. He would realize that the great white beast had found the scent of its master.

Swayne's confidence—he checked his watch—so high not twenty minutes ago, dropped off the table. That dog, for the second time in two days, was going to threaten his life.

He told Downes to give him a picture of that last truck coming his way. As she moved the lens of the drone camera, he called a quick meeting to brief on a new plan, a hasty ambush.

The Spartans still had about twenty minutes. It might be enough time. Night Runner gave him a look, eyebrows raised, asking his question in body language.

With a quick nod of the head, he gave Night Runner permission to get going. He vanished as quickly as if it had been night.

"Let's get down the hill and into position," Swayne ordered.

Greiner helped Friel to his feet. Swayne wasn't sure how to take it that Friel accepted help. Either he was too sick, or he had undergone a personality implant during the weeks he was on psycho-pass.

Nina swaggered by, following Greiner and Friel, giving Swayne a wink as she came even with him. One thing for sure, they were of the same mind. Both of them would like to see Carnes thrown into a scorpion pit.

Swayne went back to the rear of the position again, to help Carnes bring Saddiq forward. The CIA man had removed the terrorist's blindfold, for all the good that would do. Because of the drugs, Saddiq was still out of it, barely able to stumble under his own power. Carnes alternated between pushing, pulling, and cursing to keep the man on his feet and moving in the right direction. When Saddiq stumbled and fell on his face, Swayne decided he had to help out. Either that or leave the CIA man behind with his prisoner, and he couldn't afford to lose the firepower of even a single man. He grabbed Saddiq by the left elbow and waited for Carnes to pick up his right. Together they dragged the Al Qaeda leader toward the road, leaving twin skid marks in the sand. Much as he wanted to set his anger aside, Swayne saw the skid marks as just one more problem the CIA man had caused. Now somebody was going to have to go back up the hill to wipe out those marks that would betray their hasty ambush.

To make things worse, the terrorist stank. He'd peed

his pants—a side effect that Carnes had failed to mention. At last Night Runner returned from his first setup task. He still had time to deal with the skid marks before another column of dust appeared on the horizon.

Minutes later, a single truck roared into view. The vehicle that had pulled out of convoy earlier to change a flat tire raced at full speed, trying to catch up. This truck, one that Swayne wanted as his own, was their best way out of Afghanistan.

SWAYNE SET UP his ambush quickly and well. He would trigger it when the truck reached a choke point in the road. His first choice, like Night Runner's, would have been a half mile down the road. There the road curved, forcing wheeled traffic to slow down before crossing a wadi. Climbing up the near bank of the wadi would have brought the vehicle to a crawl.

They would have to make do here, though, with no incline and no curve. The track cut through the rockfall from the slopes above. Here, the driver had to stay on the track. Or else risk ripping the vehicle's underbelly.

Swayne set out to create a slowdown. After Night Runner collected their boomers and went to plant them, and while Friel kept watch over Saddiq, he and Greiner rolled a pair of small boulders to the right edge of the track. Nothing big enough to stop traffic. Just curb-sized, to force the driver to steer left, as if avoiding a speed bump. Ten meters down the road, they placed a stone near the left tire track. There the vehicle would have to swerve right, then left to drive on. The driver would have to let off the gas to slow down.

If Swayne's plan worked, the Al Qaeda troops might turn the truck over to his team without a shot fired. Since Swayne never relied on the goodwill of an enemy, or even the hope that an enemy would behave, he put Friel down the road ahead of the stones. From a spot among the boulders, he could take out the driver with a single head shot.

A last resort. Swayne did not want to shed blood if he did not have to. Two things could not happen—either losing the truck or letting an Afghan sound a radio alert to the main Al Qaeda force at the wadi ahead.

Night Runner came back to brush out Swayne's and Greiner's tracks. He then slipped into a spot across the road from Swayne. Just as the roar of a truck engine came to them from half a mile away.

Swayne made a brief radio check with the Force Recon team. They rogered in turn. He waved to Friel, who waved back from his sniper's nest—he no longer had a radio. His jaw kept him from talking anyhow.

The plan was simple. Swayne had kept the CIA man next to him to talk to the Al Qaeda fighters on that truck. But first, he had to settle something else. He shut off both their radio mikes.

"Listen, Carnes, I'm not going to fight you over the control of Saddiq. Whatever report I get back from higher, I'm going to obey. We get Saddiq out of the country, and you can do what you want."

"Fine, but first chance we get, you let me have at him—alone."

Swayne raised an eyebrow.

"I don't want to torture him, Swayne. No need to. The drugs will loosen his tongue better than electrical shocks to the gonads. You people don't have a need to know for the kind of intel I want to get out of Saddiq. He has information—"

They both looked down the road toward the sound of the diesel engine, which had suddenly grown louder. The vehicle had ground its way up the slope to level ground. The driver jammed his way through the gears, picking up speed.

"All right," Swayne said. "You can have Saddiq. I need to trust you, Carnes. Help get us through this ambush."

Carnes shrugged. *What else?*

Swayne said, "No freelancing. Just tell them to give up

and keep your ears open for anybody trying to make a radio call."

"No problem. Now let it go."

Swayne had to. The truck rolled into view. He crouched in his hiding spot, lying closer to Carnes than he wanted to. He turned on his radio mike to control the action—as much as anybody could control it once he'd sprung open a box of chaos. He made sure Carnes had a mike hot. The team needed to hear what he and Carnes had to say in the next few minutes.

The ambush started out on script. The truck passed by the hiding position where Swayne had put Greiner and Nina Chase. Swayne had given her a pistol, but told her to stay down until he gave her the all-clear. The pistol was for her self-defense only. That he'd made clear to her. In turn, she'd made clear to him, if there was no chance for self-defense, she was going to use it on herself. "I'm not going to be captured, Jack. Not even for a few minutes." She made a tent of the front of her khaki jacket, showing off the spatters and streamers of blood slung from Night Runner's sword in the early morning's killings. "I'm not going to be gang-raped, and I don't want to have to be saved from the middle of a hatchet fight." Swayne had had to admit she had a point.

He put everything but the ambush out of his mind. The driver slowed for the speed bump, passing Swayne, Carnes, and Saddiq on one side of the road, and Night Runner on the other. They and Greiner would be the main part of the ambush, forming a rough half circle behind the truck. If things went south, Friel would come into play. Swayne had chosen Friel's position so he could avoid a cross fire. The spot that would allow him to take any Al Qaeda fighters who tried to flee or fight from the front of the truck.

The truck swerved left. On cue. As the driver began to cut the steering wheel back toward the right, Night Runner used his tiny remote control to touch off the first boomer, a single concussion grenade a hundred meters down the road. The grenade, designed to create blast, shock, and concussion more than throw shrapnel, sent a boiling cloud of dust from the churned-up road. The blast looked big enough to be an eight-inch gun. Puffs of dust curled up in front of Swayne's face.

"The next ones will come closer," he warned his team. "Cover your faces."

The driver let up on the gas. Confused. His first instinct would be to slam the gas pedal to the floor.

Swayne had a counter. Night Runner let off a second boomer, just fifty meters away. Followed by a third explosion only two seconds later, just twenty meters away from the driver. As if an artillery observer was walking rounds down the road toward the truck. Anybody who had ever been in battle would infer an attack by indirect fire, either a mortar or light artillery. The pattern would lead them to believe the next round would land nearby, followed by a barrage as the entire gun battery fired for effect.

Shouted questions came from the canvas-covered rear of the truck, and answers came from the cab.

"What's going on?" Carnes said in a monotone, translating for the Spartans on the radio net and for the OMCC. "Artillery." "Go, go, get out of here." "No, stop. Dismount." "Get away from the truck." "No, keep going— drive through it."

At that, Night Runner punched off two quick blasts, one fifty meters behind the truck, the other ten meters in front.

That last explosion was close and decisive, shattering both headlights and one panel of the windshield.

"We're bracketed," Carnes translated. "Get clear of the truck, I command it." "Here they come," he said in his normal voice, reporting the obvious.

Both doors of the cab flew open, and the truck coasted to a stop in the road, the left front wheel dropping into the nearest crater. Like clowns out of a jalopy, the remaining Al Qaeda fighters poured out of the truck bed, landing on each other, stumbling and falling to the ground, dropping weapons and leaving them. Nobody wanted to be near that truck when the barrage hit.

"Now," Swayne said.

Night Runner fired a short burst of machine-gun fire through the very top of the canvas of the truck, and one body, head-shot, tumbled from beneath the flap, landing in a heap in the dust.

"Drop your weapons, and you won't be killed," Carnes shouted, standing up to cover the men with his BRAT. He too fired into the canvas to punctuate his command. Swayne and Greiner followed suit.

The shooting of four guns over their heads let the Al Qaeda fighters know that they were in mortal danger. They had jumped out of the truck, and the first things they saw were the nearby boulders where they might get cover. Now the boulders had come alive with gunfire. An enemy covered them from three directions.

The fighters froze, then some dove to the ground, their hands over their heads—they had been through this drill before.

"Don't shoot," Carnes translated. "God save us." "I don't want to die."

One man started to turn, looking toward the front of the truck. So far no gunfire had come from there. But as he began to raise his rifle, he did elicit a reaction after all. A single shot from Friel, a slap in the back at the knot of vertebrae where the neck meets the shoulders, a wound that killed him instantly and threw him to the ground.

Swayne had hoped to control the men without killings, but he could not afford for any more of the group to get the idea that fighting could save them. The deaths made a point of the futility of resisting.

Carnes followed up by shouting at the men. They acted confused.

Swayne barked at Carnes. "What are you telling them now?"

"Surrender or die. Drop your weapons or we will shoot. Lie down on your bellies. Surrender or die."

"Don't say *die*. Tell them to surrender and live."

Carnes got the point. He called to the Al Qaeda fighters, who seemed more willing to give in now.

Even so, one man at the front of the truck, one who had bailed out of the passenger's seat, chose to die. Lying sprawled in the dust, he brought up his rifle in panic, pressing the trigger, his Kalashnikov on automatic fire. A single shot by Friel, unheard in the rattle of other guns, put down the last threat. The man died, his face in the dirt, his finger still clutching the trigger, shooting up the roadway just inches in front of the muzzle, until the magazine ran dry.

"Tell them again," Swayne ordered, and Carnes repeated his commands.

Al Qaeda fighters who had lived to die as martyrs lost their zeal. They began to cry out.

"Spare us." "Blessed Allah." "I am English," Carnes translated.

Carnes and Swayne both snickered. The man claiming an English heritage had cried out in Pashto, the language of most Al Qaeda fighters.

Swayne checked his watch. It had all taken just a few ticks under a minute. So far. They weren't out of the desert yet. They had to act while the men were still in a state of shock, before they could find the courage or weapons to fight back. Or worse, to pull out a phone or radio to report.

"Round them up," Swayne said into his mike. "Watch for commo gear—Carnes, tell them to give up their radios and phones."

The Spartans had practiced handling prisoners many times in their training. Night Runner would cover any Al Qaeda fighters to the left of the vehicle, Swayne collected

those at the back, and Greiner ran up from Swayne's rear
to gather anybody on the right side of the vehicle. Friel
stayed in place so he could take out any of Saddiq's men
who tried to escape to the front of the truck.

Swayne had not heard a report. Then again, Friel could
not talk. He saw Friel make the OK sign in the air.
Swayne waved back, and the hand vanished behind the
rocks.

Carnes piled gear in a heap. The CIA man moved nim-
bly among the captives, talking in a calm but firm tone,
gathering rifles and pistols first. Then he made another
pass, picking up three cell phones and two radios.

One radio interested him. Somebody kept up almost
nonstop chatter. He listened to it and smiled at Swayne.

"Practically a step-by-step description of the search of
the wadi," he said. "They found the two wounded guys.
The company commander keeps trying to get in touch
with our friend Saddiq. Want me to blow his mind?"

Swayne shook his head emphatically. "No. Don't try to
fake anything. Just listen. These guys lose commo all the
time. The officers would try to contact Saddiq—so when
he did get back to them and started to chew them out for
not being in contact, they could say they gave it the old
college try. Believe me, it's no big deal to be out of touch
for a while, but if you try faking them out, we'll be
busted."

Carnes shrugged. "Fine. I'm going to check pockets for
phones, knives, and hidden weapons. I've already told
them to keep their arms outspread, so if anybody moves,
it won't be to scratch his nose."

Night Runner brought the driver to the rear of the truck,
and Greiner found a second man who had been sitting
erect and afraid in the cab. Swayne counted three killed
and nineteen able-bodied. A lot of men to handle, but after
Carnes had tied four sets of wrists together, Greiner set
his weapon aside and began to help. Night Runner assisted

with the rest. After tying all the hands, Greiner began throwing gear into the truck bed. Carnes ordered the men to line up, facing back the direction they had come.

Swayne checked his PDA again. The dog had won its way. The handler had let the animal have its head. Goatdog had begun pulling him at the end of his leash. A handful of men piled into a truck. None of them in a hurry.

Swayne put the picture together. The main force would stay at the wadi, gathering dead bodies and body parts, tending their wounded. A small security force would be idling down the road after the dog.

He could live with that. He spoke to Carnes: "Tell the prisoners they will not be harmed if they start walking and don't look back. Tell them we're going to take all their weapons, so they have no reason to come back this way, except later, to bury their dead."

Carnes pursed his lips.

"Tell them, just as I said."

The CIA man spoke, then turned to Swayne. "You know, the minute we're out of sight, they're going to untie each other's hands and find some way to give a signal, light a fire or something."

"Don't be so sure. Greiner, get some bad-ass duct tape. Carnes, tell each man to put his thumbs together behind him."

Greiner went down the line of Al Qaeda fighters, taping each pair of thumbs with a quick wrap. For good measure, he slapped a length of tape around each set of knots.

Carnes picked at one taped knot and whistled. "How come we never heard of this stuff at CIA?"

Because you never listen? Swayne kept a straight face. No need to start trouble now with a smart-aleck remark. Too much was at stake. They needed to get moving. An arm signal brought Friel in. Swayne ran back to Nina, calling her name so she would not fire blindly.

She joined him, and they hurried back to the truck.

Swayne saw that Carnes had collected several wraps from the back of the truck, where the Al Qaeda fighters had left them. Good, he thought. They'd need them to pull off the next phase of his plan.

"Jack?" Nina said. "Ever thought about quitting your job? A career change?"

He looked to see whether she was serious. She was, although not about his career.

"I'm quitting, Jack. When we get back. I'm leaving the news business. Maybe to find a husband. To have children, settle down, like that."

Swayne felt his stomach churn like one of the dust balls from the concussion blasts. Why he felt sick, he could not say. He decided the reason was that they had stayed too long in the ambush zone.

"Jack?" she asked. "Have you heard a single word I said?"

"Nina, keep an eye on Saddiq."

"Not a single word. You haven't heard a single word I've said."

He gave her a sober look. "Saddiq?"

"Sure." She stood over the Al Qaeda leader as Swayne gave a quick briefing to his team. The men stood in a tight circle, facing out for security. As he talked to their backs, he noticed that Nina carried her pistol at her side, the muzzle aimed at Saddiq's face.

Saddiq cared not a whit. Carnes's drug had made him drowsy in the warming morning sun. He lay in the dirt, his mouth open. Strings of drool seeped onto the desert floor, and a scouting party of ants had begun a recon of his scruffy beard and ample lips.

Carnes stood by Swayne's shoulder and said, "Looks tame as any four-year-old Sunday school kid, eh? Want to see him try doing a million push-ups? He would. Until his pecs burst like overinflated balloons."

"Get him into the truck," Swayne said, barely hiding his contempt.

Carnes barked at Saddiq in Pashto. The man rolled over onto his face and brought his knees under his chest. The CIA man helped him stand up. He spoke to him again, and Saddiq nodded, turned around, staggered, caught himself, and walked to the back of the truck. He did not even acknowledge the existence of two of his dead men on the ground, or the line of men straggling down the road toward the southeast, in the direction of Kholm, nearly fifty kilometers distant. He just stood at the back of the truck expectantly.

Swayne felt a sinking in his gut, not because he felt sorry for Saddiq. Rather, because even a violent fighter's spirit could be reduced to that of a workhorse standing idle, his weight on only three legs, waiting for Farmer Joe to harness him to the plow. Swayne had always kept a reluctant image tucked away in the forget-about-it-until-you-have-to-think-about-it region of his mind. Namely, how he would behave as a captive, should his vow never to be taken alive be thwarted. This image he had kept cloaked in the sturdy but bleary cloth he called honor. He would behave well as a prisoner. Or he would die resisting his enemy, a kind of death-before-dishonor self-image.

Just as Saddiq had doubtless vowed to fight to the death, to be an unruly prisoner, to force his captors to kill him so he could die cloaked in his own brand of fervor, a martyr true to his cause, his God, and his vicious honor.

Yet there he stood, a meek and sallow nag. Swayne saw that honor couldn't matter much if men could steal it with a needle. He'd always known that the dead neither got nor lost honor. Instead honor was a snapshot of a man's state of grace at the moment of his last breath. A battle drug could steal honor from a man without a fight.

Carnes let down the tailgate, yapped at Saddiq, and when the man had laid his face on the floor of the cargo compartment, picked up his legs and shoved him in like a fence post. Carnes clapped the dust off his hands as proudly as if he'd thrown up the last of a load of bricks.

"Gentle as cashmere," Carnes said. "Want me to tell him to eat"—he looked toward Nina and changed his menu—"dirt? He'll do it. He would do anything I said for the next hour or two."

"Mount up," Swayne ordered. What if Saddiq had such a drug? What would he have to eat if he were Saddiq's captive? He shuddered to—

"Carnes?" Swayne asked, struck by a sudden brainstorm. "Anything? You can make him say or do anything on command?"

"Anything. Want him to eat something?"

"Forget that. The drug is reliable?"

"Absolutely."

"For how long?"

Carnes look at his watch. "Two, maybe three hours more."

Swayne narrowed his eyes. "You ever seen the movie *Weekend at Bernie's*?"

Carnes twisted his mouth into a sneer that dissolved into a smile. "Gotcha. Swayne, you ever thought about changing jobs?"

"Never mind that. Let's get him into the front—you ride shotgun. Greiner, can you drive this thing?"

Greiner beamed. "If it can be driven, I can drive it."

Friel whacked him on the shoulder and made some unintelligible sounds.

Greiner shrugged.

Night Runner said, "I think he's trying to tell you that you're beginning to sound too much like him."

Friel grunted in an affirmative tone. Greiner smiled broadly at the notion Friel might finally be ready to accept him as one of the Spartan team.

"Let's mount up," Swayne ordered. He helped Carnes grab Saddiq by the ankles and pull him out of the truck bed.

Carnes pulled a pocket knife and put it to the cord holding Saddiq's wrists.

Swayne pulled the tape off Saddiq's lips. "Are you sure, absolutely sure, we can control him with words alone?"

Carnes said, "I've been using this drug for a year. I was in on the development. I've been a subject of interrogation— for training purposes, mind you. It works. In one test, they told me to condition myself not to answer the questions they would ask. They gave me evasive answers to some questions. They gave me wrong answers and hypnotized me, directing me to give wrong answers instead of right answers—things like Yankee Stadium is in midtown Manhattan. No matter how well they prepared me, as soon as they poked me with the needle, changed my diaper, and started giving the orders, I behaved exactly as they wanted me to. I did not even remember the evasions they drilled into my head—all I remembered was the truth as I knew it. I did not know how to lie anymore. Think about it, Jack. What if we used this drug before a Presidential debate—put the candidates on television wearing Depend adult diapers and ask them any question you wanted to. They would have to tell the truth. Think about it, man."

Swayne shook his head. Too scary to think about. Politicians telling the truth? "As long as you can vouch for him. If you can't, I'm going to be sitting right behind his head. Tell him that if he disappoints me, I'm going to turn him over to this young woman and let her deal with him."

Carnes spoke the words, and Saddiq lifted his gaze to examine Nina's eyes. Swayne wondered that he did not go blind in the intensity of her hatred.

Swayne reflected a moment about honor again. Not ten minutes earlier he had felt despair that drugs could take away a man's honor without a fight. Five minutes later the idea to use Saddiq as a Hollywood-inspired buffoon sprang up in his own mind, and he found it hard to argue that he had not given up Saddiq's—and his own—honor without a whimper. How would he deal with that? Later,

he decided. He put the problem away on the I'll-think-
about-that-tomorrow shelf at the back of his mind.

GREINER DROVE WITH Saddiq sitting in the middle, until
Carnes thought to ask him where he usually rode as a
passenger in a truck. Saddiq gave him a broad, sheepish
smile, as if he were afraid to mention it, and said that he
always sat by the door unless he rode with Osama bin
Laden. The Sheik always insisted on sitting by the door.
Carnes crawled over him and told him to slide across the
seat.

Swayne sat on an ammunition crate at the center of the
bed of the truck, so he could see forward and talk to
Carnes. He marveled.

SWAYNE HAD LONG since downloaded the terrorist's dossier. Saddiq had earned his reputation in Lebanon more
than a decade ago as a suicide bomber whose truck failed
to explode when he drove it into an Israeli checkpoint
outside Jerusalem. Afterward, as he ran away, drawing
fire from Israelis who exposed themselves to try to shoot
down a rabbit darting in the desert, the truck did detonate.
The explosion did kill fourteen Israeli soldiers and a
dozen bystanders, allowing Saddiq to escape.

According to his dossier, he had felt ashamed that
martyrdom—his honor, Swayne thought—had eluded
him. Even so, his attempt elevated him to hero status
among all Arabs, but especially terrorists. A young Saudi
prince by the name of Osama bin Laden recruited him for
the Al Qaeda. In a personal interview, bin Laden saw
leadership potential in Saddiq. After two years of training
in desert camps, bin Laden sent his protégé into the Soviet
Union for finishing with the KGB. The would-be martyr
sent many an Arab to terrorist heaven in other suicide
attacks. He had risen to coequal status with only a handful
of the most elite of bin Laden's lieutenants. He would as
soon drink an American's blood as look at him.

Now he sat, his hands untied and resting on his knees, like an altar boy. He kept looking from Greiner, the Marine, to Carnes, the CIA agent, grinning like Gomer Pyle trying to decide between eating a hunk of sweet potato pie and losing his virginity.

The truck roared down the dirt track toward the rest of the convoy, now parked at the wadi. The Spartans kept the canvas flap tied shut, first to hide them, and second to keep out the back draft of dust. Even so, grit drifted in from every angle, through every seam and grommet and bullet hole.

Swayne felt both sorry and grateful for Friel. Sorry because his injuries had turned his breathing to noise as the air rushed through his broken teeth to and from his lungs. Grateful because Friel didn't complain about his woes, either by making noises or in sign language. Night Runner took out a camouflaged bandanna, poured water over it, and handed it to Friel, who pressed it gently to his nose, wincing at even that slight pressure.

Swayne dealt with the dust by putting it out of his mind so he could work on the end game of his plan. No point in worrying about the middle. No way could he plan for that. Not until he saw how the Al Qaeda fighters reacted to their approach. For now, the problem was what to do should they have to fight their way past the troops deployed in the wadi.

Rather than change his own radio frequency and risk being out of touch with Zavello, Swayne asked the colonel at the OMCC to put the Marine lieutenant, Radford, up on his frequency. Once he had the young officer on the horn, he gave his tactical instructions. Using his PDA, he scratched a few general lines into the sand, uplinked it to the satellite and back to the OMCC. Zavello's technicians then retransmitted to the platoon leader, whose standard-issue equipment was not compatible with the high-tech versions in the hands of Force Recon Marines. Swayne made a mental note to address that situation in his after-action report. Time the Corps issued some of the tools in the Force Recon inventory to support troops and contact units in the field.

By the time Radford rogered his instructions, Greiner spoke up.

"Tallyho on Spot and the bandits, Boss," he said.

Swayne craned his neck, squirming into the space beside Saddiq's shoulder so he could look out the windshield.

A half mile away, the huge white dog continued to pull its handler across the landscape. It did not walk in the roadway proper because Saddiq's scent would have drifted downwind a short way. So it was tracking six meters or so to their left. The truck followed along, keeping to the roadway.

The dust now became their ally. Greiner and Carnes wrapped scarves around their heads and covered their faces, except for their eyes. A good disguise and a natural one. Saddiq's face they left uncovered. Swayne wanted the Al Qaeda leader's men to recognize him. He needed the man's fearful reputation. His dossier showed that he was not above killing one or two of his own men to set an example. Nobody ever resigned from Al Qaeda. The only way to get out of the organization was through terrorist heaven, by suicide attack, or in battle with the infidel. Or else through terrorist hell, usually torture and execution for failure to perform to standard. Saddiq, then, held the keys to hell. The ordinary line soldier would never want to come to the Al Qaeda leader's attention. He would not ask the man why his face was uncovered. He would assume that Saddiq was tougher than the average soldier, unfazed by dust.

They drove by the tracker first. Carnes told Greiner, "Wave at the guy. Not too excited, just a little wave." He spoke in Pashto, and Saddiq gave a short whistle and pointed back toward the wadi.

"What's happening?" Swayne asked.

Greiner checked his left rearview mirror. "Nothing—no, wait. The dog has smelled out Saddiq. It's practically dragging the guy this way."

"Don't slow down," Swayne cautioned. "Not for anything."

Greiner said, "Do I move over for this truck? I mean, we have the big guy with us. What would it look like?"

"Good point," Carnes said. He switched to Saddiq's language. The Al Qaeda leader leaned out the window and spat a command, waving his fist. The oncoming truck veered off the track, making way for Greiner's vehicle.

"Keep checking them in the mirror," Swayne said as they drove past. Meanwhile, he turned his attention toward the larger group in front.

A mile away, he could see on the ground what the XD-11 had showed him from its orbit above and to the southwest. The trucks had pulled off the road, tactically alternating one to the left, the next to the right in a herringbone pattern. On the upside, that left the road open down the center. On the downside, it gave the Al Qaeda soldiers a view of them from both sides of the road.

The soldiers had formed roughly into four groups of about forty scattered up and down the wadi. Swayne asked Downes to play back pictures from the last half hour on his screen, moving the images at ten times normal speed. After just three minutes, he could make a fair guess as to what would happen next. The Al Qaeda fighters had searched both sides of the wadi, staying dispersed, their weapons at the ready. Each time they found dismembered bodies, the groups would form defensive perimeters, wait a while, then resume their search.

Now, looking at the pictures in real time, Swayne could see that two of the groups gathered around the wounded men who had fought the Uzbeks. Generally, discipline had relaxed. The way it did when soldiers realized they were in no danger—either from attack or from ass-

hewings from a ranking officer like Saddiq. Now they
were reacting to the needs of their bodies, their fatigue,
their need to urinate, drink, eat, smoke. A few Muslims
prayed toward the west, the direction to Mecca.

One close-up showed a group of soldiers pointing and
shouting. They had spotted the truck—or perhaps somebody in the group with the dog had called ahead on the
radio. In any case, after the first reaction, the soldiers went
back to their routines. With renewed urgency, Swayne
noted.

"Is this as fast as you can go?" Swayne asked. He
wanted to be clear of the parked trucks before the troops
began to assemble and mount up.

Already the Al Qaeda officers had heard from the dog-
handling party that Saddiq was riding in the truck to join
them. They had begun trying to renew contact with Saddiq, making radio reports about the dead bodies in the
wadi. They kept asking for instructions.

"Want me to have Saddiq answer them?" Carnes asked.

"No," said Swayne. "Keep them in the dark. Let them
believe he lost his radio—whatever they want. You let
them start chatting, and they might just tell him they
thought he was captured by the CIA or something. That
might there's a case where you don't want Saddiq telling
the truth. Once you started a conversation, you couldn't
just stop talking."

Carnes looked over his shoulder. "I guess you know
what the soldiers might do?" He was asking more than
telling.

Swayne didn't take the bait. He did know what would
come next. The officers would get their heads together—
not on radio—to figure out a safe course of action. Meaning one that did not get them in trouble with their leader.

After a few minutes, they came back on the air and
reported that they would conduct a final search, sending
men in a huge sweep outside the area already swept. They

assured their leader, in case he was listening but could not transmit, that they would find the forces responsible for the havoc in the wadi.

Swayne supposed they might find the remains of two flying wings or they might not. They would find boot prints of Night Runner and Friel, boot prints and a drop zone. That would boost their sense of urgency. They would take to their trucks and head toward the nearest foreign border, Uzbekistan's.

Getting past those trucks was not going to be a drive in the park. Swayne wanted to do it before all those men and guns had assembled in one spot, especially if that was what Saddiq would expect to be happening.

With less than a half mile to go, Swayne decided he could breathe easier. The Al Qaeda platoons would not be likely to assemble, even if the order was given in the next few seconds and they marched to their trucks at double time.

He went over the latest, updated version of his plan with Carnes. Saddiq, still deep under the influence of drugs, was all smiles. Same as Carnes.

At a hundred meters, a guide stepped out onto the track. The man was acting like a reserve traffic cop at a concert, directing the truck to a parking spot.

"Slow down," Swayne said, putting a scarf to his face, frowning at the smell of sweat and garlic in the surprisingly soft wool.

The traffic guide wanted Greiner to go right. That would not do. Swayne wanted a witness to Saddiq as they passed through. He wanted that witness to pay attention to Saddiq alone, to end up gawking and speechless. So he would not see the smallest detail that might betray Greiner or Carnes.

"Go left. Easy, take it easy," Swayne urged. "Don't piss him off."

The guide backpedaled out of the roadway, staying in front of the truck's bumper.

Greiner said, "Guy must not have got the word that the boss is in the area."

"So, give him a hand signal," Swayne said. "Point at Saddiq."

Greiner carved a rainbow in the air and poked a finger at Saddiq, practically tapping him on the head.

The guide didn't get it. Clearly tired of the driver's antics, he threw his hands into the air and stormed around the front of the truck to get to the passenger door. Greiner kept idling forward, turning the wheel to get back onto the road.

Without turning his head, Carnes spoke to Saddiq.

The guide stood up on the running board of the truck. First his hands hooked onto the frame, then his face came into view. As soon as he recognized the passenger, his eyes showed white all around the pupils. Saddiq cuffed the face with the back of his hand, and the man fell off backward into the dirt, rolling and scrambling to stay clear of the rear dual wheels.

Carnes spoke again. Saddiq leaned out the window and growled at the man.

Carnes barked at Saddiq in a hushed voice. Saddiq parroted the remark in tone and the volume, too softly for the guide to hear. Carnes gave him another instruction, and Saddiq repeated his command, this time shouting it.

"Drive on," Carnes said. Then he continued to speak in Saddiq's language.

Saddiq put his head and shoulders out the window. He shouted back to the guide. Other men sat up in the cabs of their trucks. Carnes muttered. Saddiq yelled.

"Drive on in a normal speed," Carnes said. "If anybody starts to step out in front of the truck, wave them away. Show them your fist—don't give anybody the finger—too Western."

When they had cleared the parking area and begun driving down into the wadi, Swayne finally stopped holding his breath. His eyes met Night Runner's, and they allowed each other a nervous grin. They might get through this after all. Night Runner sat on the troop seat on the left of the truck, his sword in hand. If he needed a firing port, he would cut it with two or three quick strokes.

On the right troop seat, Friel clutched a strap hanging from one of the overhead ribs, his eyes closed to deal with the pain of the bouncing. Nina sat on a pack in the center of the cargo compartment, ready to flatten facing the rear. She held her pistol. If anybody tried to get into this truck—

Swayne used his pocketknife to cut a one-inch slit in the canvas, so he could look down the wadi through his improvised knothole. He did not like what he saw.

He turned and saw Carnes, the scarf pulled from his face, grinning broadly. Something was up.

Swayne said, "It looks like an ant war back there. What did Saddiq tell them, Carnes? They're not coming after us, are they?"

"Relax, Swayne. He told them to saddle up and get back to the caves. He said he was going to find the infidels on his own."

Swayne shrugged and shook his head. He still didn't understand the sense of urgency among the Al Qaeda fighters. He saw Carnes grinning like a Halloween skull.

"What else?"

"I told them—Saddiq told them he was going to line up everybody in the last truck back to the caves and shoot every other man in the head."

Once again, Swayne realized that one of the things he did not like about the CIA man was that tendency to do things with a flourish. He couldn't just tell them to go back to the caves, or even to wait in place. He had to turn it into an elaborate war story he could tell once he got back to Langley.

But, Swayne supposed, it didn't matter. As long as the Al Qaeda troops put some distance between themselves

and Saddiq, things would be fine. Let Carnes have his war
story.

Swayne braced himself, taking staggering steps past
Nina Chase, the packs, and the weapons they had thrown
into the back of the truck. He pulled the flap aside enough
so he could watch the Al Qaeda fighters evacuate the
wadi. He didn't want to see any change in plans. Not now.
The nearest group was less than a hundred meters away,
far too close for Swayne's piece of mind.

"Shit!"

Carnes and Greiner said the word at the same time.
Saddiq said something else, or perhaps the same word in
his own language.

Swayne turned, and through the opening to the cab and
out the windshield, he saw a soldier step in front of the
truck. The man carried a Kalashnikov rifle. He swung it
toward the truck, and even before he had come level, began firing on automatic.

Everything happened at once.

Greiner mashed the accelerator.

Swayne shouted for everybody to duck.

The CIA man lunged toward Saddiq's lap.

Bullets shattered the windshield from the outside.

Swayne drew down on the opening and fired through
the windshield from the inside.

In the corner of his eye he saw a glint of Night Runner's slashing sword.

Nina screamed, and Friel grunted, wanting to know
what was going on.

Night Runner stood up on the troop seat and stuck his
machine gun and the top half of his body out the slit he
had made.

More bullets struck the truck, this time hitting metal,
making a noise like a massive air wrench loosening the
lug nuts on the wheels.

Night Runner fired a short burst, his body bouncing on
the canvas roof of the truck like a trampoline.

Swayne cursed, not so much because he had missed, which he had, but because the soldier in front of the truck looked familiar. He could not place him.

A cry of pain came from the right side of the truck, as the right-rear dual wheels ran over somebody in the track. Swayne supposed it was the shooter.

Carnes shouted, "Saddiq is out. He's getting away."

Figures, Swayne thought. So much for Carnes's drug— what did he call it? Truth serum? No, trust serum? Now what the hell were they going to do?

"Stop the truck," Night Runner shouted.

NIGHT RUNNER DUCKED back inside as Greiner hit the brakes, tossing him forward. He braced himself against the cab, mindless of the rap on the elbow it gave him.

"Greiner, Friel, stay in the truck," he shouted again, knowing that he had to be the one to give orders, because he had seen what went on. "Captain, Carnes, out of the truck and help me pick up Saddiq."

Carnes yelled, "He's going to get away."

"No," Night Runner said. "He's down." He handed off his machine gun to Friel. "Cover us."

At the back of the truck, Swayne was pulling on the ropes of the flap, trying to remember where he had seen the face of the man who'd stepped out of nowhere to wreck an almost perfect plan.

"Here, Captain," Night Runner said, and as Swayne stepped aside, Night Runner cut off the flap from left to right in a single stroke. He and Swayne jumped down and met Carnes at the rear of the truck.

"Shit!" Carnes said. At the feet of the three men lay Saddiq, both his legs crushed, a bleeding, ragged, bubbling tear in the front of his jacket, the same sheepish grin on his face.

Carnes pulled at his own hair. "Shit! Shit! Shit! Run over and shot. I'm never going to get anything out of this guy now."

Swayne muttered, almost to himself, "Did anybody recognize the shooter?" Night Runner gave him a quick head shake and bent over Saddiq. Carnes looked at him as if he were crazy even to care who the shooter was.

"Spartan One, this is Falcon 36, over."

Swayne went blank for a second. Then he realized that Falcon 36 was the Marine lieutenant, Radford. "Go ahead, Falcon 36."

"Lady here says it was one of Saddiq's Uzbeks. One of the guys who got caught in the cross fire between the Uzbeks and the ambush last night."

Swayne remembered. Downes had recognized him. The Uzbek was one of the traitors. A little detail that had gotten away from him. After the ambush, Swayne had not given the guy much thought, or much credit as being a threat. Now look what one overlooked detail had done.

"Tell the lady many thanks," Swayne said, his voice flat.

FRIEL PULLED UP two backpacks and propped the BRAT over them. He looked out over the tailgate from behind his makeshift nest.

He didn't feel a moment's compassion, either for Saddiq or the snot-nose CIA bastard. Both of them had something to do with the fact that he was going to need a face transplant after they got back to the world. Then again, he did not have time to worry about either of them. A whole army of ragheads was gawking at them as if they were a drive-in porn movie.

Friel's impulse was to take out about thirty of the bastards standing in the road between the trucks. One burst of ten would do it—or one hand grenade would get them all. A smile stabbed him across the face, although the duct tape and the swelling kept it from showing.

He knew better than to start shooting, though. Even without the captain telling him. The ragheads weren't going to figure this one out for a while. They were not going to start shooting toward Saddiq. Saddiq was their Zavello-with-attitude, and Friel couldn't even imagine any of them taking potshots in the direction of that guy.

So he waited. For the first time since he could remember, he wasn't spoiling for a fight. He hoped like hell that he hadn't knocked the meanness out of himself on his hard landing. Or worse, that hooking up with Night Runner and his team hadn't turned him into some kind of girlie-boy.

Just the thought of it made him want to start shooting. Kill him some ragheads. Send some terrorists to terrorist heaven. Nail some camel drivers to the—

Another smile tried to blow his face off his head. He was fine. He was back. Now, if only his head wouldn't swell up and explode.

SWAYNE HELPED THROW Saddiq into the cargo compartment. The Al Qaeda fighter clenched his jaws but did not make a sound. Carnes had said the drug did not dull pain. Saddiq had some gonads. Swayne pulled off his own pack to get at the medical kit. If he didn't treat the sucking chest wound, Saddiq wouldn't last twenty minutes.

"Carnes, get into the back with us. We may need your gun."

The CIA man said, "I'll need to get my AK."

Night Runner said, "I'm going to check damage to the engine."

Swayne began cutting off Saddiq's shirt.

"Nina," he said, "come over here. Stick a finger into this wound."

Nina gave him a look. *Like hell I will.*

"Do it. Now, Nina. Henry, what are the Al Qaeda troops doing?" He remembered again that Friel could not tell him.

Night Runner understood. He answered, "They're milling around, trying to decide what's going on. We have some time, but not much."

Carnes yelped his way into the conversation. "Negative, we got no time at all. One of the trucks. It's moving this way."

Carnes clambered into the back and over the pile of backpacks.

"Greiner, move out," Night Runner said into his radio as he swung up into the back. "We're losing diesel."

"Great," Swayne muttered. "What else?"

"Both front tires are hit. We'll be running on flats," Night Runner said.

"Shit!" said Swayne. *What else?* he thought, not daring to ask the question aloud.

Runner answered it anyhow. "And some engine oil."

The truck began to roll, more roughly than even before, the flat tires bunching and flopping at each turn. Nina's finger plunged in and out of Saddiq's wound, and Swayne saw that she was not going to be able to stomach much more of this. He said, "Somebody give me a chunk of that bad-ass duct tape." He dried the skin on Saddiq's chest around the wound. The terrorist leader had begun to labor for each breath.

Night Runner somehow found a moment to hand him a patch of tape. Being careful not to let it touch Nina's hand, Swayne stuck it on Saddiq's damp, pink chest skin. On his order, Nina pulled out her finger. He slapped the tape flat. The center of the tape bubbled out and sucked in, but did not leak.

"Roll him over on his side," Swayne said. If there was any hope of Saddiq not drowning in his blood, it would be if his one good lung stayed inflated.

Swayne had seen grievous war injuries to his comrades, and he had caused more than a few to his enemies. Still, his stomach clenched when they turned Saddiq's torso, because his boots never changed position. He didn't have to tell Night Runner, who began applying tourniquets to each crushed leg close to the groin.

Swayne saw a bloodier, larger, exit wound. He cut

away the back of the shirt, and Nina, who kept wiping her finger off on her jacket sleeve, recoiled.

"I'm not putting my finger into *that*."

Swayne saw that her finger would not do any good anyhow. The bullets must have tumbled inside Saddiq's body. Or perhaps struck a rib on the way out, blowing a chunk of bone through his back. Night Runner covered the exit wound with the palm of his hand, while Swayne dug a field dressing from his kit. He dried the skin again, stuffed a bandage beneath Night Runner's hand, and covered the wound area with a square plastic bandage made for the purpose. He taped down the edges with surgical tape.

It was the best he could do. No telling the damage inside the man's chest. He shook his head.

"I saw that. What?" Carnes wanted to know. "Is he going to die on me?"

"You saw the same wound I saw. What do you think?"

"He's going to die," Carnes wailed. "Shit!"

Swayne had other concerns, namely whether he and his team would suffer the same fate as Saddiq. The one truck had left the rest, at first moving tentatively. Nobody in the larger group knew quite what to do about the situation. Somebody had reported the Saddiq sighting to the officers. Carnes reported they had tried to get his attention on the radio—Swayne could hear the excited jabber on the small speaker.

They had heard the shooting of the Uzbek who had come out of nowhere. Surely one or more pairs of binoculars had seen the American fire drill going on at the truck. Swayne had to assume the worst. They had just witnessed the kidnapping of their leader.

As Swayne's truck drove away, the first truck picked up speed. The soldiers in the wadi boarded their vehicles, and the chase was on. So far, nobody in the pursuing trucks dared to shoot at the vehicle with Saddiq in it. Swayne wanted to keep it that way. But Saddiq had also

passed out. No longer could they rely on him talking to
his men, faking them out.

Under the guise of reminding his team, he said for Carnes's sake, "No shooting until I give the command."

Greiner reported, "We're losing fuel and power. I can
practically see the temp gauge going up and the gas
gauge going down—the lost oil. Want me to nurse it
along or—?"

"Pedal to the metal, Greiner," Swayne ordered. "Until
I tell you to stop or the damned thing seizes. When I do
tell you to stop, you make it a quick one." He looked to
Night Runner. The gunny shrugged. *Why not?* Swayne
had to smile. He had forgotten that he and his men could
communicate without words. Runner seemed to know
what he was going to try.

Carnes tapped Swayne's elbow. "Can you let me in
next to this guy? I have to try to get some information
out of him."

Swayne gave him a sardonic grin, but did not make a
remark, other than the one in his expression: *You sure
you're not worried about us hearing?*

Carnes gave him a wicked snicker. "What's it going to
matter if we're all dead anyhow? At least I could radio
the information back, salvage something out of this debacle."

Then again, maybe not. Carnes couldn't stir Saddiq
from his state of lost consciousness, couldn't stop his head
from lolling on the metal bed of the truck, couldn't stem
the flow of fluids from his mouth. Carnes shook his head.
The best he could do was find a dirty towel inside one of
the backpacks. He used it to prop up the Al Qaeda leader's
head to keep it from banging on the heavy metal decking.

Carnes tried to arouse Saddiq, speaking to him gently
in his own language. He wet a bandanna, daubed at the
terrorist's face, and cut the nylon ties that bound his
wrists.

Swayne shook his head in disgust at the pathetic efforts

of the CIA agent to play good cop to the Al Qaeda leader.

"Captain!" Greiner called from the cab.

Swayne could hear the engine lugging down already.

"How bad is it, Corporal?"

"Bad. Maybe . . . a mile . . . left in her. No more." Greiner punctuated his report with grunts as he fought the bucking wheel for control of the steering.

Swayne could feel the front wheels plow deeper into the sand as the rubber tires began to flop off the rims. He could smell the stench of burning oil on the exhaust. They would have to abandon the truck. He picked up his PDA and scrolled to a map screen to get a fix on the terrain. He needed a miracle escape route. Or at least a piece of ground his tiny force could defend.

What he got was an earful from people trying to get his attention all at once.

"Captain . . . sir? Not going to . . . get a mile . . . after all." Greiner—*grunting*.

"Captain Swayne?" Alvin the Chipmunk Downes—*trilling*.

"Spartan One, this is Falcon 36, over." Radford—*begging*.

"Spartan One, this is Eagle One, over." Zavello—*growling*.

"Swayne, dammit." Carnes—*bitching*.

"Jack." Nina—*pointing*.

Friel—moaning, as he pointed in the same direction as Nina.

And Saddiq—suddenly awake and chanting.

Swayne had always marveled that two things about combat had always evaded Hollywood. First, the chaos of people trying to be heard, everybody's priority a matter of life and death. Second, the chaos cubed by the noise of the battlefield, a racket so terrible that nobody heard nohow.

His own people were giving him the first. The Al Qaeda fighters were about to give him the second.

Swayne, no matter how many times he faced it, had never mastered the chaos. He had earned the reputation of being cool under fire. Not true. He felt the agitation as much as the next man. His only advantage was that he understood he could not waste time fighting the urge to panic—if you did, that panic became just one more of your enemies. If he could force himself to ignore the panic, he could deal with his other problems. So he tried to take in the entire battlefield, tried to listen past the racket and see past the chaos. He set quick priorities, then took quick action. The way to handle panic was simply to give it a low priority—then plan to deal with it after the battle.

First he must deal with the soldiers in those trucks, where Nina pointed. Seven trucks—all with good engines—roared up the near edge of the wadi, bent on catching up to the invaders trying to kidnap Saddiq.

Friel had pointed at the eighth truck, which had pulled off the roadway and disgorged a heavy-weapons detachment. Swayne saw several machine guns and at least half-a-dozen RPGs—the shoulder-fired rocket-propelled grenade launcher, deadly and relatively unchanged since the Vietnam War.

Carnes had glued one of the Al Qaeda radios to his ear. "They're giving orders to each other to fire over our heads, trying to make us stop," he called out.

Zavello said, "If you can make it to the top of that incline you're on right now, you can make a stand."

Zavello had read the terrain, had anticipated Swayne's need of the terrain, had given him a solution to his need. The colonel had seen the desperation of their situation.

Swayne could hear the anxiety in the crabby colonel's voice. He tried to keep the tremor from his own voice as he rogered the colonel and said, "Greiner, can you make the hill?"

"I think . . . I can . . . I think . . ."

Swayne knew what Radford wanted to talk about. He

wanted permission to respond to Swayne's crisis by bringing his platoon forward. That could not happen, except in the cavalry movies. Radford was too far away, at least ten miles. He could not get into the action in time, except to lose more men. No, Swayne and his tiny group would have to rely on themselves. He handled Radford with a terse reply: "Falcon 36, stand by. Stay in position."

"Falcon 36, wilco." Radford did not hide the dismay in his voice, but his response told Swayne the man understood his orders and would obey them. One more thing handled.

Downes heard an opening and spoke up. "Captain Swayne?"

"This is Spartan One. What's your standoff time?"

"Six seconds, ten tops."

Swayne could not suppress a flash of a grin. Overnight, she had picked up the art of brevity. "Spartan One, roger. Stand by for my instructions."

"Roger, wilco, over and out."

Another grin. Later, if they survived this fiasco, he would work with her on her radio procedure.

He caught Nina looking at him oddly. *Forget jealousy, Nina.* Over her shoulder he saw the trucks had bunched up. They also began to spread out across the desert and come after them on line. Each truck full of Al Qaeda fighters wanted to be the ones to rescue Saddiq.

Beyond the line of trucks, he caught the flash of weapons firing. First machine-gun fire, then RPGs began to tear up the ground around them. But no closer than two hundred meters. The weapons platoon commander did not want to risk his career—or his life—by having an accidental round kill Saddiq.

Carnes looked out at the explosions and nodded his head, giving Swayne information he had figured out for himself. "The company commander is telling him to shoot even wider. He's afraid of hitting us."

Swayne felt only too happy that they would be willing

to waste ammunition. But then, they were traveling in trucks, which meant they likely had plenty to spare.

The heavy weapons were not a problem, for now. The other seven trucks had closed to within a kilometer, perhaps less than a half mile. He turned toward the front of the cargo compartment and stuck his head and shoulders into the cab.

"How are we doing?"

"Not good," Greiner said, straining the words between his teeth.

Swayne did not need the report. Smoke had begun to roil from beneath the hood, gray smoke, darkening to black. The incline had begun to level off, though. Swayne saw they were in a tiny pass, that the ridge dropped off on the other side, that the road snaked down toward another wadi.

"Stop here?" Greiner asked.

Swayne covered his mike because he did not want Zavello to hear. "Keep going."

A rush of heat hit them both, and the black smoke turned orange.

"Keep going?"

"Coast if you have to. I have a plan. But I need a hundred meters. Twice that would be even better."

Greiner laughed, and Swayne saw not humor, but relief in his face. The kid was giddy. He believed that his boss actually had a plan. More than that, he needed to believe that his captain had a plan for the team—and the others—to survive. Hauling on the steering wheel, pulling himself completely out of the seat, he stood on the accelerator to milk the last of the truck's waning power.

Flames billowed from the front of the truck, but it kept rolling. Swayne saw that it would soon get an assist from gravity. He had only a few seconds. He turned back toward the troop compartment and hollered instructions into his open mike so that Zavello, Downes, and Radford would hear his plan as well.

Zavello wanted him to dig in and defend on the ridge. Swayne had decided his team was too small a force to do that. The trucks had spread out across the desert. If the Marines began shooting now, all those Al Qaeda fighters would already be dispersed into an attack formation, difficult to hit, able to overwhelm. Worse, they might not be so careful about shooting Saddiq's way.

But because the terrain closed in on the roadway at this tiny pass in the ridgeline, the trucks would have to converge again. Taking on the mass of Al Qaeda fighters gave the team a better prospect of winning the fight.

To his credit, Zavello did not contradict him on the radio. Zavello had battle experience all the way back to Vietnam. He knew what it was like to have chair-borne commanders second-guessing the officers on the line.

By the time Swayne had finished briefing his troops, the front of the truck had dipped down the slope. He looked toward the Al Qaeda attack convoy and saw that it had dropped out of view beyond the crest of the ridge. They might have thirty seconds, one minute tops. Even so, over the noise of their own truck, he could hear the roar of the pursuit as it closed on them.

"That's it," he hollered. "Let's go." As he, Night Runner, and Friel jumped from the back of the truck, he caught the look on Carnes's face: *You call that a plan?*

Indeed, Swayne's scheme began to unravel the moment they abandoned the truck. First, Swayne turned to see that Nina had jumped with them, completely contrary to what he had told her. He gave her a harsh look, and she returned it tenfold.

He snarled at her. "You could get killed up here."

She tossed a quick glance at the fireball of the truck rolling down the hill and rolled her eyes at him. *As opposed to what?*

No point in arguing with her, he thought. Besides, Friel had landed hard again. Any jolt would have rattled his brain and set off the fireworks in the nerves of his basketball-sized face. He knelt on all fours, still clutching the BRAT. From the way his body spasmed, Swayne realized he was fighting back nausea as strings of pink drool stitched from his mouth to the sand.

"Henry, tell me if you're going to throw up," Swayne said.

Friel glanced at the sky and shook his head.

FRIEL HOPED NOT anyhow. He had to get a grip, had to suck it up and choke it down. He saw that the cap had grabbed the babe. They ran to get into position. Up the hill to the side of the road. To get some standoff distance. The first cover they could find at least a hundred meters from the road. That's what the cap had briefed.

Trouble was, Friel could not run. Afraid his head would fall off. He had enough trouble just trying to balance it on his neck. Somehow, it had grown to twice normal size. Hell, maybe three times. Friel did the best he could. He knew it wasn't much. He had been at a picnic one time. As a kid. At the downtown juvie detention center. They made him do a sack race in the park. He said no puke would ever make him do it again. Yet here he was. Running like he was in a sack race, only without the sack.

"Henry, do you need any help?" Night Runner said.

Friel pointed up the hill. *Get going, Gunny.* He had stopped trying to talk. Hurt too much. The chief got the point.

Friel shuffled as fast as he could drag his feet.

Swayne had told him to keep to level ground. The gunny and the captain would go as high up on the hill as they could. They knew he could not make the climb. When they'd told him not to try, he'd felt insulted. Now he felt happy that they had cut him some slack.

He had run only fifty meters and thought he could go no more. The sound of truck motors beginning to crest the ridge gave him a kick in the pants. He might get another thirty meters.

He made only ten before coming to a shallow gully, just a meter deep and a meter wide. Three stinking feet. Yet he dared not try to jump it, for fear his head would pop like a zit. His head. It felt light. He sat down to let the dizziness pass. He dared not faint. Only partly on purpose, he toppled into the gulch.

Looking up at the sky, he could see the earth turn. Rotating very fast today, he thought. Getting dark early too.

Damned Afghanistan, he thought. If he ever got out of this godforsaken place alive, he vowed, he was never in hell coming back. And if he ever did go to hell, he figured, this was the place he'd be waking up in.

Did he ever return, no, he never returned. Poor-er Henry . . .

NIGHT RUNNER SAW Friel go down. He had sprinted to the top of the ridge, high enough to be able to see down into the gully. Friel lay sprawled on his back on top of his machine gun.

Night Runner crouched, thinking he might have time to dash toward his man. If he didn't—

"Leave him."

Swayne. Night Runner made eye contact with the captain, who had found a firing position two meters downhill. Beside him lay the woman. She clutched a 9-mm pistol, useless in the coming battle.

Swayne had a point, though. The first truck had barreled over the crest of the ridge. If Night Runner tried to cross the open area to help Friel, he would be spotted and blow the slimmest of slim chances they had to succeed.

ZIP TO NONE, thought Swayne. Bad enough to have only five guns against upwards of 150. Now they had lost Friel and his light machine gun. All they had was Swayne's bonehead plan. In other words, no chance in hell.

If it were dark instead of mid-afternoon. If they had

some air support. If, somehow, they could summon a helicopter to—

Forget if, dammit! If frogs had shock absorbers, they wouldn't bump their asses every time they landed. He had to snicker. That was one of Gunny Potts's garbled expressions. How long ago had it been that they lost the gregarious Potts in battle?

Potts had never quit. Swayne could not. They did have a plan—even a weak plan was better than none. They had weapons. There would be no surrender.

Nothing to do but play it out.

Night Runner had already planted the last of their boomers, only two—the others he had used up in faking the artillery attack. Swayne looked down at the road. Two piles of stones marked the spots where the gunny had put them.

The flaming truck had not stopped rolling yet, but Greiner had stopped trying to steer it. Flames engulfed the cab. Greiner, his clothing smoking, bailed. Carrying his light machine gun, he ran to the back of the truck to help Carnes unload.

Swayne bit his lip. The two were exposed. If that lead pursuit truck were to stop now and dismount its soldiers, one sharpshooter with a rifle could take them both out.

Leave Saddiq, he said under his breath. He did not give the order, though. Carnes would not obey him anyhow. What's more, the Al Qaeda fighters might well hesitate about shooting at three men when Saddiq was one of them. Sitting up here above the action, he was not much different from Zavello back at the OMCC, except in scale. Greiner and Carnes had a plan too. Swayne knew he would be better off—they would be better off, if he left them alone to play it out.

Carnes jumped down from the truck bed. He and Greiner reached back up into the smoky compartment.

The first Al Qaeda truck in convoy slowed nearly to a stop. Swayne switched off the safety of his rifle. He would not allow anybody to take on his man point-blank.

On the ridge the first three trucks of the convoy had now bunched up, all of them nearly stopped. They would not try driving down into the wadi, fearful of an ambush.

Unless—

Swayne saw Carnes and Greiner drag two floppy legs out of the truck's bed. Then came Saddiq, landing hard on the ground, as the truck continued to roll away. Swayne cringed at the impact of those broken legs against the ground. The Al Qaeda leader did not know how lucky he was to be out cold.

Carnes and Greiner picked up Saddiq, showing him full-face to the Al Qaeda force. A nice move, Swayne thought. Dead or alive, Saddiq might prevent his men from shooting.

The first truck roared off down the slope in pursuit as Carnes and Greiner dragged Saddiq into the wadi, his legs dangling behind him like those of a string puppet.

Saddiq's men were going to be heroes. They were going to try to rescue him without firing a shot.

Of the seven trucks now on the ridge, one had started down the slope toward the inferno. Three idled forward across the crest, and another three still inched forward, climbing the grade, two of them side by side, jockeying for position on the road, forced to converge by slopes on both sides.

The first truck came even with an insignificant rock pile and vanished in a cloud of dust, as Night Runner set off the first boomer. Although it relied on concussion rather than shrapnel, the boomer burst the saddle fuel tanks and set the truck afire. The blast stunned the Al Qaeda fighters inside, and nobody got out, except for two soldiers riding at the back of the troop compartment. The explosion heaved them from the truck, and they lay still on the ground where they hit. The truck continued to roll forward in flames. It steered left, toward Friel's position, and Swayne held his breath.

As the driver-less truck picked up speed, the wheel turned more sharply left, and the truck rolled over. More fuel spilled, and the flames grew higher, soon engulfing the truck and its human cargo. Swayne hoped the men were out cold.

Perhaps fearing a land mine that must have destroyed the first vehicle in convoy, the second truck's driver ground gears until he found reverse. He backed into the third vehicle, trapping his soldiers inside.

Night Runner set off the last boomer, which was behind the third truck now. Its blast immobilized the terrorists in the third truck, who got its full effect.

So far, nobody in the convoy had responded with gunfire, perhaps thinking that they had struck a land mine. Since Swayne and Night Runner did not have a machine gun, he did not want to give away their position with so many Al Qaeda fighters still able-bodied and well armed.

So far, less than a minute had passed. At the back of the convoy, drivers had begun to turn off the track, a common tactic—if the terrain allowed, it was better to scatter and drive away from an artillery impact zone.

Swayne aimed his 40-mm chunker at the canvas of the last truck in convoy. While the first round was in flight, he loaded a second HE grenade and shot it at the next-to-last truck. The first grenade struck the rearmost dual tires and flattened them. Other than some broken eardrums, little damage, he supposed.

The second grenade hit the canvas as troops were dismounting. Swayne had always dismissed the chunker. He found the ammunition too heavy to carry much of it—he seldom packed more than half-a-dozen rounds on a mission. It was a good noisemaker, but he doubted its lethality. Until the 40-mm round hit the canvas, blowing shrapnel outward and downward like an artillery round set to airburst. The six soldiers who had already dismounted simply fell to the ground. Those who remained conscious clawed at their faces with their hands. Nobody else climbed out of the truck's cargo compartment. The driver stepped down, walked four feet, and fell over.

So far, nobody among the Al Qaeda fighters had fired a shot, not even in panic. A good sign they assumed it was an artillery attack, Swayne thought.

As he thought it, one man lay on his back, pointing his rifle into the air, firing on automatic. Perhaps in panic, or maybe sensing danger, he thought that shooting blindly into the air might bring down an unseen aircraft.

"Carnes," he said into his mike. "Don't react to that shooting. It's not aimed fire. By now they must be sure that we are directing air strikes at them."

Leaders among the Al Qaeda fighters tried to rally their soldiers. But most of the men were following the few that had begun running away, downhill, away from the ridge. Toward safety. Walking in the tracks of their trucks.

Swayne crept to the top and lay beside Night Runner. The heavy-weapons detachment, still a kilometer to the rear, had mounted their truck again and it was on the move—back toward Kunduz. Away from the strikes that had caused so much black smoke at the top of the ridge.

A lot depended on what Swayne did in the next few minutes. Despite the wreckage, he could see nearly a hundred Al Qaeda fighters still alive. Many helped the wounded back the way they had come, and many not wounded helped themselves. Even so, nearly half remained behind on the ridgeline. He could see their officers and noncoms try to rally the survivors for an assault down the hill. They had guts.

Swayne knew his team would still have to fight to get out of Afghanistan. The Al Qaeda fighters had enough honor to try to recover their leader. *Honor among terrorists?* Was that an oxymoron? No, these fighters were faithful to each other and to their commander. He dared not take them lightly. Hate their tactics, despise their objectives, but give them credit for their bravery. For their honor.

He sorted through the options left to him and his team. Hoping was no option. The Al Qaeda fighters would go after Saddiq. The Marines, although they had whittled the odds, would have to take on a huge force. Swayne knew that this Al Qaeda force was going to test his ability to manage a battle as no other combat had yet tested him.

The terrorists showed they would make it hard. They deployed using one of the most basic small-unit tactics. Forty-eight fighters—Swayne had counted them by now— spread out on a line across the slope. They kept an interval of five to ten meters—fifteen to thirty feet—between soldiers as they walked downhill toward the spot where Greiner and Carnes had dragged Saddiq into the wadi. Swayne thought that Carnes might remain there with his prisoner, but Greiner would not dare to raise his head at that spot. He would move off to the side and come up where the enemy least expected him.

The troops *could* focus their fire if Greiner or Carnes tried to shoot at them. The gunfire would be too dense for either one to even raise his head. Other squads could charge ahead at full speed to outflank and overrun the position.

Unless Swayne and Runner butted in. As Swayne knew they could. From the hill, he was like a battle cop directing traffic. A puppet master directing the outcome, even a god of battle deciding who should live or die.

As the line of the Al Qaeda fighters ran on, Swayne asked Greiner whether he had put some space between himself and Carnes.

"A hundred meters enough?" Greiner asked.

"Fine," Swayne said. He then told Greiner to pick as many targets as he could hit with a single, long burst. "Then put your head down and dig in. Don't even try to move until I tell you to." He reminded Carnes to stay out of sight and not to shoot, except under his order.

Carnes replied in a huff, letting Swayne know he had tired of getting the same reminder. Too bad, Swayne thought. If he had been a trained Force Recon Marine, he might trust him.

Swayne looked to Night Runner, who simply said, "Sniper time?"

Swayne sighed. He knew all the honorable reasons that justified doing what they were about to do. This was war. These men would try to kill his men if he did not kill them first. If he and Night Runner shot poorly, they would lose this fight, disgrace their uniform, betray their country. Lose their honor. They had to commit murder to save lives.

Greiner opened up with a burst of twenty. He hit three of the men exposed on the slope.

Most of the Al Qaeda fighters returned fire on Greiner. Swayne guessed that they just wanted to shoot at something, anything, even if they could not identify a specific target. That kind of thing happened when men were struck hard. They had seen their friends die in their trucks, consumed in flames. Until Greiner shot at them, they could not see to strike back.

Swayne took on shooters. He had the high ground. They lay sprawled behind what little cover they could find. They lay exposed to Swayne. Offering their backs.

Because they did not hear where his shooting came from, they could not defend themselves, and he killed four of them in five shots. Night Runner, because he was the better marksman, killed three and wounded three of the men trying to maneuver against Greiner.

The Al Qaeda fighters did not lose their discipline. Green troops would fire blindly when men around them began to drop, even if they could not see their shooters. These fighters held fire, trying to ID targets. He and Night Runner stopped shooting as well, not ready to give away their position. Swayne told Greiner to pull out of his spot.

As Greiner dashed to safety, half-a-dozen terrorists opened up on him. Under the cover of their renewed

noise, Swayne and Night Runner took out two more soldiers apiece.

More confusion. Because they had dispersed, the Al
Qaeda fighters could not see that their men had been shot
from behind.

Swayne asked, "Carnes, do you have any shots? Clear
shots?"

"Affirmative. I have two."

"Take them. Make them quick."

Two quick shots from Carnes's position rang up two
more casualties and brought a new response from the Al
Qaeda fighters. Some soldiers turned their guns on Carnes.
Others rushed his position, running in front of their own
men. One attacker fell victim to his own soldiers' guns.
Swayne and Night Runner shot down three others.

By Swayne's count, fewer than thirty Al Qaeda fighters
remained. But they kept the pressure on Greiner and Carnes. He had to admit, they were brave and honorable men.
They closed on the wadi faster than he expected, closing
to within fifty meters of Carnes. They no longer worried
about hitting Saddiq, their concern for him lost in the
madness of the firefight.

Snapping off quick shots, Swayne and Night Runner
struck down four more fighters. The rest continued their
blitz on Carnes's position.

Until one of the many factors that Swayne, would-be
god of battle, could not control came into play.

FRIEL BEGAN HACKING. He awakened from a drowning
nightmare and found himself drowning. He couldn't remember going to sleep, but sleeping on his back had been
a bad idea—blood and spit ran down his throat. Too much
blood. Drizzling into his lungs, making him cough, filling
his stomach, making him nauseous. Never before had he
panicked under fire. Now he felt a terror he had never
dreamed of.

Not from the enemy soldiers shouting nearby. Rather,

because he was going to throw up. In his sleep, he'd nearly drowned in his spit. Now he was going to drown in his own puke because his face was taped shut.

He tried leaning over and putting his head down. That did not stop the spasms in his gut. In only a few seconds, it would be over. Already, he tasted the salt. He tried pulling at the tape on his face, knowing that it was pointless— he was the one who had given bad-ass duct tape its bad name.

Bullets snapped over his head. For some reason, a firefight had sprung up around him. In all directions.

Well, shit. There were better ways to die than to drown in vomit. He found his machine gun. He saw he had a hundred rounds belted. More bullets than time—he could not fight down his stomach much longer.

He stood up and saw that he was at one end of a line of ragheads. How did that happen? How had they surrounded him without his knowing?

Firing the machine gun on full auto, aiming as well as he could without putting his fat cheek to the stock, he attacked.

"EVERYBODY UP AND shooting," Swayne hollered. "Now!"

Even with the damage Friel had done in his surprise attack, and the powerful effect of four other guns shooting from three positions, Swayne knew his Force Recon Team was in danger of getting wiped out. Somewhere between twenty and thirty terrorists remained. Now they had targets. If they could not see Swayne, Night Runner, Greiner, or Carnes, they were spread out. And they could see Friel. Finally, an enemy. An enemy staggering into the open.

Friel hunching over his gun.

Friel dropping to his knees.

All the while, Friel shooting.

Friel shooting wildly as he lay down in spasms.

"He's hit!" said Swayne.

"No," said Night Runner, up and running at full speed down the slope. Of all things, Night Runner had pulled his sword. What the hell did he think he could accomplish with that? There were too many Al Qaeda fighters for hand-to-hand combat, too many—

Swayne realized the problem. He knew he must keep trying to pick off any Al Qaeda fighters exposed, especially anybody shooting at Friel or Night Runner. Even so, he felt as if he was all out of ideas.

Except for one.

"Bonnie, can you hit the center of the formation?" Swayne said into his PDA. "Wherever that is?"

"Roger, wilco, over and out," said Alvin the Chipmunk. "Inbound in . . . ten seconds . . . nine . . . eight . . . get your heads down . . . six . . . five . . . four . . . three . . ."

If this last-ditch effort had any chance of success, Swayne knew that he had to pump it up as best he could. He shot his last four 40-mm chunker grenades at the Al Qaeda scattered on the slope, lobbing them like rounds out of a small mortar.

CARNES HAD NO idea what was happening until the pathetic Saddiq sat up and pointed at the sky.

"Dear Allah," he said in Pashto. "They have picked the wrong targets. The fools are striking the convoy instead of the White House."

Carnes followed the line of Saddiq's arm and finger. An airplane. An odd-looking airplane. Like the CIA's Predator, only smaller, much smaller.

He couldn't figure what was going on—Swayne had not said anything about an airplane or air support. Carnes waited for the craft to shoot its Hellfire missile, but it did not. Then again, this machine was smaller than the missile itself.

Saddiq cried out, more in anguish than the pain of his wounds. "You fools, you fools."

He fell over backward, out cold.

• • •

AS SWAYNE WATCHED, the small craft struck an Al Qaeda firing position of at least three guns, the fiery explosion shooting flames a hundred feet into the air, as the XD-11 drone, called the Dirty Birdie, flew into the ground and was disintegrated by its onboard demolition system. The light but lethal explosive composition had been used as part of the construction materials. Once the self-destruction mechanism had been armed after launch, the XD-11 was set to explode if it crashed or was hit by ground fire. Downes had told Swayne the charge also could be detonated by remote control. The system was installed to prevent the technology from falling into enemy hands. Alvin the Chipmunk herself had given Swayne the idea to use it as an unmanned kamikaze craft.

Swayne's grenades added enough noise to complete the effect.

Once more, combat surprised him beyond his expectations. The exploding drone and chunker grenades reminded the Al Qaeda fighters that they could be taken under attack from the air at any moment. He counted ten men who threw down their weapons, stood up all at once, their hands in the air, and walked toward Night Runner to surrender. Another half dozen ran away without weapons. Of the four Al Qaeda fighters left, three tried to hit the zigzagging Night Runner. Greiner, Carnes, and Swayne picked off each of them in turn. Two more fighters stood up to join in the surrender.

Night Runner ignored them all. He threw down his own rifle and raised his sword over Friel's face.

FRIEL DID NOT see the surrender of the Al Qaeda fighters. He did not care. For he had fallen victim to a surrender of his own. Panic had won him over in a way no enemy soldier ever had. He threw down his machine gun and tore at his face with his fingernails. But he could not peel the bad-ass duct tape from his mouth.

Friel knew the drill. Oh, yeah, he knew too freaking well. From advanced field surgery training. He had been taught how to wire or splint shut a broken jaw. He knew the dangers of nausea. If you couldn't cut the wires or get the split off quickly enough, you had to break out the teeth. Or cut a guy a new mouth.

No way would he let that happen. He would shoot a guy first, even the captain. Better yet, he would shoot himself. Gagging, he reached for his machine gun, but found it too heavy to lift. Then he saw why.

The gunny. Night Runner stood over him, his boot pinning the BRAT to the ground.

The gunny. The only man that he would trust to do what must be done. The man who had nearly killed him on the last mission, the one into Iran. The gunny stood over him brandishing that toad-sticker of his.

Night Runner knelt beside him. "Henry?" he whispered.

Friel knew that Night Runner was offering him three choices. Only Night Runner in all the world was man enough to do that. The cap would have jumped right in without asking what he wanted—that was an officer for you. Greiner might have stood there, watching him die in his own vomit—that was an FNG.

Not Night Runner. Night Runner asked: *What do you want me to do?*

Friel's stomach clenched. He had to decide.

A hand up to tell Night Runner to leave him alone to drown?

A finger across his own throat?

A finger across his own mouth?

The spasms hit him in the gut so hard he could barely find enough strength to give his signal.

EPILOGUE

HONOR. WHAT WAS it? Swayne asked himself after the mission had ended. What did it mean?

To Saddiq, honor meant killing Americans. If he had a hand in the killings, honor would be his in the terrorist afterlife. If so, Saddiq now basked with seventy-two virgins on a heavenly beach. Greiner and Night Runner had recovered one of the undamaged Al Qaeda trucks and loaded up the ailing terrorist leader. He had awakened briefly to tell a fabulous story: that four U.S. airliners were to be hijacked and flown into the World Trade Center Twin Towers, the White House, and the U.S. Capitol. The mission had failed, he said. Instead, he cried, one of the planes had flown into his own convoy. At evening, as their truck neared the border with Uzbekistan, Swayne and Carnes decided they must report Saddiq's delirious tale, no matter how preposterous. A somber Zavello came back within minutes to report the truth of September 11 in America. No sooner had Zavello spoken than Saddiq awakened, babbling in his own language. Then he died, a smile on his face.

To Carnes, honor was a tool. A device you wore to suit

the occasion. Swayne asked Carnes to interpret the terrorist leader's last words. He refused. Swayne could understand why. The CIA man blamed himself. And perhaps Swayne. If he could have gotten that intelligence information earlier, he believed he might have prevented the attacks. The man thought he might have been the savior of his country. An arrogance that Swayne had never seen before, not even in the CIA. Before entering the zone defended by Lieutenant Radford and his platoon, Swayne stopped the truck to coordinate the passage. Before telling Greiner to drive on, Night Runner leaned from the cargo compartment into the cab to whisper in Swayne's ear. Carnes had stepped out of the truck, not to urinate, as Night Runner had thought. But to walk away. Into the night. Back into Afghanistan. Night Runner asked with his eyes. Swayne shook his head. No, he did not want the gunny to go after the CIA man. They had done their job in rescuing him from Saddiq. If he did not want to go back to face his superiors, they should let him go. Let him have the slim honor of self-exile or whatever Carnes needed.

To Night Runner, who had battered Friel on the mission into Iran, honor was to allow Friel to decide how to live or how to die. Friel understood Night Runner's honor. He signaled that he wanted to live, even disfigured. He drew his finger across his mouth, and Night Runner saved his life by slashing his face, cutting a wider mouth to expel the contents of his stomach and to let in the air. The pair would be brothers forever. Warrior brothers.

To Nina, honor was a guy thing. As with most guy things, perverted, base, superficial, macho, misguided, and flat-out dumb. She did not speak to him after he refused to respond to the remarks about settling down. He knew she would have nothing to do with him anymore. Unless he took her aside. Unless he explained himself. Unless he explained that tone in the voice of that other woman, Bon-

nie Downes. Unless he offered her what she wanted. But
how could he?

For to Swayne, a part of his world, the most important
part—that which he sustained in the place called heart and
soul—had come undone during the mission into Afghanistan. Behind everything else, honor had urged him on.
Honor made him a good Marine, a good officer. He had
held his own honor above that of terrorists like Abu Saddiq. Above con artists like Carnes.

Yet if he was so superior to them, how did he reconcile
shooting men in the back? Survival of his unit? Survival
of himself?

He was no virgin to killing. He had directed air strikes.
He had painted targets for laser-guided bombs. He had
tossed grenades into groups of unsuspecting soldiers. He
had seen their faces as they died—or he had stood off so
far that he could not see their faces at all.

But until today, he had not shot them down deliberately
from behind. He had not executed men by shooting them
in their backs.

That was the problem for him. He could say that terrorists had killed thousands of innocents at the World
Trade Center, the Pentagon, and on the plane that crashed
into the Pennsylvania countryside. But did that justify his
cold-blooded murders? Yes, the Al Qaeda fighters had had
weapons, but did that justify? Yes, survival did depend
on the killings, but did that justify?

Yes, he decided. Because he could not continue to serve
if the answer were otherwise. Killing like that had to be
done. That day, Swayne took his place alongside other
soldiers who had already learned their lesson about honor.

Honor was a word. It could not set a broken arm or
Friel's broken face. It could not relieve the pain of a
wound. It did nothing for the dead, like Saddiq. Or the
living, like Carnes. Or even himself.

Honor, like glory, was a wonderful thing, if a man

could sustain the illusion. If he could see it on the giant movie screen and believe it.

Honor was a shield. A soldier used it to protect himself against realities such as Swayne had seen—the backs of his enemy in the sights of his rifle. He had seen through his shield at the moment he carefully, deliberately pulled the slack out of his trigger, felt the recoil against his shoulder, saw the convulsions in his target, and the trembling of one stiff leg before the body went slack.

Swayne finally understood what his grandfather had tried to tell him again and again. That he did not belong in the uniform of a fighting man.

Swayne always believed the man had tried to insult him, had tried to tell him he was descended from a cowardly father. But no, that was not the case after all. Senator Jamison Swayne had been giving him another, even more urgent message.

Quit, he had been trying to say. *Get out while you still have your illusions.*